The Butcher on Colfax

J. T. Tierney

CURTISS STREET
PRESS

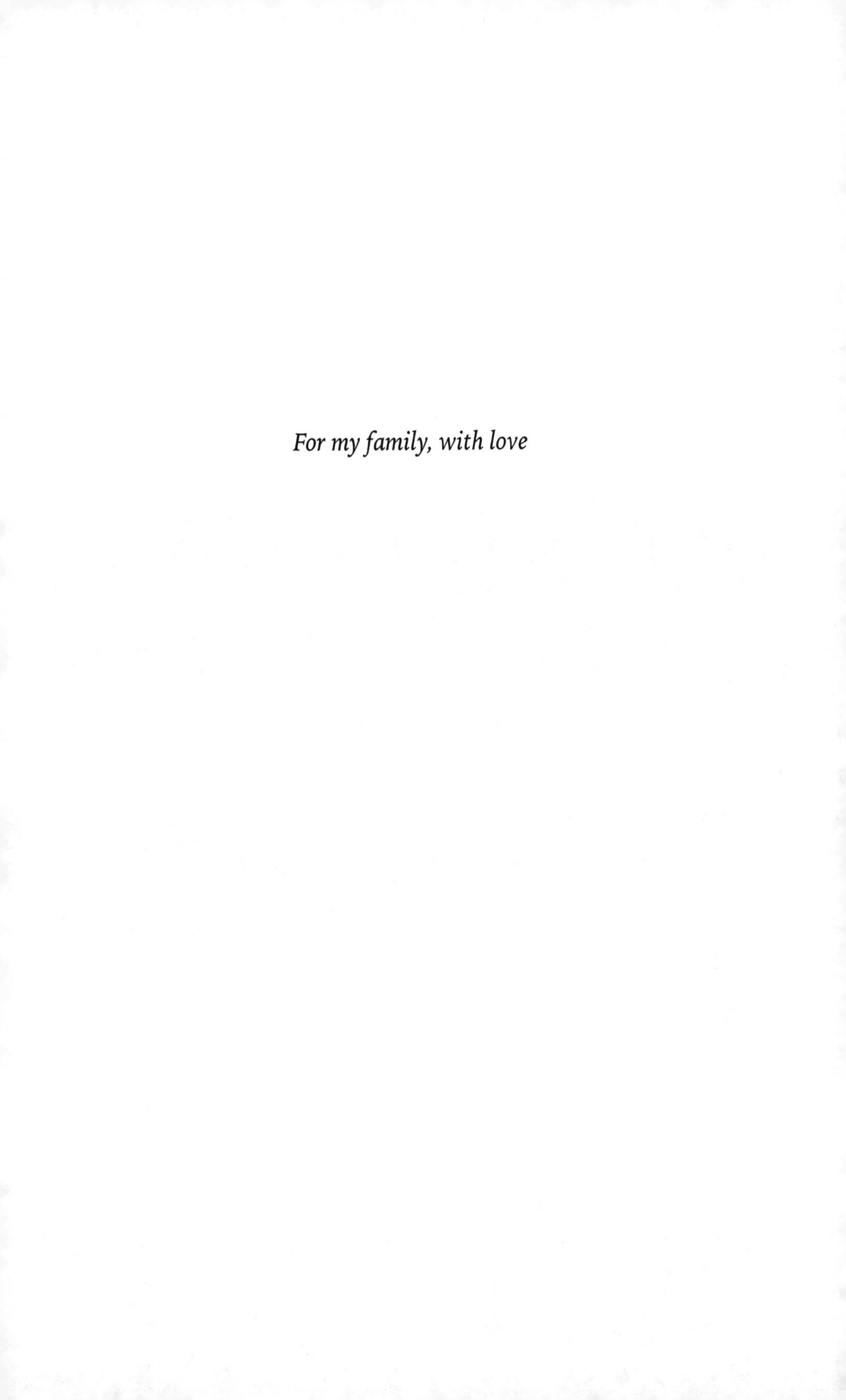

For my family, with love

Chapter One

Hundreds of men toiled alongside him at the rail, their arms flashing sharp knives and cleavers in a blur of motion—carving, splitting, gutting under the harsh glow of gas lamps—each as part of a relentless machine of steel and death. Six days a week from dawn to dusk, Emmett rasped hair from the cold, hanging carcasses of hogs that trundled past him in a ceaseless procession. Some days Emmett filed the hair off legs, some days off the neck and shoulder. But the work was an unchanging, mind-numbing stream of flesh and bone that left him reeking, his muscles screaming for respite. Night after night, the grim parade of butchered beasts haunted his dreams.

For six years—since 1884, when he had bid farewell to schooling and to his fifteenth year—Emmett Kelly had been a scraper at this Armour meatpacking plant in Chicago. But in recent months, a deep, restless yearning had taken root within him. He had become desperate to escape the life that had become his cage. And that day, he finally declared his emancipation. "Enough of this," he said to himself. Emmett Kelly would not be chained to this bloody rail any longer. So, at day's end, with his week's earnings clutched tight in his fist, he stood before Mr. Hausner, his foreman, and spoke his piece. "I won't be back on Monday."

Hausner's tone was a mix of ridicule and curiosity. "And what grand plan do you have for yourself, Kelly?"

"I'm setting my sights on Colorado," he announced, the decision firm in his heart.

Hausner laughed. "Startin' to have notions, are ya? Goin' out to find your fortune in silver?"

"No, sir," Emmett replied, his resolve unshaken. "Mining's not in my blood. I'll find something else."

"Denver's got meatpacking, should you miss the blood and guts," Hausner cracked, thinking himself quite the wit. He always talked about his aptitude for *sherzhaft*. But all the men under him thought his humor was as dull as a blunted cleaver.

"I'll keep that in mind," Emmett said, though the thought of returning to such work chilled him to the bone.

With a dismissive wave, Hausner dismissed him. "Godspeed to you, boy."

All the way home, the telling of his decision to his kin weighed heavy on Emmett's soul. He foresaw his da's scornful derision and his mam's sorrowful acceptance, yet he couldn't deny the call of his heart. And how could they fault him for wanting to pick up and search for something better? Each of them also had wandered—all the way from Ireland—for the same shot at a better life.

And now, with the two of them at opposite ends of the scarred table, Emmett laid out his plan. The old man ran a handkerchief across a beard as grey as the ash of peat, sopping up droplets of soup collected there. Emmett's father regarded him with eyes that spoke of hard years and harder judgments. "You think you're too grand for us now, is that it?" he had challenged, his words cutting deeper than any knife at the plant. "You think you're a step above buttermilk." He rendered his usual verdict of Emmett's worth. "You'll come to nothing, boy. Mark my words. You're nothing but a laughingstock. A washout." His dismissal stung, but it didn't sway Emmett. He was determined to forge his own path, far from the shadow of his father's disdain and the stifling air of the tenements.

The old man himself was no Andrew Carnegie! Nothing wrong with being a teamster, driving a horse team, but it wasn't exactly a roaring success story. What had the old man been doing when he was eighteen? Digging potatoes? Salting herring? Cutting peat? Again, he was no one to judge.

"You'll never make it," his father growled, as if stating it yet another way would finally get his point across. He hawked some phlegm into his muckender, then gazed down at the cloth to inspect the new pattern this latest secretion had created on top of the soup stain. Looked like the coat of a mottled pony. Returning his attention to Emmett for one final hostility, he scowled. "Face it. You don't have what it takes to succeed in this world."

Enough of him. Let that be the last put-down Emmett ever heard from him. Emmett turned to his mam, who was fifty-eight years old, but appeared seventy-five. Her life had been hard. Hopelessness and fatigue etched her face. Condemned to dreary domestic life and the drudgery of looking after others, she nevertheless tried her best to maintain a light demeanor. "They'll turn ye into a gunslinger out there, Em," she teased.

"Doubtful, Mam," he countered with a half-smile. "I hear Denver's no longer any wilder than it is here."

They spoke of possibilities and plans, his heart growing lighter with each word. "It's opportunity I'm after, Mam. A chance to carve out my own destiny."

"And what of work?" she asked, her concern a tangible thing.

"I'll find it. No shortage of jobs there. And who knows? I may start my own business."

"Doin' what?"

"Don't know yet. I'll have to see what needs doin'."

"When would ya be goin'?"

"Soon. No point delayin'. I'll be takin' the train through Omaha and Cheyenne. They say those towns are sights worth seeing."

His mother's smile, though tinged with sadness, warmed him.

She said, "Then go with our blessings, son. Just remember, wherever you roam, you're a Kelly, and you carry the name with you."

Da looked up, then hawked another glob of phlegm into his handkerchief.

Chapter Two

The train hissed and snaked as it crossed the bridge over the Missouri and weaved through Omaha's complex rail yards. The man Emmett had been talking with for much of the last several hours said to him, "Good luck to ya in Denver. You'll do fine. As I said, no shortage of opportunity there."

"Thanks for the encouragement—and for the lively conversation. … One last thing: is there an inexpensive hotel here in Omaha you'd recommend?"

"You might try the Paxton at 14th and Farnam. More affordable than most. Goodbye now."

Emmett gathered his bag, clambered down from the train car, and made his way out of the station. He didn't think of himself as easily surprised, yet what he saw confounded him. Back home, wood blocks or bricks paved the principal streets. Here, dirt and dust served as road surfaces, the city having made little progress toward paving its streets. As he carried his canvas Gladstone bag to the Paxton, he marveled at the number of saloons. From what he could tell, if you were to close down all the saloons, brothels, and tobacco shops, about half of Omaha's businesses would be gone.

Emmett left his belongings in his tiny hotel room, ate a quick meal at the Paxton, and explored the town. He wandered past saloons emitting the tinkly sounds of gambling and the rowdy laughter of drinking men. On a whim, he dived into a rum hole called "The Morgue" and, feeling bold, ordered a cheap whiskey instead of his usual beer. The barkeep poured him a glass. "This here, we call 'Coffin Varnish.'" It was about as undrinkable as it sounded. He figured he might be better off sticking to beer.

The night's entertainment was a racy stage show that was cut short by a fistfight that had started from a gambling feud. Emmett slipped out of there, soon finding himself in another saloon down the street, where he struck up a conversation with a fellow roughly his age, who turned out to be from Ireland. This Tom Quinn most recently had lived in New York for six months and also was on his way to Denver the following morning. They became fast friends over multiple beers.

After telling Quinn the various reasons for his own migration west, Emmett asked, "And what's behind your decision to go to Colorado?"

Tom looked down into his suds. "Nothing at all like your reasons. Never knew my father, I didn't, and liked my work back in Cork as a carpenter. My older brother had moved to New York, and I followed him there about five months ago. He was my only reason for being there. He … he died on a job site not two weeks past. With him gone, staying there lost all its meaning for me. And going back to Ireland? Didn't seem the right time for that, not just yet. So, I figured I'd try Colorado. Denver's booming, so I hear, and there's no shortage of work for a carpenter."

"What happened to your brother, if you don't mind my askin'?"

"He got crushed by a swinging load of an electric crane. ... Drives me mad, so it does, thinking on what happens every day in big city factories, foundries, machine shops, electrical works, construction sites. You name it. Men losing their lives —snagged by moving belts; struck dead by a flywheel or by a shard from a bursting grindstone; crushed when they're pulled into the guts of machinery. ... Some of it's down to sheer daftness or carelessness. But most are 'cause the bosses couldn't give a fig about keeping their workers safe. I'm telling ya, Emmett, it's no wonder at all men are banding together in labor unions ..."

Tom's commentary trailed off when two Poles drinking nearby made loud, derogatory comments about the "bog trotters" down the bar. Emmett put his glass down on the mahogany, plastered a smile on his face, and started toward them.

Alarmed by what seemed to be unfolding, Tom said to him, "What are you doing?"

"I think that one fella's loud mouth just got his smeller broken," Emmett replied. Approaching the nearer of the two men, he extended his beefy arm as if to offer a handshake, but then smashed it into the man's nose, triggering a rush of blood. The man's hand flew to his face. His look of surprise made Emmett laugh. The man's angry glare quickly turned into action as he pounced, overwhelming Emmett with punches and knocking him to his knees. Emmett noticed the other, larger man approaching, signaling real trouble.

Suddenly, from the side, a boot hit the larger man in the crotch, doubling him over to Emmett's level. Emmett gouged the man's eyes, forcing him to jerk back upright. Looking up, he watched Tom deliver a powerful blow to the first man, almost spinning his head like a top. Fighting to stand, Emmett then slammed a bar stool down on the larger man, who was still reeling from the eye gouge.

The burly bouncers descended like storm clouds, yanking the brawlers apart and tossing them out into the cool night air. Outside, the fight sputtered to a halt under the stern gaze of a club-wielding constable who barked threats of a night behind bars if they didn't scatter. Emmett brushed the dirt from his jacket and probed the steady trickle of blood seeping from a deep cut above his eye.

Gasping for air, Tom dabbed at his mouth with his sleeve and managed a wry grin. "You're a wild one, Kelly," he chuckled. "Hanging around you might just be the death of me."

Emmett flashed a crooked smile, which quickly turned into a wince as he discovered his lip had split open. "Aye, but there's worse things than scrapping. Turning the other cheek tops that list."

"I'm not one for fisticuffs myself; seems a pointless exercise. But I wouldn't leave a mate to swing solo in a melee," Tom said, eyeing the jagged gash above Emmett's eye. "You might need a few stitches for that souvenir."

"I'll keep a watch on it. How about you? How's your side?"

"That one fella landed a roundhouse. Feels like he cracked a rib. Breathing's all bockety now."

"Rotten luck, Tom. Sorry about that. But I thank ya for divin' into the mess to help me."

"Wouldn't call it a pleasure."

Emmett clapped Tom on the shoulder. "Catch you on the train tomorrow then? We'll lick our wounds together," Emmett said, then shuffled his way back towards the Paxton Hotel with the night swallowing his silhouette.

Chapter Three

By the time the train pulled out of Omaha, Alice Butler was beyond exhausted. Her travels had taken a toll on her. The rail to Dublin; the ship from Dublin's Kingstown port to Liverpool; two nights at the awful boarding house there; the ten days of dark, noisy, smelly bunk dormitories in the iron-hulled ship's steerage class; the lines at Castle Garden; the chaotic effort to find Nora in the crowds at the dock; the long day of gaping and gawking around New York City, absorbing the outsized proportions that made Dublin and Liverpool look tiny as Loughrea by contrast.

Exhausted and numb, she was. Numb from weeks of travel. And dazed by the barrage of wonders she'd witnessed along the way: the bright, cloudless American skies; New York's towering buildings and sprawling bridges; the sheer numbers of people; the lush, rolling farmlands that eclipse even Ireland's green; the endless towns and cities; the boundless open spaces.

But at least this train was comfortable. Although she and Nora couldn't afford to ride in a Pullman car, Alice felt their travel in a second-class car was luxurious enough. Their train had vestibules, wooden seats with reclining backs, and kerosene lamps giving off dim, flickering light at night. *If this is second-class,* she thought, *then no need to strive for the top of the heap. This will do just fine, thank you very much!*

Alice had spent much of the train ride so far napping, taking in the scenery, and doing little pencil sketches to send home to her mam and da, as well as reading and writing letters. She had just pulled from her bag the letter her sister Nora had sent to her in Ireland two months ago from Boston, where she was working as a domestic for a posh family on Beacon Hill:

"I'm up at the crack of dawn to light the fires, and I'm the last to turn in, with everything tucked in for the night. I'm kept busy six days a week, always on my toes, even through the night. Sundays and Thursday evenings are my brief respites. Most of my time is spent on the drawing-room floor—greeting guests, serving meals, polishing silver, and washing up. I handle it all!

Though my three-dollar weekly wage are scanty by Boston standards, it's a fortune compared to what I could make back there in Loughrea. Saving isn't too hard either, since my food, lodging, and uniform don't cost me a penny. The hardest part? The deep loneliness. I run the house but miss out on the warmth of home, the laughter and companionship that comes with it.

When Thursday evening or Sunday afternoon roll

around, I am so eager to get together with Bridget Gleeson. We have the best time! She has started to talk of going West —have you heard of Denver, in Colorado?—where she says there is more opportunity, even for young Irish women. Bridget knows a girl who went out there two years ago and says there are jobs galore and you can barely move for all the available men! Her talk has my own head spinning with the thought. I think I'm going to do it.

So, what I'm writing to say, my darling Alice, is that you should come over. Life here is like painting with rainbows. There's not always a pot of gold at the end, but the riches are more than are to be had in Loughrea. We can be together and have adventures. And together, we can send extra money home to Mam and Da.

I've enclosed the amount you'd need for passage to Boston. Please, please, please, my sweet Alice. Please come."

Alice folded the letter and put it away, then turned her attention to Nora, who was seated next to her and who'd been flirting for the past four hours with a handsome young salesman across the aisle who'd boarded in Ottumwa, Iowa.

As the train began to slow for Lincoln, where he'd be getting off, the man turned to Nora and said, "Allow me to thank you for the pleasant time I've had."

"Not at all," Nora replied. She ran her fingers through her auburn hair and smiled.

"I hope you have enjoyed it, as well" he said.

Hearing that, Alice almost burst out laughing. The cheek-iness of him!

"Oh, very much so," Nora said, giving the man a wide

smile accompanied by a batting of her big brown eyes. Seeing that, Alice did laugh.

"I'm so glad I succeeded in pleasing you," he said with a grin that, Alice thought, strangely bordered on the lascivious.

Nora was undeterred. "How could you not please me! Spending time with you was like turning coins into bills! "

The young man looked so pleased with himself he was about to burst with pride. As he exited, he tipped his hat and threw Nora what Alice supposed he thought was his best smile. When he was safely out of earshot, Alice said, "What a billy noddle that fella was! And how in the Lord's name did you learn to be so flirty?"

"I got out and about a bit with Bridget Gleeson. Enough to learn American men are more open to bold women than the fellas back home are. They like forward women here. I calculate you'll be bold as brass yourself in no time."

Could that be true? Would she turn brazen and saucy? Would she find this country's men appealing? Alice wondered. She'd just seen two of them board this car back in Omaha. The first, with forearms like ham hocks, had a deep, fresh cut above his eye and a split, swollen lip. The second, a tall and attractive man with dense brown hair, had a swollen jaw and a bruised eye, and he clutched his side as though it hurt. They were now about five rows back. If these rough, unsavory characters were representative of the men Alice would find in America, then God help her soul.

For now, all she wanted to think about was the scenery. The train had lurched and swayed and screeched as it navigated all the rail switches on the way out of Lincoln. But soon the ride smoothed out, and the countryside rolled into gentle ups and downs, with groves of trees becoming more spotty. Occasional spaces of tillage were still to be seen, but nothing like the rich farmlands they'd seen in Ohio, Illinois, and Iowa. Soon, even the occasional farms were left behind, as the train glided along open prairie that, the young man had said, would stretch now all the way to the Rocky Mountains.

What would Da and Mam think of this immense grassy plain, with its dusty, sun-dried coloring—its parched and withered grasses faded to a pale, sapless yellow, stretching as far as they eye could see. And overhead was a great blue vault of sky with a searingly strong sun. That was another thing Da and Mam were unaccustomed to seeing. Whereas back home, there were a hundred different ways of describing rainfall, out here, there'd have to be a hundred different ways of describing the light of the sun.

The gentle rocking of the train and the rhythmic clickety-clack of the wheels hitting rail joints gradually lulled Alice to sleep and Nora soon after.

Chapter Four

When the conductor announced that the North Platte stop would be extended by a half-hour to tend to a problem in the locomotive, Emmett and Tom got off the train and walked along Front Street, such as it was, until they hit a small cafe.

A thickly mustached man served them coffee and couldn't stop himself from commenting on the cut above Emmett's eye. "You'd best think about having somebody patch up that gash, mister. That looks pretty bad."

Emmett drew a bowie knife from his boot and laid it on the table. "And you'd best think about minding your own business." Emmett was just having fun with the man, but the poor fella couldn't have guessed that from the situation.

"Now, there's no need for that. I was just bein' friendly. Expressin' concern."

"Much obliged, friend. My companion here is just a bit

touchy," Tom said with a smile, then joked, "As you can see, his gal recently gave him a bad lickin'."

The man's mustache and matching eyebrows bounced, and he said, "I guess she did. She clipped you pretty good."

Emmett smiled and said, "She won't be messin' with me any more." Then he wiped both sides of the blade across his sleeve and slipped it back in his boot. The mustached man looked shaken by Emmett's remark and went off to get their hotcakes and bacon.

Tom laughed when the man was out of earshot. "You have a wicked sense of humor, you do, Emmett. I thought that auld feller might faint at the sight of that Arkansas toothpick. And you sure left him wonderin' about the dispatch of that feisty girl."

Emmett's eyes twinkled. "A wicked sense of humor serves a man well. A big knife serves him still better. After our incident in Omaha, I decided that I won't go around without my blade any more. Ya never know what you're going to encounter."

On their way back to their train car after their quick meal, the pair stopped where two attractive young women from the train cast disapproving looks at a group of boys throwing rocks at the funniest little creatures imaginable. The animals looked like squirrels, smaller than a rabbit, perhaps a bit bigger than a rat. They appeared to live in underground burrows marked by domed mounds of packed earth at their entrances. The rodents would stick their heads out of the holes, then emerge fully, their tails smartly cocked up in the air, look around and bark defiantly at anyone nearby. But if someone got within ten yards or so, their courage would fail them suddenly and they'd bolt down the hole, quick as lightning. Sometimes, one would pop his head out for an instant afterwards, for one last angry bark. The rock-throwing boys were having great sport, but no luck. The rodents were much too fast and clever a match for their throwing arms.

"You shouldn't try to hurt those poor animals. They're not doing any harm to you," one of the young women said to the boys. When she turned and noticed Emmett and Tom, she grimaced, then turned back to the boys and added, "Fortunately, they're too fast for you."

Hearing that, Emmett again drew his knife from his boot and winked at Tom. Drawing his arm back slowly, he then snapped it forward, sending the blade spinning through the air, end over end, catching one of the unsuspecting critters right in its warblin' chest. The mouths of all the onlookers—the young women and the little boys alike—dropped open in amazement.

One of the boys said, "Mister, I ain't never seen nothing like that! You're darn good with that knife!"

"It pays to know how to throw a knife, lad," Emmett said. He pointed at the dead animal. "What are those critters called? I've never seen one."

"Them's 'prairie dogs,' mister. They're all over the place out here."

"They sure as hell are!" He laughed. "But now there's one fewer of 'em." The train whistle sounded. Emmett said to the boy, "Run and get my knife, will ya, lad?" The boy scurried off to get the knife and when he returned, Emmett gave him a penny, wiped the knife blade on his pants, and said to the boy, "Remember: it's good to know how to use a knife."

Alice's shoulders shook, as if from a shiver, and she followed Nora up the steps of their train car, saying, "That little boy said it right: 'I've never seen anything like that!'" She was referring not only to the precision of the knife throwing, but to the gratuitous taking of life. It was so unnecessary. And for what? Sport? To impress the boys? To impress Nora and herself? The whole thing made her a little nauseated.

As they boarded the train behind the women, Tom asked Emmett, "When did you learn to throw like that?"

"When I was still in school. My mates and I spent most of our time throwing knives at targets or playing mumblety-peg. Then, when I was working in a meatpacking plant, the men would sometimes have throwing contests during our short lunch breaks."

They'd reached the row where the two young women were taking their seats. Emmett stopped, removed his cap, and looked at the one who had spoken to the boys outside. She had dark hair, brown eyes, a slender neck, and pale white skin. He swallowed and addressed her. "I can tell by your brogue that you're here from Ireland, miss. You might be unfamiliar with American cuisine. I suspect those prairie-dogs are mighty fine eatin'. Probably like squirrel in taste, and that's a favorite delicacy in parts of America. You might even be able to get one for your supper when we get to Cheyenne."

She replied, "And I can tell by your faint accent that you have some Irish in you, as well. Tell me, is it always your custom to be so brass-necked in the way you address strangers, especially women?"

"My intention is only to be cordial, miss. Cordiality: that's my watchword." Emmett put his cap back on and moved on down the aisle. He heard one of them say to the other, "The impertinence of that hooligan!" *Ah, good,* he thought. *I got a rise out of them.*

Emmett and Tom fell into a silence as the train pulled away from North Platte. Emmett began to notice some temporary breaks in the sun-blanched uniformity of the parched plains. Sometimes a long, low line of bluffs shortens the view on one side of the car or the other. Their varied shapes interested him. Some of the bluffs were steep and rock-faced, a flat-topped ridge against the sky. Others had channelled, wrinkled fronts, where torrents of water had at one time coursed down and eaten into their now bare and arid sides. Those sand hills looked like someone had raked fingers down a mound of his mam's colcannon.

Sometimes, the broad shallow Platte was beside them. Along its banks, thick groves of stunted copse occasionally appeared. Or sometimes the train would pass nearer bluffs, not a mere distant ridge bounding the view across an expanse of prairie, but hills close by, or within a mile or two of the railway's course—barren and stony hills, with single trees of dark-green foliage, pines or cedars, thinly scattered up and down over their sides and hollows.

Emmett felt mesmerized by the landscape passing by his window. But the distinct sharp sound of rifle shots rang out, interrupting his trance-like state. He heard one of the young Irish women forward of them yell, "Jaysus! What now?" Emmett wondered the same.

He and Tom scrambled toward the sound of the gunfire,

only to discover an absurd sight through the window of the door at the back of the car: two fancy men wearing bowler hats, bow ties, and six-button waistcoats, stood on the platform, passing a Winchester back and forth, each taking turns firing off into the distance.

Emmett heard someone yell, "Antelope!" Like everyone else in the car, Emmett looked out the window and saw a herd of about twenty animals—smaller than deer, but similar in appearance—running a race with the train, about fifty yards off.

Emmett didn't know much about rifles—or about shooting one—but figured it mustn't be very easy to shoot a running animal from a rocking train. And these two men, whoever they were, certainly weren't sharpshooters. Some of the bullets cut into the ground amazingly wide of the mark. But every now and then, a bullet would rip up the turf very close to an antelope, making the creature bound into the air in wild terror, provoking great guffaws from the dandies.

A tall, older man standing near them muttered to Emmett and Tom, "Those two feckers couldn't hit a pronghorn if it was sitting on the seat next to them." The boys laughed in appreciation of the man's joke, and together the three watched the fusillade continue for about five more minutes.

Then, at last, the animals turned away from the train, heading off toward the bluffs, escaping without wound or scratch—to the delight of many in the car, especially the two young women, who cheered their escape from the bullets' paths.

Chapter Five

When the train rolled to a stop in the town of Julesburg, in the far northeastern corner of Colorado, Emmett and Tom stepped off the car to look around. The tall, older man who'd spoken to them about the poor marksmanship of the fancy men also had disembarked and stood beside them. After gazing about, the heavily bearded man muttered, "It's a fuckin' pity."

"What is?" Tom asked, turning to look at the man, who was easily six and a half feet in height. His reddish-brown beard was ragged and untrimmed. He had a thin face, from which a great nose protruded, emphasizing the cheekbones and making his eyes seem larger than they were.

The man nodded toward the dilapidated buildings stretching away from them."Fifteen years ago, this pathetic collection of run-down shacks was a real town. Thriving, booming. Men called it 'the roughest on this side of Hell,' and it deserved its reputation." He pointed to the dusty, rutted road adjacent to the tracks. "This here was the main street. All up and down it was houses for dancin' and gamblin' and drinkin'. And all of 'em was filled. You had to muscle your way through the door, there was so many men in this town. The only females around was the young girls who did the dancin' and other entertainin'. Those girls musta made a fortune! Most of the men was wild Western types— either miners from the mountains or bullwhackers from the plains—"

Tom interrupted him. "Now you're losing me, friend, and I don't want that, because I'm findin' the picture you're paintin' to be mighty entertainin'. But help me. What's a bullwhacker?"

"Why, a bullwhacker drove teams of oxen to bring supplies westward from the Missouri, carryin' on the trade of the country. He'd walk up and down the line of oxen on a bull train, makin' sure each ox was pitchin' in, doin' its job. He always had to be on the lookout for them long horns that would swing out at him when least expected. His feet would get stomped, his boots shat on."

"Men still doin' that work?" Emmett asked.

"They's a few still around, but 'cause of these railroads, there ain't as many of 'em now as once was." He looked at the two young men who comprised his audience and said, "I'm Jedediah Pinsker. I shoulda told you my name right off."

Emmett and Tom introduced themselves to their new companion, then Tom said: "You were talkin' of bull-whackers."

"Yup. A good one had to be fearless of Indians, 'cuz redskins were a constant problem. He had to be able to stand any hardship of life." Jedediah paused, straightened his tall, thin frame, and stroked his long beard as if in deep thought. "A bullwhacker was generally of fine physique, in full feather, a handsome specimen of manhood. He showed a magnificent beard and mustache. Was partial to flannel shirts." Another pause. A twinkle came to his eye. "And he was capital company, if ya could pocket some hard fuckin' swearin'. Most bullwhackers could cuss the feathers off a buzzard."

Emmett and Tom took in Jedediah's hirsute face and flannel shirt and then guffawed at his funny way of tellin' them he'd been one of these bullwhackers. "How'd you get into bullwhackin?" Tom asked.

"I heard about the life from an uncle of mine who'd done it. I was a young man in Sheboygan, Wisconsin, when he came to visit my father. He worked on the Fort Pierre-to-Deadwood Trail. He painted the job in a mighty rosy hue. So, I decided to give it a try and stuck with it for almost ten years."

Tom smiled. "Where ya headin' now?"

"I'm heading back to Denver. From Omaha. My older sister died, and I was there for her burial."

"May she rest in peace," Tom said. A long pause. "What do you do in Denver?"

"I got myself a provisions shop there. After I quit bull-whackin', I settled down and worked on a cattle ranch for a while, then opened a small hardware store in Omaha. When my wife died, I sold the store and moved to Denver, startin' over there."

"Business good, Mr. Pinsker?" Emmett asked.

"Call me Jed. ... Son, in Denver, suppliers of any sort

can't keep up with demand. That town is swelling faster 'n a cowboy's cock at the sight of a naked whore."

The whistle blew, and the three men clambered back up into their car. Their conversation continued for a moment inside. The older man finally said, "I assume you boys are spending the night in Cheyenne?"

"Yes sir," Tom replied.

"Let's reconnect when we get there, and I'll show you fellas around."

Emmett stopped Jed. ""Beg your pardon a moment, Jed. I'd wager you've seen your fair share of scrapes and bruises. What's your take—should I seek out a doctor in Cheyenne for this gash over me eye?""

"That's a real cut you got. Let me get a better look at it." Jed moved closer and inspected Emmett's brow. "Nah. I don't reckon there's much to be done about it at this point. But you'll have yourself quite a trophy scar there to credit you for whatever trouble you got into."

Chapter Six

Being small, distant, and the color of their surroundings, the pronghorn antelope easily had escaped their attention previously. But now that Tom and Emmett had been sensitized to their presence on the high plains, they noticed lots of them—sometimes in herds of twenty or thirty—and pointed them out to each other. They spotted coyotes, too. Always alone, always slinking away at a stealthy canter from the train—shy, and looking as if they were ashamed to have been spotted.

Everyone in their car was abuzz with excitement at seeing the mountains. Tom and Emmett got swept up in the anticipation and joined in the lookout. Heads stuck out of windows and bodies swung out from the platforms. One boy cried out, "There they are!" But what he'd seen was merely a bank of dark clouds. Several more false alarms sounded before the mountains truly appeared—a solemn line of blue peaks, white at the top, with masses of vapor breaking over them.

As they reached the outskirts of Cheyenne, the young men were surprised that the town appeared far more substantial than any they'd been through since Omaha. It was well laid-out, with good wide streets, and building going on everywhere they looked. Cheyenne was as far as they could continue on this rail line. Tomorrow morning, they'd have to take a different railroad heading south from Cheyenne to Denver.

When the engine pulled to a stop, they gathered their belongings and stepped out to the surprisingly impressive train station, where they gawked at a boodle of people that seemed a most curious mixture: fastidiously dressed tourists from New York and Boston; long-bearded, sleepy-looking miners with blue shirts and trousers tucked into their high boots; Chinamen with bamboo hats, like inverted wash-bowls; aggressive young cattlemen from the ranches farther north; amiable-looking Indians, draped in blankets of scarlet and blue.

Jedediah came up behind them. "I assume you boys haven't a baldy notion where you're bedding down for the night."

"You'd be right," Tom said.

"Follow me. We'll head to the Eagle Hotel. I've stayed there a number of times, and it's mighty commodious."

Outside the station, Tom and Emmett couldn't get over what a large and agreeable town Cheyenne was. Would you look at this!" Tom marveled. "I didn't expect even Denver to be this grand, much less the city of Cheyenne in Wyoming!"

Jed said, "I tell ya, boys, it's fuckin' amazin'. Twenty years ago, this town was a puckered little arsehole. Now look at it. It's got everything, even a goddamn opera house." He paused and ran his fingers down the sides of his long beard. "Most important, though, it's got the principal car shops for the entire Union Pacific railroad. When the city signed that contract with UP, it put itself on the map, changed itself from a little shit-hole into this. Otherwise mighta ended up like Julesburg." He swept his arm in a broad arc. "As I say, fuckin' amazin'."

After they'd dropped off their gear in their rooms, the three joined up again. Jedediah said, "I don't know how experienced you fellas are in the ways of the West. But my guess is you've got some learnin' to do. So, listen up. Here's an important thing to know, especially in a town like this: don't look a stranger in the eye for long. Don't stare. Starin' at a man is likely to invite a bad fight or worse. Just keep your eyes movin' around. Don't alight on anyone in particular. If you catch someone's eye by accident, look away."

Emmett found this advice curious. "Why's that, Jed?"

"Can't rightly say why. It's just the way it is. Folks out here accept each other, no matter how different in look, dress, or other aspect. A stare implies there's something wrong with its object. That's disrespectful. Insulting. So, make no curious stares. Them's not wise. That's near as I can come to an explanation. But don't doubt the truth of what I'm sayin'."

"Thank ya for the advice."

They went into a gamblin' saloon familiar to Jedediah. The older man ordered a whiskey, his two companions beers.

They took their drinks over to watch the doin's. Some of the gamblers played cards. Others stood over a small billiard table of some sort, playing a game they called rondo. Elsewhere, men placed bets at roulette wheels. Tom couldn't fathom why folks would bet at games like this that hung on pure chance. To him, that made little sense. He said so to Jedediah.

"Son, you make a good point. I guess them kind of games offer an even playing field. You don't need no skill, so anybody can win. Most of them have few rules, and even them's is basic. So, a man can jump in with no experience and still have a chance at victory against other players or the dealer. Plus, a fella doesn't need to be in the best mental or physical shape to play. Whether you had a hard day in a silver mine or on a cattle ranch, whether you're in low cotton or loop-legged drunk—none of that matters. It don't affect the outcome of a game of pure chance."

Tom watched the men casually tossing their money around, as if they had plenty to spare. There was a certain nonchalant daring about them, a trait often attributed to Westerners. He found it curious how in this world of gamblers, appearances gave nothing away. Whether decked out like a bandit or dressed to the nines, all of them were equally eager to stake their cash.Jedediah resumed his commentary.

Jedediah continued. "Now, if you like games of pure skill —I'm thinkin', say, checkers or chess—you'd better be in top mental condition when you take on an opponent. And those games are exhaustin', both while you're playing and afterwards, worrying whether you're making the right choice or thinkin' about the bone-headed moves you made."

He then pointed to the multiple tables of poker players. "Then you have popular games like poker, which are a mix of skill and chance. If ya want to win at poker, you need to develop certain skills—like readin' other players, or carryin' out specific strategies, or understandin' how particular combinations of cards may affect the outcome. When I was younger, I was partial to poker for all them reasons. Now, in my wiser years, I'm content with pure games of chance because there's less likelihood of a fight breakin' out over 'em."

Just then, players at one of the poker tables leaped to their feet in alarm as one of the men loudly claimed another was "a cheatin' son of a bitch." The accused man stood to protest the allegation, and the first man cracked him over the head with a beer bottle. He went down in a flash. A couple of cards stuck out of his sleeve. "There's proof the fucker's a swindler!"

The downed man's companions carried his motionless form out of the saloon, and in short order activities resumed throughout the room. Tom said, "I wouldn't be surprised if that blow killed him. Fractured his skull."

"Might well have done," said Jedediah. "But that there's frontier justice! Nobody'd dream of chargin' the assailant. It's like we used to do: hang horse thieves without botherin' to take 'em to the sheriff first. A fella doesn't last long out west if he's caught stealin'—or cheatin' at poker. And few will blame the man who takes it upon himself to deliver a punishment." Emmett found all this exhilarating. He liked the idea of swift justice, delivered directly by the aggrieved. Chicago could benefit from some of that!

"Finish your beers, boys. We're movin' on," Jedediah said, throwing back the rest of his whiskey. The trio made their way down the street to another establishment. After ordering whiskeys for each of them, Jed turned to them. "This here's a keno room. Keno is a gambling game that originated in the Far East. Chinese workers who helped construct the transcontinental railroad introduced keno to towns along the route. Men in Cheyenne are absolutely crazy about it."

They stepped into the elongated, narrow room, dazzlingly illuminated at the far end where the tables were situated, while the opposite end remained shrouded in darkness. The room was occupied by at least fifty men, with around two dozen actively engaged in the game. A significant number of them were visibly under the influence of alcohol. The air was filled with a cacophony of oaths and curses.

Tom was awestruck by the scene before him. One man sported diamond studs and what appeared to be a pricey French silk hat, yet he wore no shirt collar. The adjacent man was clad entirely in leather, adorned with a sizable gold ring and a chain. For comfort, he had removed one boot and rested his bare foot on the table. Jedediah noticed the leather-clad man casting a piercing glance in their direction. Turning, he caught Tom staring at the man. "What did I tell you, son? A stare like that will land you in trouble." Tom promptly averted his gaze, and the man in leather let the matter slide.

Just then, a tremendous clatter started up at the front of the establishment. Sounded like men throwing handfuls of birdshot at the mirror behind the bar. That made no sense. The three men went to see what was happening. "Ah. Just as I thought," Jed said. "We've got ourselves a 'Cheyenne zephyr,' boys!"

"What the hell?" Tom exclaimed, as sand pelted the building's front windows. The rattle was unlike anything he'd ever heard.

"It's a gravel storm. A sand-auger," Jed said. "Fierce winds pick up the dirt and sand, hurling it around so hard and fast it could kill a man. And has done!" Even during lulls when pebbles weren't strafing the windows, lighter sand still did. Emmett marveled that the window glass was able to withstand the onslaught. He commented to that effect and Jed replied, "Yes, glaziers are mighty busy tradesmen in the wake of storms like this." Eventually, the winds died down. The men had another drink, then headed back to their hotel.

Jed lifted his hand, all bone and sinew, to his face. He spread his thumb and index finger and ran them down the sides of his mouth, smoothing his mustache into his beard and dislodging some sand in the process. "You boys are dreadful good company. I enjoyed the evening with you. But this old bull-whacker's not the late-night carouser he once was. And the train to Denver leaves pretty fuckin' early in the morning. So, I'm gonna take my leave now and see ya then."

Chapter Seven

The mountain range formed what looked like a massive, impregnable wall, with a saw-like top edge, silvered with snow in places, even in late summer. The train passengers stared wide-eyed at the peaks as they glided by them on the high plain. The gradual appearance of industrial activity announced the approach to Denver. Soon, the number of rail roads multiplied until there were too many to count, and within moments the train pulled into Denver's Union Depot.

Alice and Nora were full of excitement but also trepidation. This was a whole new life they'd taken up. What would it be like? Would they be able to make a go of it? Nora, already having some experience in America, had fewer fears than Alice did, but both felt uneasiness about what lay ahead. After they disembarked, they found themselves walking through the station almost side by side with the two young men they'd encountered at the North Platte stop.

"Hello, ladies," the taller of the two men said. "I hope you enjoyed your journey from Cheyenne,"

Alice wasn't eager to engage in conversation, but didn't want to be impolite. "We did. Thank you."

Emmett leaned forward so that he could see around Tom and catch the girls' eyes. "Are you staying in Denver or passing through?"

"We intend to settle here," Alice replied. "And you?"

"Us, too."

"Perhaps we'll see each other again. Good day." Nora said, then pulled Alice by the arm and led her off toward a different exit.

"Why did you do that? They were being polite." Alice said.

"I don't like the looks of them. They're not the kind of men we want to associate with at the start of our new life in Denver. We'll set our caps for a higher class of men."

They stepped outside into bright, hot sunshine. Stretching before them, as far as they could see in the three directions open to view, was a city dense with brick buildings —mostly three to five stories tall, but some, in the distance, eight to ten. Looking sharply to their left or right, they saw smokestacks of industrial enterprises spewing dark coal smoke. The sounds of streetcars, electric cablecars, coaches, wagons, and carriages filled the air. Pedestrians hailed each other with greetings of familiarity. People bustled and hustled in every direction.

Alice and Nora gaped at the scene. "I had no idea it was going to be this big, this prosperous," Nora said.

"I didn't know at all what to expect. Certainly not this!"

A short, thin man approached them. He had dark, beady eyes, close together as an earthworm's. "Hello, ladies! Welcome to Denver! Is this your first time here?"

"'Tis," Nora said.

Talking a mile a minute, the man said, "Let me welcome ya to Denver! The Queen City of the West! I see ya have luggage with you. Where would ya be heading in town? Will ya be needing a boarding house? You've—"

"We're—" Nora tried to interrupt him, but he talked right over her.

"—happened on the right person. I have a carriage here and can easily and cheaply convey you to several different nearby boarding houses so you can inspect each for its suitability to your needs."

"That's kind of you, Mr. …"

"Jones. Franklin Jones, miss. At your service."

He started to pick up their bags, when the two young men from the train appeared again at their side. They stepped in front of the thin man, stopping his progress. Emmett said to the women, "We found a carriage for the four of us, and we can drop you off at the Home for Working Women. The telegram from Aunt Margaret said that's where you should stay."

The scraggly man protested at the intrusion of the two young men who now towered over him. "Now, wait a minute, you two. I'm taking care of these women. You stay out of it." If he'd been able to watch this scene unfold from a distance, he might have realized how laughable his protest was. Unless he had a gun, he had little chance of prevailing against these two robust young men.

Emmett turned on the man and broadened his shoulders like a hawk spreading its wings. "Mister, I suggest you skedaddle." The man didn't move. "Git!" Emmett barked. "Before I beat you senseless or hail a police officer to cart your conniving carcass away."

At that, the man looked around nervously, put the ladies' bags down, and hurried away.

"What do you think you're doing?" Nora said to Emmett, her voice dripping with indignation.

"We're saving you from a swindling, or worse."

"Whatever do you mean?"

Emmett said, "We're thinkin' that fella's a right chancer, a shark. His sort are always skulkin' about train stations in every big city 'cross the land, lying in wait to pounce on the green and the unwary. They'll sweet talk you with promises of cheap fares to wherever it is you're headed, or offer to sort you out with a place to kip if you're still on the fence. And then, before you know it, they've lifted your wallet and everything else you own, or worse, they've handed you off to one of their cronies, who'll fleece and bamboozle you till you haven't got two pennies to rub together."

The women were flabbergasted. Alice tried to speak, but nothing came out. Finally, she asked, "What was that nonsense about a telegram from Aunt Margaret?"

"I wanted to convince the man that we were with you and weren't about to be put off from accompanying you where you were going."

"And the 'Home for Working Women'?"

"When we saw that man approach you, we suspected he was a gouger, so I asked that policeman over there for the name of a good boarding house for newly arrived young women."

Alice stepped forward. "Thank you, Mr. ..."

"Kelly. Emmett Kelly. And this is my friend, Tom Quinn. And whom do we have the pleasure of meeting now on more friendly terms?"

"I'm Alice Butler, and this is my sister, Nora."

Tom took off his cap. "Pleased to meet you both."

Nora was still amazed by this intervention. "Would you tell us how you know about these schemes?"

Emmett said, "I've read news reports of such things in the Chicago newspapers. The police there issue warnings to residents to be wary when they travel."

"Thank you for coming to our rescue," Alice said.

With a gleam in her eye, Nora teased. "How do we know you two aren't the real fraudsters?"

Emmett smiled. "You don't, of course. Perhaps you'll have to trust us." He turned to Tom. "What do you think? Should they bank on us?"

"Me, they can trust. I'm not so sure about you." He made this comment in a joking manner and the other three took it that way. But it was, in fact, an honest statement: Tom Quinn did have an uneasy feeling about Emmett Kelly. He couldn't put his finger on why. But it was there.

Chapter Eight

As the taxi carriage conveyed them from Union Depot to Capitol Hill, Nora and Alice couldn't get over the broad, clean streets; the sophisticated electric-streetcar system; the impressive civic buildings; the elegant residences with handsome shade trees; and the tall mountains, visible from almost any vantage. Cement sidewalks lined every street they saw. Bright, green turf on either side of the walk enhanced many of the streets and avenues. Together with long, straight lines of trees, the grass formed an agreeable feature of the city's landscape. "Sweet Jesus! Would you look at all this!" Alice hadn't expected Denver to be this grand.

Thankfully, Nor and Alice weren't heading to some incommodious rooming house for women. Nora's friend from Boston, Bridget Gleeson, had made it to Denver a month earlier and initially had stayed at one such place. She'd written to Nora about the dreariness of living cheek by jowl with others, the scant furnishings, the utter lack of charm. Bridget had soon lucked into alternate accommodation—room and board in a private home. She wrote to Nora about a similar arrangement she'd learned about at the home of an older Irish couple, John and Mary Flannery, at the corner of 17th and Logan Street on Capitol Hill. At Bridget's urging, Nora had immediately contacted the Flannerys and arranged to let a room in their home.

When the taxi carriage arrived at the Flannerys', Mary Flannery greeted Alice and Nora enthusiastically. She was a woman of about fifty, large without being fat. Her forearms and hands showed a fine play of muscle and tendon, suggestive of time spent with the washtub and the rolling pin. Her face was broad, with large features, barely lined by wrinkles, and beaming with shrewd good humor.

Mary showed them to their room and told them to take their time freshening up after such a long train ride. Exhausted as she was, Alice was nonetheless excited by what she was seeing. She marveled at the quality of the house construction, the fine furnishings and appointments, all the decorative touches and comforts, the electric lights and gas stove. "Nora, is this what normal people's houses are like in America?"

"I don't know. I can't say. The only private American homes I've been in were those owned by my rich employers, those are much nicer even than this," Nora said. "But I agree with you that this is surprisingly comfortable and enchanting. This puts Ireland in bad light. And this is a frontier town!"

When the girls emerged from their room forty minutes later, their hostess greeted them each with a small glass of applejack brandy to soothe their "train-rattled nerves," and to put them in the frame of mind for an evening of good talk. Linens, china, silver, and fine glassware graced the dinner table. "Oh, my goodness," Nora said, "I hope you didn't go to all this trouble for us."

Mary smiled. "I must admit I don't pull out all the stops like this every day. Don't be thinkin' this is our normal way of dinin'. But my instincts tell me you two girls could use a treat after your long journey."

Alice looked over the beautifully set table. "We're much obliged, ma'am."

"Please call me Mary, girls."

"'Mary,' it is, then. ... I'd love to ask you a question, Alice said.

"Feel free to ask me whatever you like."

"Is this a typical American home? ... I mean ... It's so much grander than the way most people live in Ireland. And I know this is 'the land of opportunity,' but—"

Mary laughed. "I know what you're saying, Alice. I don't know for sure what 'most' American homes are like. It's a big country, and I've seen only bits of it. But I think things are changing so fast in America that a house like this is more and more typical."

Her eyes wide and her brows arched, Alice looked at Nora. "Janey Mac!"

When Mr. Flannery returned home from work, the four of them settled down to a remarkable meal—a great platter of roasted chicken, mashed and sweet potatoes, peas and turnips, sliced tomatoes and hot biscuits, with a beautiful red jelly, two kinds of preserves and two kinds of pickle.

Mary passed Mr. Flannery a glass of brandy and he gave her a grateful smile before turning his attention to the girls. "Well, now, I hope you're finding everything to your liking?" he inquired, raising his glass to them.

Nora, her mouth already full of mashed potatoes and gravy, eagerly nodded. "It's all so delicious, thank you!"

"I'm glad to hear it," Mr. Flannery replied with a grin. "Mary's cooking is top-notch, isn't it?"

Alice nodded in agreement, her green eyes sparkling with appreciation. "Absolutely. We feel like we've been transported to a fancy banquet."

As they ate, Mary regaled the girls with stories of her own journey to America about forty years earlier and how she met Mr. Flannery. She also told them tales of raising their three rambunctious children in Denver, including a particularly amusing anecdote about their younger son getting stung on the nose by a bee when playing mumbledypeg. That story reminded Alice of the incident in North Platte where the young man from the train killed the prairie dog with a thrown knife.

Mr. Flannery chuckled heartily and said, "Well, you two are in for quite an adventure here in America. There are lots of men in Denver, and not all of them are refined." He wiped his mouth with a napkin and smiled. "And I must warn you, dear girls, that my wife can be quite the protector. She'll be watching over you like a hawk, keepin' a wary eye on any young fellas who come knocking at our door."

Mary playfully swatted her husband's arm and protested, "Oh, hush now, John Flannery! I merely want to make sure the young women who stay with us are safe and happy, No need for any nonsense from boys who might come around."

Mr. Flannery laughed again and winked at Nora and Alice. "What Mary regards as 'nonsense' from boys may be different from what you two regard as such."

Alice now laughed and said, "There won't be any lads coming around here for us any time soon. Besides, we'll have our hands full finding work and getting settled."

Nora said, "Oh, I hope that's not true, Alice. I wouldn't mind a fella coming around. And I wouldn't mind puttin' up with a bit of nonsense."

John Flannery laughed heartily at that, but Mary Flannery's grew stern. She held up her hand to secure the girls' full attention before speaking in a low, measured tone. "Nora, my dear girl, you mustn't go wishin' for trouble now. Menfolk can bring both joy and heartache, and sometimes it's hard to tell which is comin' your way."

Alice felt a shiver run down her spine at Mary's words, wonderin' at the truth in them.

Chapter Nine

Emmett and Tom had found lodging at a rooming house in a neighborhood called Auraria, south of the confluence of Cherry Creek and the South Platte River. The rooming house was a dreary place. The smoke from the railroads left a constant haze on the windows, the rooms were as bare as a barn, and not a hint of privacy was to be had. But it was dirt cheap.

The surrounding area had suffered a devastating flood a few years earlier. Many residents and businesses had left the neighborhood, making it affordable for new migrants like them. Its remaining buildings were mean brick structures two or four stories high, their flat, dirty faces set flush with the sidewalk. The neighbors included three-cent lunch counters, other rooming houses, Chinese laundries and shops, gipsy fortune-telling booths, petty drug stores, and about two saloons to the block.

And, as Emmett and Tom had been told, the job opportunities in the city proved endless. Within a couple days of their arrival, they felt overwhelmed by the options they'd already encountered. Jobs were to be had in smelting, meat-packing, sugar refining, residential construction, the building of infrastructure (streetcar lines, municipal water and sewer, telephone), mills of various sorts (flour, pottery, brick, paper, cotton), ice houses, machine works, a boot and shoe factory. And they understood those to be only a portion of the choices available.

Tom immediately found work as a carpenter, the demand for such tradesmen being extraordinary in this booming town where there was new construction everywhere in sight. Emmett took the first job he came across—at a brewery. His immediate concern was simply to find steady income, no matter how low. All he needed at the start was assurance of some money coming in; he had no intention of getting by on the income from employment alone. He kept constant lookout for ways to supplement—indeed, far surpass—that income.

The first time that he sent out his laundry through the regular channels provided by the rooming house, he noticed that the bill for it was higher than he'd have paid at any of the nearby Chinese laundries. He guessed that the residence's manager made a slight profit on the house laundry as a return for gathering it up and distributing it again.

Sensing a money-making opportunity, Emmett made a canvass of nearby laundries and found one that was willing to do work at a low rate on a poundage basis provided he turned in at least fifty pounds a week. He at once organized a laundry syndicate at the rooming house, and took away from the rooming-house management nearly one-half of its laundry business. This enabled him to earn about five dollars a week in a single afternoon's effort. The housemaster investigated and found out what had happened, but had no real recourse. The men had a right to send their laundry where they pleased. Emmett had made an enemy of the housemaster, but that didn't bother him in the least.

Neither Tom nor Emmett liked being at the gloomy, barren rooming house during their scant hours of evening leisure each day. So, Tom usually headed out to be with carpenter friends or exploring the city on his own. For his part, Emmett, was intent on finding a way to make his evenings profitable by spending them in a nearby billiards hall. He made a careful study of the regular patrons of the place, and identified all of those whom he was sure he could beat before he ever offered to play a game. He always played rather badly at first, so as to encourage his victim, and always won by a spurt at the end of the game.

Emmett soon discovered another profitable evening destination that quickly became one of his favorite haunts: The Larimer Lunch. This establishment, while not the most refined of Denver's lunch rooms, boasted a modest charm with its half a dozen white-topped tables, a small steam table, and a counter displaying an assortment of slowly withering delicacies. The glass case showcased an array of pastries, including case-hardened doughnuts that patrons enjoyed dunking in their hot coffee.

Behind the counter stood two impressive nickel-plated urns, one for coffee and the other for hot water, along with a milk tank equipped with a long-handled dipper. The window

44

display featured inviting piles of oranges and grapefruit, flanked by vibrant rubber plants in green wooden buckets. The latest news from *The Denver Post* hung prominently on the wall, while the room was adorned with well-used spittoons, as smoking was permitted and widely practiced by the patrons. Although the food at The Larimer Lunch was satisfactory, with ham and eggs, baked beans, beef stew, and coffee comparable to other lunch rooms in town, it wasn't the culinary offerings that kept drawing Emmett back.

The true allure of The Larimer Lunch lay in its role as a social institution for the local community, particularly the livery drivers and policemen who frequented the establishment for their suppers. This small, tight-knit group had been gathering for years, fostering a warm atmosphere of camaraderie. Discussions about horse races, baseball, and prize fights were commonplace, with bets being made and stories shared. Occasionally, tables would be pushed aside to make room for a lively crap game on the floor, usually with a modest five-cent limit. Even when fights broke out, the losers typically remained good-natured, borrowing streetcar fare and cigarettes from the winners. Emmett quickly found his place within this social circle,his engaging storytelling and enthusiastic dice-rolling, complete with colorful language, endearing him to his new companions. At The Larimer Lunch, Emmett had discovered a place where he belonged.

Chapter Ten

By the end of his first month in Denver, Emmett had already had two different jobs. He'd left the brewery to take a job in a pickle cannery. Although both jobs left him pungent after a day's work, neither was as bad as the hog line at the Armour plant back home, which truly left him with a lingering stench. And he didn't mind the work. Compared to his most recent employment, the jobs seemed to him ridiculously easy. Tom liked to torment Emmett about the pickle job, asking him why he didn't want a "manly occupation" rather than "standing all day next to aproned women in a pickle plant." At first, Emmett had found the taunt amusing, but over time it rankled.

One day after work, Emmett noticed a posting on a telephone pole near the boarding house. It advertised an opportunity at the Marquis Canning Company for a "capper and tipper." He'd watched others do that work at the pickle plant, so knew how to do it. The ad said the job would pay $2.00 per day, which was more than he now earned.

What's more, Marquis was close by—across the South Platte in the Colfax neighborhood, southeast of the Highlands. Emmett checked his pocket watch. He figured there might still be someone there. It was an easy walk, though he could hop on a cable car, if one came by. Fifteen minutes later, he stood outside the handsome new three-story Marquis building. Nearby, he could see, was a store called Röhr's Meat Market and Grocery. And stretching out in both directions were a variety of other businesses—where one could buy dry goods, boots, drugs, furniture, and one could obtain the services of realtors, bankers, printers, and undertakers. A vibrant commercial area.

Emmett knocked on the Marquis door, waited a moment, then pounded harder. A man in his sixties swept the walk in front of the meat market nearby. He said, "I think they's all gone home for the day. Whatcha lookin' for?"

"I came to see about a job they posted a notice for."

The man regarded him. "You're lookin' for work, eh?"

"I have a job now. I'm just wantin' somethin' different. And better payin'."

"So happens I'm lookin' to hire a man. I'm Oskar Röhr." He reached out to shake

Emmett's hand. "What's your name, son?"

"I'm Emmett Kelly, sir."

"Come into the store. I'll get you a beer and we can talk. You drink beer, don't ya?"

"I sure do, Mr. Röhr."

"Call me Oskar." He led Emmett into the market, where the sawdust on the floor was still to be swept up.

"What kind of help you lookin' for?"

"As you can see, meat ain't the only thing we have in here. I'm now sellin' all sorts of things including canned foods and fresh fruits and vegetables. I'm gettin' busier, and the extra hands I have now ain't enough to keep up with the work. I need help with all kinds of things. A little of this, a little of that: keeping items in stock and on the shelves; helping customers; tracking sales; sweepin' and cleanin'; taking the buckboard to get supplies and goods that don't get delivered; cuttin' meat; dealin' with carcasses. As I say, all sorts of things."

All the jobs Emmett had had to this point had involved performing repetitive tasks all day long. The job he'd gone up to the Highlands to pursue at Marquis canning—a capper and tipper—would've mean the same kind of mindless labor, hour after hour. But this position at Röhr's market was one with much more variety to it. Emmett couldn't calculate how much the thought of a job like that pleased him.

Oskar watched the wheels turning in the boys' head boy as he drank his beer, and asked, "The 'dealing with carcasses' throw you off? If so, you wouldn't be the first. I've had lots of men wave off a job offer when they hear they've gotta do that."

Emmett laughed. "No sir. That don't bother me. I came here from Chicago, where I worked the past three years at a meat-packin' plant. I can deal with carcasses."

"What animals ya work with?"

"Hogs, mostly."

"We got fresh pork here. Whatever cut ya want. We also got dried pork—hams, bacon, salt meat. And, as you can see, we also got beef, chicken, mutton, and more. You'd be branchin' out! You good with a knife?"

"The best." Emmett smiled. "What would ya be payin'?"

Oskar Röhr regarded the boy. "I reckon I could pay you $2.25 a day."

Emmett about fainted. That was a dollar more than he was earning now. Income like that would make a huge difference in his life. But he remembered another bit of advice Jedediah had imparted to him and Tom in Cheyenne: "Always push hard when you deal with an employer. They'll try to underpay you. That's their concern. Your responsibility is to push them for more. Don't let any man take ya for a fool."

Emmett looked Mr. Röhr in the eye. "And I reckon I could do a job requiring so many different tasks and skills for $2.50 a day."

Oskar laughed. "I'll soon go broke if I pay ya at that rate. But let's give it a try." He extended his hand to Emmett for a shake. "I should warn ya that I don't countenance theft of any sort. If I catch ya stealin' from me in any way, I'll have ya arrested or I'll cut your hand off. Probably the latter. And don't think I wouldn't."

Emmett shook the old man's hand. "You can trust me, Oskar. I'm an honest fella. When can I start?"

"Monday. Be here at 6 in the morning."

After leaving Oskar Röhr, Emmett considered heading to Larimer Lunch for some companionship and gambling. But he was hungry and felt like being alone. He stopped in a little place called the White Café, which lived up to its name with a white tiled floor and white enameled tables and resembled the operating room of a hospital. It was manned by a single morose-looking Greek, who shouted Emmett's order through a little window and presently handed him across the counter, in exchange for five cents, two egg sandwiches and a mug of weak but steaming coffee.

As Emmett devoured his food, he paged through a magazine an earlier patron had left behind. He always relished magazine advertisements more than the articles. In particular, he enjoyed the long and eloquent advertisements for for correspondence courses and other methods of self-improvement. These were his favorite reading because he regarded them as such humorous buncombe.

They told how common men like himself had risen to wealth and fame. "You can do it too," they assured him. There was no career—from chiropodist to xylophonist—they did not offer him. There was no handicap they could not help him overcome. Was he a boorish fellow? They would teach him the secrets of etiquette so that he might mingle with peers and millionaires without reproach. Did he lack conversation? They would fit him to talk of more diverse things than anyone ever thought of. Did he wish to entertain? They would teach him to play the piano by ear in ninety days. Was he a puny fellow? They would show him how to grow bulging muscles like the pictured man with the leopard skin about his middle. Did he lack power in the crucial tests of love? They would endow him with puissant and fertile loins. Cogently, plausibly, offering proof to all and money back to the dissatisfied, they preached that a resolute man may make himself over in the image of power and success.

Yes, the image! That's what most appealed to Emmett about the approaches offered in these advertised courses. Their common lesson was this: one need not be a good man or a smart man or a particularly skilled man to succeed; one need only equip oneself with the accoutrements of success, the veneer of it. Image is everything, and reality bends to it.

But Emmett believed there was another element to success, too. No great man ever got to the top on brains or effort alone. They schemed and connived and stepped on others to get there. To him, that was the only path. And only the wisest of men recognized that.

He often argued with Tom Quinn about the path to success of America's great men. Tom would say, "Look at any of the big men in this country. Look at Rockefeller, Andrew Carnegie, Thomas Edison ... What were they? They were ordinary poor fellows, and they worked hard and studied and saved money and used common sense. That's all there is to it."

Emmett would laugh at what he regarded as Tom's naivete. "Go on, go on! Next, you'll be telling me that if I lay on my belly in front of the fire at night and study hard for years, I'll become a great man like Abraham Lincoln. ... Can't you see that you might lie on your belly and study till the floor wore out under you, and you wouldn't be any more of an Abraham Lincoln than you are now? And it wouldn't make a darn bit of difference what you studied either? It's all a matter of luck, cunning, and manipulation of others. 'Honest Abe!' Ha! I'll bet ya' a deuce that 'Deceptive Abe' or 'Deceitful Abe' would have been the more appropriate moniker!"

Tom would shake his head at this, saddened by his friend's attitude.

Chapter Eleven

In the stripping room, Nora was one of about eighty women, each parked at their own identical work stall. The light barely skimmed the surface of the expansive, square room, not that it mattered much. The work was so mind-numbingly repetitive, you could almost do it with your eyes closed. Ten hours a day, Nora sat in her stall, leaned against a piece of rough board, her lap full of tobacco. She'd pull out the stem from a leaf, throw it on a scale, then tie it when she had a pound. She had to be careful to cut the stem without tearing the rest of the leaf, but aside from that, the work was easy. She often thought that a monkey could do it.

Even if the setup allowed for chatter, Nora doubted her workmates would have much of interest to offer. Glancing around, she observed a mosaic of women—various ages, some a little stupid, others not quite at the top of their game, be it due to poor eyesight, a physical quirk, or otherwise physically below the standard strength and dexterity required to keep pace with a machine. That's why most of them worked there, where no machinery was to be seen.

The pay was lousy. The air was heavy from the nicotine exhaled by the mellowing leaves, and thick with the dust of pulverized scrap and brittle edges. And there was constant pressure from the supervisor to strip more pounds of tobacco each day. All of those were reasons behind Nora's decision to leave that job and find different work. When she picked up her week's pay on a Saturday evening, Nora told her supervisor she would not return Monday morning.

But that meant finding another job. For the next few days, she walked the streets of downtown Denver, checking for help-wanted signs. She scanned the newspapers for employment notices. Nothing appealed to her. A chance conversation with a girl her age on a streetcar got her thinking about working as a shop girl.

Eager to pursue the idea, Nora asked her, "Where should I try?"

"Try the two biggest first—Denver Dry Goods and the May Company. You might have to start out as a cash girl or a wrapper." Appraising Nora more closely, and noting her long legs and natural S-curved torso, added, "But I bet you'll be a shop girl in no time. … Oh, this is my stop. Got to go. Good luck to you!"

The idea held enormous appeal to Nora. She knew that Denver's shops and stores were every bit as varied and cosmopolitan as those in Boston or New York, fully equal to those cities in the range of luxury merchandise available, including the finest furniture and fabrics, all the latest fashions. Plus, there was better social status accorded to shop girls than to women who worked in factories.

The next morning, Nora took extra time working on her hair and her general appearance. She decided to try for the popular Gibson Girl look. She already had the figure, the youthful features, and the ephemeral beauty. She figured she could pull off the rest, so she worked her auburn hair into an elaborate pompadour. She dressed in her nicest shirtwaist and trim skirt, her best shoes and overcoat. She regarded herself in the mirror and concluded she was ready to start her new life as a young woman working in the commercial trades.

She showed up at the Denver Dry Goods employment office on California Street in search of a job as a shop girl. Just as the young woman on the streetcar had predicted, they hired her as a wrapper. But the hiring officer said, "With your height and your attractiveness, you'll be a shop girl before long if you're a good worker." And that turned out to be true.

But over time, Nora's earnings disappointed her. The low pay was a favorite topic of conversation among the shop girls, and there were multiple theories among them as to its cause. Maddie Johnson claimed the employers assumed the girls were only partly self-supporting and needed the work only for pin money. "But that's true of only a few of us," Nora protested.

Emma Norquist and Minnie Benson had theories that dovetailed and supported one another. Emma said, "Lots of girls want this job because it has a higher social position than that of factory or domestic work. So we lose because folks in this society are startin' to go crazy in their desire for social esteem. The bosses offer low wages because there's no shortage of girls ready to take the job if one of us leaves. Usually, there's a waiting list."

Whatever the cause of the low pay, it was undeniably true that for the vast bulk of sales girls, the wages paid weren't sufficient for self-support. Lucky were those girls who had families they could fall back on. Others went undernourished.

Nora was shocked one day when the conversation turned to how some of the girls supplemented their income by selling themselves. She hadn't thought of it before, but once the other girls laid out the facts for her, she felt foolish for not noticing what was going on around her. How obvious! Employment in a mercantile house meant lots of opportunities. The larger stores were in the busiest part of downtown, so the girls found it easy on their breaks to meet men.

"Is this mere gossip, or do you know of girls who've seized such opportunities to make extra money?"

"Remember Martha?" Minnie asked, eliciting nods from the others. She turned to Nora. "Martha worked at the ribbon counter at four dollars a week. She had a mother and two sisters who were dependent upon her, and her mother was always pushing her for more money. So, Nora began to 'make money on the side.'"

Emma spoke up. "Gert's another example. She used to work here as a sales girl. A man used to come in to chat with her. After they'd been seeing each other a while, he offered to set her up in an apartment on Capitol Hill. She accepted, and now she's a kept woman, but still works as a sales girl over at the May."

Minnie nodded. "And over at the May, the employers not only seem to tolerate girls who sell themselves in one way or another, but they encourage it. It allows them to keep the wages low."

Nora couldn't imagine how bad things would have to get for her to contemplate following such a path. She hoped never to reach that point. But as she thought about her own loneliness and the prospect of spending another Saturday night alone, she couldn't help but wonder if a little extra income might be worth the company of a gentleman caller. After all, a girl had needs—and if those needs weren't being met, well, who could blame her for getting creative?

Chapter Twelve

Saturdays were the one night each week when Emmett and Tom reliably spent the evening together. They had a standardized program of dissipation they followed—the same sort followed by millions of other American men every Saturday night, just as regularly as many of them went to church the next morning. Tom and Emmett would wander among the saloons and cafés, drinking beer or whiskey, gambling a bit, until about eleven o'clock, and then adjourn to Denver's tenderloin district, centered at Twentieth and Market streets, where the brothels were so plentiful they crowded one another out.

Every door and window seemed to have its own sentinel —a woman either leaning casually against a frame or peering out. These women were a mixed bag: some looked like they should be in school, all fresh-faced and naive, while others wore their years and wild nights like badges, makeup caked on in an attempt to cover up. Dress code varied from the somber in black shifts and nude stockings to the whimsical, sporting bleach-blonde curls, donning frocks that would fit better in a schoolyard and socks to match. By day, the scene was merely sordid. But at night, the street had a sinister beauty; a hideous lust impregnated the air, intense and mysterious.

Tom displayed a somewhat reluctant attitude toward these Saturday night expeditions. He almost always went along, but sought to create the impression that he was interested chiefly as a professional observer of life who must not overlook its seamy side. Emmett, by contrast, was frankly enthusiastic and eager. So, on these Saturday nights, when he and Tom had their fill of drink (and Emmett, of gambling), they would join the bands of other tipsy revelers, roaming from house to house, often turned away from the doors for lack of room.

In time, they came to give their patronage mostly to one establishment, known as Mrs. Barker's, which had an especially good reputation for its cleanliness and order. Its proprietress was an extremely able woman, well past sixty years of age. With her bony frame, severe grey hair and spectacles, she bore an incongruous resemblance to a stage representation of a New England spinster. She was proud of the reputation of her establishment and of the police protection it enjoyed, and she ruled her ten girls as strictly as though they had been the inmates of a house of correction. They were never allowed to come down stairs in their kimonos or to swear or to make too much noise. When callers arrived, Mrs. Barker herself would receive them, very graciously, and then she would go to the foot of the stairs.

"Ladi-e-e-e-s !" she would call sweetly. "Gentlemen here!" And the ladies would all come trooping down in evening dress.

Drunkenness was strictly prohibited at Mrs. Barker's, and any vehement display of convivial feeling in the parlour was apt to bring from her a discreet reprimand. By practice of these excellent methods, Mrs. Barker had acquired a regular clientele of a good class, including several high-ranking state officials of whom she was especially proud. She called many of her longtime patrons by their first names. When one was about to go home after a sociable evening, she always gave him a cigar, wished him a polite goodnight, and invited him to call again soon. The atmosphere of her place was not only homelike, but almost moral.

Her parlor, in keeping with all this, was neat and respectable-looking, with its heavy furniture upholstered in red plush, its thick large-figured carpet, its silk-shaded lamp and discreet, heavy curtains. Behind it was a slightly larger room with a hard-wood floor suitable for dancing, and a mechanical piano which issued a melody when fed a coin.

Mrs. Barker had gathered about her a group of women who were carefully chosen for looks, but extremely various in other ways. Elsa Lipowski was a large bovine Polish woman with eyes like a Guernsey heifer and a mind not more than ten years old. She had slipped into her profession soon after passing Ellis Island and had only a limited command of English. A sharp contrast to her was Gladys Weston, a rosy Connecticut girl with bright blue eyes that twinkled when she laughed. She was betrothed to a Cheyenne-based railway conductor, who came to Denver to see her whenever he could, and at such times Gladys was not accessible. Both she and her fiancé were saving money, and as soon as they'd set aside enough capital, they were going to open a bakery shop and settle down to respectable money-making.

Tom's first venture at Mrs. Barker's was with Florence Pindell—a tall blonde woman with a pleasant, low voice. She and Tom got along famously, having a most pleasant time together, so Tom tended to gravitate to her on following trips to the Barker house. Emmett was partial to a different type. Like iron drawn to a magnet, Emmett quickly found himself at the side of Sadie Ferguson—a slim, shy, and awkward girl of about eighteen, dressed in starchy white, such as country girls usually wore on Sundays, with shining new patent leather slippers. Her face was remarkably pretty, with a china-white complexion, a large amount of dark brown hair and long, sly-looking eyes. She was the newest of Mrs. Barker's ladies—excited, eager and confused, exactly like a débutante at her first ball. Emmett quickly became Sadie's duly recognized "friend," and their "relationship"—the soon-routine ritual of sexual congress, a shared cigarette, and lazy pillow talk—would last for many years.

Chapter Thirteen

Alice didn't want to be a domestic, though the demand for them in Denver was great and she could easily have found work doing that. She didn't like sewing, so she also avoided all the stitching trades. And although jobs were plentiful in commercial laundries, she was adamant that was work she would not do.

She worked for a cracker company for a while, having thought it would be fun to bake crackers. But she had been unprepared for the huge factory setting she found herself in, and she didn't stay in that job long. The same thing with work she found at a candy company. She'd known of a candy maker back home in Ireland who had a lovely little cottage business making confections of all sorts. How wonderful it would be to do that! But what Alice encountered at the Denver confectioner was nothing like what she'd expected. If anything, the place that made candy was an even bigger, more industrialized plant than the cracker company. The atmosphere indoors was cloudy from boiling kettles and cooling candies. Most of the workrooms were steamy, dark, and narrow, with windows tightly closed to protect the confections from the coal smoke outdoors.

When Alice left that job, too, after only a week, Nora gently tried to break it to her that the kind of artisanal or craft work that was still common back home in Ireland had vanished largely in America. Alice would have to stiffen herself to the fact that if she didn't want to be a domestic, she would probably have to work in a factory setting of some sort.

Alice thought about that. She figured Nora was right. But she didn't want to work in a factory producing food. She knew her view was antiquated, but to her, factory production of food was ... somehow not right. She thought not only that food should be fresh, but that as much of it as possible should be prepared at home—or by small-shop specialists. What's more, she didn't like what she'd seen in the cracker factory: rats and mice, and their droppings, and vermin of other sorts. She guessed any workplace involving food would show the same problem. And she didn't want to be reminded constantly of the possible sources of contamination of the food she consumed. In any case, her attitude on the subject also ruled out work at the pickle plant, the macaroni factory, and a dozen other places.

When Alice heard from a neighbor lady that the Colorado Telephone Company was hiring four new operators, the news piqued her curiosity and interest. She applied right off the reel at the company's central office, where she spoke to a Mr. Leo Wilkinson, the manager. His first comment after running his eyes up and down her was about her age and height, both of which he deemed acceptable. "You're young enough and tall enough."

Alice wondered at that. What could he mean? She thought at first he was expressing some personal interest in her, but then decided not. "Thank you, sir. I didn't know my age and height would be an advantage."

"They are. So is the fact you're a girl. We used to hire teenage boys for this work, but they often proved rude and unruly, so we turned to girls instead. They're naturally more polite. And all our telephone girls are young. Most are seventeen or eighteen. I don't think we have anyone over twenty-three at the moment. We find girls your age are flexible, adaptable, and able to work at high speed."

"And my height?" She felt bold. "Why did you mention that?"

At this point, they were watching a number of operators at a switchboard, with thousands of "jacks" or holes for inserting the plugs in which wires terminated. Small lights glowed intermittently. Quick movements of hands covered the board with connections, then cleared it again. A constant low buzz of questions and replies arose from the bank of seated girls.

"As you can see, the height of our switchboards reaches thirty-six inches. Short girls can't reach that high. Even someone as tall as you can only reach the upper row of jacks with difficulty, unless she stands or stretches in her chair. But that slows a girl down." He then took her in another room and subjected her to various tests designed to determine the speed of her reflexes and the accuracy of her hand-eye coordination. "You're fast and precise. I think you'd do well. The only problem is your accent."

"My accent?"

"Your Irish brogue. You must be from the West. Let me guess. County Galway?"

Alice blushed. "How did you know?"

"When you arrived, you said you were 'intereshted' in applying for an operator position. It's not uncommon for folks from Galway or Mayo to turn an ess into esh before a consonant. So, fist sounds like fisht, and arrest like arresht."

"I never knew that—or noticed it."

"You wouldn't, I guess. You grew up with it. Anyway, do you think you could work on that? Try to be conscious of it and change it?"

"I would, sure I would."

"In some parts of the country, especially the East, the telephone companies won't hire girls with foreign accents. Operators are their direct link to the public, and the managers think an accent doesn't project a positive image. Even native English speakers are given elocution training to make sure their speech matches the image the company wants. We sometimes do that here, too. But in your case, your voice is clear and pleasant, your pronunciation and articulation distinct." He smiled at her. "And I myself am partial to Irish accents. I think they're lovely. So, I'm inclined to hire you. Let's talk about wages and the hours of work."

"Thank you, sir."

"I could start you at $14 a month."

"Oh ..."

"You're disappointed in the wage."

"In truth, I was hoping for more, I was."

He smiled. "Perhaps you don't know that the typical work day for an operator is five hours. So, that's not a bad wage for half the hours of work."

"Why only five hours?"

"The work here is intense. We've found a five-hour shift is best for the girls, given the fluctuating number of calls—peaks at eleven and again between two-thirty and three-thirty. To manage this, we stagger operator schedules throughout the day, with some working split shifts for better coverage. The night shift runs from ten at night till seven in the morning since call volume is lighter. Sundays require every operator to work in rotation, more frequently for those on split shifts. Initially, you'd start on a split shift, with the option to move to night or regular day shifts later. Is that all acceptable to you, Miss Butler?"

She didn't hide her excitement at the offer. "'Tis, Mr. Wilkinson. Thank you. I'll work hard for you, I will."

Chapter Fourteen

"I'm happy for you," Nora said that evening, when she was told of Alice's new job. "When do you start?"

"Monday!"

"Exciting! Let's celebrate this weekend."

"What would we do?"

"There's a vaudeville show at the Broadway. I would love to go."

"Could we afford it?"

"Aye. We couldn't afford their regular productions, but the vaudeville shows they host are within our range."

That Saturday evening, the girls donned their best outfits and set out for the theater, which was in the grand, nine-story Metropole Hotel at 18th and Broadway. They bought their tickets and then stood outside to enjoy the evening air before going in for the show. After studying the dodger for a few minutes to see what kind of acts would be in the show,

Alice glanced around at the other patrons gathered in front of the building. She saw a familiar face. "Look, Nora. It's Emmett Kelly, that fella from the train."

"And there's his friend Tom, over there." Nora waved and caught Tom's eye.

Soon the four were thick in lively conversation, talking over each other as they hurried to share impressions of their new home town. Their excitement at seeing familiar faces in a city where they still knew so few people shone on their faces.

Just as they finished exchanging greetings and the barest of information about their new lives in Denver, an usher emerged to toll a bell, signaling patrons to find their seats. The four made their way to the grand Romanesque entrance of the theater. Tom, not wanting to lose the thread of their newfound camaraderie, suggested, "Let's gather after the curtain falls to continue our chat. But just in case we lose each other in the crowd, would you mind telling us where you've moved to now?"

Nora's eyes sparkled. "We're at Belle Birnard's Parlor House on Market St."

Tom's head spun around. "That's a brothel!"

Nora laughed. "I wanted to see if you lads had found your way around town. Appears you have!"

Tom's face glowed bright red.

Nora laughed harder. "I'm toyin' with ya', I am."

Alice jumped in. "We board at the home of an older Irish couple. It's at the corner of 17th and Logan Street on Capitol Hill. The streetcar goes directly by the house, so it's very convenient. And we're the only boarders. It's quite cozy." Tom smiled at her enthusiasm.

Inside, the four split apart, each pair heading to seats on opposite sides of the theater. But they had in common the view of an East Indian scene painted on the main curtain. The overall decoration of the interior space was far more exotic than anything Alice had ever seen. She reached over and squeezed Nora's hand. "This is so exciting. Thank you for thinkin' of this!" The lights went down and the show began.

When it was over, the four of them met up again outside the theater, and the fellas offered to walk the ladies home. As they started to head up 17th Street, Emmett asked, "What turn of the vaudeville did you like best?"

Nora laughed. "You'll think I'm low brow, but I liked the slapstick comedies. And the dog tricks."

"The ballroom dancers!" Alice said.

Tom chimed in. "I enjoyed it all. Except for the French opera singer. She made me want to get up and leave!"

"I liked the magician the best," said Emmett. "I find illusions fascinating. There's something wondrous about fooling people."

Nora decided to change the subject to what interested her more. "So, where do you two live?" She wanted to calculate the chances of their running into one another again.

"We're in Auraria. In a boarding house. About twenty of us in there. Bog-standard, but the price is good," Tom said. Nora was disappointed. She never got over near Auraria.

Upon exchanging details of their livelihoods, Nora's nose

wrinkled ever so slightly when Tom mentioned he was a carpenter. She swiftly masked her reaction by shifting her attention to Emmett, her curiosity unabated. "And yourself? What keeps you busy?"

Emmett, with a trace of pride in his tone, responded, "Well, I've had me hand in a few pots before settling into a grand spot at a meat and grocery market. I'm taking to it well, for the work's never dull and it's right over in Colfax. Handy enough for getting to and fro without a fuss."

"What's it called, the market?" Alice asked.

"Röhr's. It's on 15th Street, near the intersection with Boulder."

"We'll stop in sometime, won't we, Nora?"

"We will, sure. We will."

As they approached Logan Street, the girls answered questions about their own jobs. Then there were universal declarations of intent to try to see each other soon. When the lads left, Nora said to Alice, "Will ya be goin' out of your way to see Emmett?"

"Oh, I doubt it. But he seems like a decent enough sort. Maybe not the smoothest stone on the shore, but I 'spose I'm not a piece of Connemara marble myself!"

"Go on with ya! You're all wool and a yard wide."

"How about you? Feel a spark for Tom? I think he likes you."

Nora let herself swoon. "Oh, he's so handsome. And tall! I'd love it if he'd come courtin'." Then she paused to consider. "But I don't know that I'd want to be with a man who works a trade."

"Jaysus, when did you become so high and mighty?

You're a shop girl! There's nothing wrong with that, but I don't know it's such a lofty position that it gives you the right to look down your nose at others."

"I suppose that's true. Maybe I spent too much time working in posh Boston houses—or have been at the store too long. I think my head's been turned by the kind of men I see every day. It's true, what the girls told me: there are slathers of well-to-do businessmen who come through the store, especially when they're on their lunch break. It's amusing to watch all the girls tending to their appearance as noon approaches. Some of them are truly audacious flirts."

"Have you met any nice men?"

Nora blushed. "Aye. A few."

"Oh now, you brazen hussy, you!" Alice jostled her sister with her shoulder.

"This one fella has come back three times! The third time, he didn't even buy anything. He said he only came in to say hello to me!"

"Did he tell ya his name?"

"Oh, he did, now. His name is Patrick Flaherty. Born in Boston, but his people are from The Big Smoke."

"Is he a handsome fella?"

"He's some lash, he is." Then she paused for a few beats and made her eyes huge. "But a fella named J.P. Ritter has been in five times!" Nora said, bursting into giggles.

Alice laughed, too. "Oh, Jaysus. I see Mr. Quinn is going to have some competition. Poor Tom. ... Why does this Ritter fella go by his initials?"

"His name is John Patterson Ritter. He goes by J.P. He says he doesn't like the name John, so he prefers to use his initials. When I found out that his grandfather is Thomas M. Patterson, the U.S. Senator from Colorado, I teased him, saying, 'I bet you only go by J.P. so people will ask you your full name.' And, oh, did he turn scarlet! I knew I'd hit that nail on the head." Nora threw her head back and laughed.

Chapter Fifteen

After having happened upon Alice and Nora Butler at the vaudeville, Tom felt a strong desire to see Nora again. He liked her, wanted to spend time with her. But he thought it best not to angle right away to be alone with her, so he persuaded Emmett to approach the girls together for an outing as a foursome. They took the ladies to the Elitch Zoological Gardens that had opened a couple years earlier in the Highlands, the first zoo west of Chicago. Tom had never been to a zoo and was eager to go. But mostly, he was eager to have an outing—any outing!—with Nora.

The four of them were in absolute awe of the two lions and the bears. They laughed at the monkeys, and delighted in the way some of the timid, smaller mammals—the marmots and the ferrets—would play hide-and-seek with the crowd of human observers.

The whole atmosphere fit the impression he wanted to make on Nora. Everywhere one looked was a magnificent parade of respectability—of humanity made as perfect as soap, shoe polish, razors and a zealous regard for the opinion of others can make it. Nora and Alice themselves wore pretty frocks, and Tom and Emmett wore new, stiff white collars. The four walked carefully and slowly so as not to muss themselves up or perspire too heavily.

Around them were many married couples accompanied by well-laundered children, who were constantly being rescued from mud puddles and poison oak. Emmett tried to be humorous by making comments about some of the married men having been trapped by their wily female partners.

Pushed by Nora to explain his real views on the matter, Emmett said, "Marriage looks like a trap to me, like being locked up. And all the mushy stuff people say about it is just a bunch of pretty lies to hide the truth about what it means for a man—a life behind bars."

With a touch of irritation, Alice said, "It's not men who face difficulties. It's women who are in a bind! Society says you've got to marry and settle down with some man or else get a job. I'd rather work and be independent. I've yet to meet a man in this town that I would want to marry."

Emmett laughed and teased, "Tom and I are tough. Don't feel you have to be so protective of our feelings!"

She ignored him. "The problem is that the jobs available to women never have any future in them. Men have all the good jobs. And it makes me angry to see men with less than a spoonful of brains making many times as much as I can ever hope to make!"

Alice's commentary produced a long period of quiet

among them. Tom finally broke the silence with a story about a carpenter friend of his who was planning to marry the young lady he'd been courting for the past year.

He said, "If I were entering into marriage, I'd want to be certain I could provide comfortably. I wouldn't be content if my wife were having to spend her days scrubbing floors, doing laundry, and cooking meals. I wouldn't want to impose that kind of tiresome life on someone I care for."

Nora felt ashamed of herself for having looked down her nose at Tom's work as a tradesman. She smiled at him and squeezed his arm. "You're a good man, Tom Quinn. A kind, thoughtful man."

EMBOLDENED by that flattering comment from Nora and by the good time she seemed to have that day, Tom next invited her to go on an outing alone with him—for a picnic in a nearby park. He had in mind a simple little meal involving no fuss. The main point, after all, wasn't the food, but spending time alone with Nora. Tom said he would pull together the picnic lunch, but Nora wouldn't hear of that.

With Mary Flannery's help, Nora prepared chopped ham sandwiches as well as sandwiches of crisped bacon and lettuce. She tediously transformed hard-boiled eggs into deviled eggs, mashing their yolks up with sundry other ingredients. She cut oranges, peaches, and plums were cut for a dessert, along with slices of a home-made chocolate cake.

At the park, Tom and Nora spread a lawn blanket under a canopy of maples that provided ample shade. They chatted amiably about everything and nothing. She fascinated him and even awed him a little. Although he had enjoyed some success with girls back in Kinsale, he had never set his cap for any such striking, confident young woman as this. Indeed, he could scarcely conceive of himself winning her. She had the self-assurance of an aristocrat, even though he knew she must be from a family at least as humble as his own.

Despite her bearing, she was as drawn to Tom as he was to her, and she took keen delight in being with him. When they headed home from their park picnic in a taxi carriage, she let herself lean heavily against him in the luxurious languor of weariness that a big meal and a long afternoon of lounging in a park can bring. When he draped his arm over her shoulders, she welcomed his touch. As he kissed her with unmistakable passion, she eagerly reciprocated, matching his fervor with her own.

Chapter Sixteen

M r. Leo Wilkinson, Alice's supervisor at the telephone company, had been correct when he described the work there as demanding and exhausting. Alice had thought that with only a five-hour shift, she would use some of the remaining hours in each day working part time at another job. She tried that for a while, but soon found that her physical constitution simply could not sustain that. So, she found other ways of spending her available time each day.

At Mary Flannery's urging, Alice decided to learn bridge. It seemed that nearly every married woman in town spent their afternoons playing bridge, just as the men gathered for poker games at night. Even young, unmarried women who had been "out in society" for a couple of years without finding a husband often joined in. Mary Flannery laughed, saying, "It's like the whole town's obsessed with cards!" The bridge clubs met at different members' homes each week, with the women fiercely competing for prizes like dessert spoons. Alice quickly developed a reputation as a bold bidder, but her clever playing style often paid off, and she proudly brought home several electroplated spoons to display in the Flannery house.

She also took up her pencil drawing once again—a pastime for which she had no real training but for which she felt a passion nevertheless. A group of prominent female artists in Denver had formed the Denver Artists Club, an organization dedicated to increasing public awareness of the offerings of local artists, and to educating the public about developments in the wider world of art—nationally and internationally. It was precisely the kind of community activity to which Alice was attracted. Although she lacked the talent to join the ranks of its artists, she was willing to pay the annual dues of two dollars to be able to attend lectures and exhibits.

Alice also frequented the newly formed public library, then operating out of a wing of Denver High School. Although it was not large, it already had a surprisingly good collection and an impressive array of subscriptions to journals and periodicals. Alice spent a lot of time there, where she puttered about, dipping into this and that, occasionally finding something that caught her interest for a few hours.

That was how she'd first become a disciple of various purveyors of wisdom about the health benefits of certain foods, the best means of food preparation, the most favorable combinations of foods for easy digestion, and the like. She didn't understand why folks chose to remain ignorant about food and its relation to the causes of disease and death. To her, it seemed clear enough that the amounts and kinds of food people ate, and how they prepared it, affected their vitality. In her view, most folks were so ignorant they wouldn't get the same answer if they counted their nose twice. No wonder they let themselves remain in the dark about the harm they did themselves by what they ate.

The librarian introduced Alice to the exciting new work by Mr. Wilbur Olin Atwater of Boston. With hard-won financial support from the U.S. Department of Agriculture, Atwater was doing research into how the ingredients of food materials are used by the human body and the kinds and combinations of foods that are best for human health. However terrible and disturbing some of this information might be, Alice was grateful to have it. Over time, she prided herself on the fact that her understanding of the subject was becoming increasingly sophisticated.

She became a particularly ardent advocate of the view that people should eat less meat. At dinner one evening with the Flannerys—an evening, fortunately, when the meal featured only the slightest portion of meat—Alice held forth on the subject: "If people would eat less meat—in fact, eat less overall, but especially less meat!—they could reduce the amount of fevers, eruptions, headaches, bilious attacks, and many other ailments which are produced or aggravated by too gross a diet."

Mary Flannery had put her hand to her throat in alarm, and John Flannery had looked around uncomfortably, then taken a long gulp of his water.

Alice continued, so caught up in her topic that she was oblivious to her dinner companions' discomfort. "Think how often people in this country sit down to tables loaded with perfectly fine food, fresh and of the best quality, that has been so ruined by the treatment of it that nobody wants to eat it. To me, often the worst offenses involve meat slowly simmered in fat 'till it seems like grease itself. People might cure themselves of eating it if they'd look at all that fat after it's congealed into cold grease. Makes me shiver to think of it."

Alice took pride in the fact that she followed what she preached with respect to the kinds and amounts of food she ate. She generally went without lunch and always resolved to eat nothing until dinner time. But some days, by late afternoon she would become so ravenously hungry that she would feel faint. The thought of a couple hours stretching between her and dinner seemed intolerable.

One day, she was downtown when such a hunger pang hit her. She went into Baur's at 15th and Curtis. Baur's specialized in ice cream and pastries and cakes—and in light and dainty luncheons for tired lady shoppers. The counters where the pastries were sold were near the door, and passing them was an ordeal for a hungry woman resolved to restrain her appetite. Cream puffs and chocolate éclairs and Eskimo pies and caramel layer cakes leered voluptuously from their glass cases. Long rows of women, many with children in tow, were eating delicious things with perfect abandon.

Alice sat herself at the counter, the tempting odors of the baked goods tickling her nose. Could her resolve stand in the face of such an assault? Summoning all her discipline, Alice ordered a cup of tea and a lettuce sandwich. She spied a woman a few stools down who must have weighed two hundred pounds and had three chins. She was eating a Boston cream pie with a snowy decoration of whipped cream almost submerging it. Alice watched the woman devour the pie with an almost alarming gusto. Cream smeared the corners of the woman's mouth, and Alice couldn't help but notice how her fingers greedily scooped up every last crumb that fell onto her plate. The contrast between the woman's indulgent feast and her own meager lettuce sandwich could not have been starker.

As Alice sipped her tea and nibbled on her plain sandwich, she couldn't help but marvel at the woman's capacity for food. The layers of cream and sponge disappeared into the woman's mouth with astonishing speed, as if a vacuum cleaner was at work. In that moment, Alice felt a pang of envy mixed with disgust. How could someone derive such pleasure from indulging in such excessive amounts of food that offered so little real nourishment?

The woman caught Alice's gaze and conspicuously let out a satisfied sigh, patting her ample midsection contentedly. Alice couldn't help but be drawn to the woman's unusual aura, which swirled around her like a tantalizing perfume.

As if sensing Alice's judgmental thoughts, the woman flashed a mischievous smile and beckoned Alice over with a delicate hand. Alice hesitated for a moment before giving in to the intrigue, rising and moving down the counter. Seated next to each other, they were like two sides of the same coin —Alice, with her trim figure and contemplative gaze; and the woman, exuding an air of uninhibited freedom that seemed to defy all societal norms.

The woman leaned in closer, her eyes sparkling with

amusement. "Don't worry about it, dear. I know I'm fat. I'm working on it."

Alice said, "Oh, that's good. I can make some suggestions for what you might eat to lose weight. If you—"

The woman laughed. "Oh, no. You misunderstand. By 'working on it,' I mean I'm working to stay fat—or get fatter. I find it's the only thing that deters my husband from wanting to have sexual relations with me. Believe me, being fat is far preferable." She let out an enormous laugh, then paused while Alice absorbed her message. Finally, she added, "I see from the absence of a wedding band that you're unmarried. Some day, if you marry, you'll understand. Then, you may prefer to be fat, too."

Chapter Seventeen

After they'd been in Denver about six months, Emmett and Tom abandoned their usual Saturday evening routine, choosing instead to visit Jedediah Pinsker at his store, which they hadn't been back to since their first week, when they'd briefly stopped in to say hello. Full of goods geared toward those who wrested their existence from hard western occupations—things such as mining tools, camp equipment, buckskin and canvas clothing, bowie knives, and firearms—Jed's store was a wild thing to behold. It was doing a bang-up business, and the boys entertained themselves checking out the wares until Jed finished taking care of the customer he was helping, then put the "closed" sign on the door. He grabbed a bottle of whiskey and three glasses. "Get those chairs there, and we'll sit out back and enjoy the cool evening air."

When they were seated, Jed said to them, "Tell me what you fellas are doin' for work."

Tom was all aglow talking about his carpentry work. "Denver's bursting at the seams with building, Jed, to where you can't swing a hammer without nicking another wood butcher. You're well aware. To be a carpenter now is to be sitting pretty. I'm pulling in $3.25 a day! Never in my wildest dreams did I think I'd be earning that straight off here in Denver. It's solid proof, coming here was the right call!"

Jedediah lifted his glass towards Tom's in a hearty toast, then swung his gaze to Emmett. "How about yourself, lad?"

Emmett shared his own tale of dabbling in various jobs before landing at Röhr's Market. "It's grand, truly. Suits me well. And it's given me a real eye-opener to the slog of runnin' a place like yours, Jed. Hats off to ya for makin' a go of it here. It's clear it's no small feat."

Jed smiled. "It's not. You're right. I'm not sure I'd ever have gone into the retail business if I'd have known what I'd have to deal with. Long, hard hours. And my average customer is a chawbacon or clodhopper—or a foppish city fella who has even less sense. In any case, none of 'em has any way of assessing the quality of the goods they're huntin' for. Their eyes only care about the price. So, I'm at a disadvantage against the shoddyocracy. That's what I call my competitors out there selling shoddy merchandise at low prices. And, of course, there are the long days that take a toll on me. They don't often end up with me enjoyin' a glass of whiskey with friends."

Emmett and Tom soaked in his words. It meant a lot to them to have someone like Jed Pinsker consider them his friends.

Emmett looked across at Jed. "You're right. I sympathize

with what you're sayin'. The competition among merchants is fierce here, Jed. I've learned that. What was your word? 'Shoddy-something'? We face that at the market. For example, nearby markets sell 'kosher' meat that we suspect isn't kosher. How can the customer know? They can't. … But that's not all. We're pressured on all sides by those wanting more than they deserve."

"What do you mean?" Tom asked.

"For one thing, there are the trusts. They keep prices high and thwart competition. The people are the ones who suffer. Think of all the things that everyone has to pay more for because of the trusts—meat, sugar, salt, oil, tobacco, matches, anything made with steel or transported by rail—"

"Even whiskey!" Jed frowned, holding up his glass.

"It's wrong. Just plain wrong," Emmett said.

"I agree with that, Em. … But, you said 'pressure on all sides.' What are the other forces?" Tom said, wondering where this was going.

Emmett wasn't certain he wanted to get into this on such a nice evening, but in he went. "The labor unions. They're another huge problem."

Tom's eyebrows jumped. He felt his blood pressure rise. "What? How are the unions a problem?"

"They're pushing up the cost of everything—coal, bread, chairs, tobacco, newspapers … Anything you can think of," Emmett remarked, noticing Tom's growing frustration, but pressing on regardless. "Even the buildings! Your mighty carpenters' union is jacking up the prices of everything this city builds!"

"'Jacking up the prices'? And what's that supposed to mean?" Tom retorted, his brow furrowing.

"It means you lot in the union are lining your pockets at everyone else's expense," Emmett shot back, his temper flaring. "Don't play dumb with us. You're earning more and pocketing benefits that the rest of the non-union termites can only dream of. By insisting that contractors hire union labor, you're inflating costs for all. A shopkeeper has to hike up his prices just to cover what he's shelling out for his store's construction!"

"Well, here's my two cents," Tom countered, undeterred. "Maybe those non-union carpenters ought to sign up with the union, then! They'd see the same perks we do! And as for the public paying a tad more because of union labor, I see no harm in it. We'd all be better off in a community that cared a more for its own, even if it means the price of goods and services goes up a bit."

Jedediah sat back in his chair and took a big swig of his whiskey. He enjoyed this whole scene immensely. It was like watching young wolf pups scrabble with each other.

Emmett blew out a breath, his patience wearing thin. "You actually reckon the carpenters' union is looking out for you? You're away with the fairies, Tom! It's not some benevolent society fighting for its members! It's a business, through and through. The bigwigs at the top are lining their pockets with your dues! And why, pray tell, are you so keen to hand over your hard-earned cash to the union, just to make those fat cats richer?"

At this point, Jed interjected himself into the conversation. "Are you fellas sure you want to carry this on?" His amusement at the conversation wasn't so great that he couldn't see trouble ahead.

Tom ignored Jed. "My 'hard-earned money'? The good wage I earn is thanks to the union! Because I'm a union member, I get paid more than I would if I were out there on my own." He was exercised now.

Jed decided to intervene and change the subject. This was getting too hot. He loved conflict even more than the normal man, but he didn't like seeing his young friends go at each other like this. He didn't see any advantage to letting it go on. He stood and poured more whiskey into their glasses. "Enough work talk, you two. Let's talk about women. Have you boys had a chance yet to check out the available mattress busters?"

After a long pause, during which he tried mightily to dampen the ire he'd built up, Emmett finally spoke. "We've been by some of the houses on Market Street. The wares are pretty good at Mrs. Barker's. Do you have another place you'd recommend?"

Jedediah smiled. "There're so many to choose from. But, to my mind, you can't go wrong by finding your way to Mattie Silks. She runs the best brothel in Denver. Tell her I sent ya. She'll take good care of ya."

Maybe the boys didn't bury the hatchet at that news, but at least their thoughts turned to things other than the costs and benefits of unionism.

Chapter Eighteen

Over many months, Emmett had learned the ropes at Oskar Röhr's market. He liked the work and enjoyed talking to the customers. One afternoon, he was busy cutting bacon for one of their regular customers. Emmett noticed a young couple walking around the store. They seemed to be keeping their eyes on him and Oskar as much as on the store's wares. When he made eye contact with them, each of them looked away. He finished wrapping the customer's bacon just in time to see the young man reach to a shelf, remove two cans, and drop them into the opaque reticule carried by his female companion. The two continued to look around the store for a few minutes, then the man asked Oskar if he happened to have any canned fish.

"We're all out at the moment."

"Thank you. We'll try somewhere else." The couple started for the door. As they were about to open it, Emmett hurled his bowie knife in their direction. It stuck into the wooden door frame, quivering a foot from the man's head.

"Stop right there, you two." Emmett yelled. "I saw you take those cans of beans."

Oskar hurried to the door as Emmett armed himself with another knife. The man said, "You must be mistaken, friend." He opened his voluminous coat to Röhr and also pulled its pockets inside out. He shrugged.

"Look in the woman's bag, Oskar," Emmett said.

The couple tried to resist Röhr's efforts, but when Emmett stepped around the counter with the other knife in hand, they relented. Röhr reached into the woman's sack and pulled out two cans of beans, a box of macaroni, and two bars of soap.

"Ah, you were up to even more thievery than I saw!" Emmett said. "Oskar, I'll hold these two here. You go to the call box and get a policeman over here."

"Now, there's no need for that," the man said. "We'll pay you for the goods. We'll pay you double the cost of the goods."

Emmett shook his head. "No, you won't. We're going to press charges against you for petty theft. If we let you go, you'd do the same thing to other merchants around town. Lowlifes like you hurt all shopkeepers."

It didn't take long for a constable to arrive and take the couple into custody. Oskar praised Emmett for his quick action and his fine knife-throwing. "That's the third time now that you've saved us loss from malefactors. Thank you, Emmett. You're alert to wrong-doers, and that's a valuable trait in a shop assistant. You're a good man. I'm grateful for the grand work you're doing for me."

For Emmett, the feeling was mutual. He liked Oskar. Emmett could imagine someday having a life like his. He fancied the autonomy Oskar had as a merchant—being his own boss, making his own deals with suppliers, setting his own prices. In what other occupation, Emmett wondered, would a man have that much control over the circumstances of his work? It was also true, of course, that as a small merchant, Oskar didn't have much in the way of buffers. All the financial risk was on him. So was all the stress. And the time commitment involved in keeping a small business going was truly staggering. Sometimes Emmett wondered how a man Oskar's age managed to do it. He couldn't imagine his own father putting in the kind of hours Oskar did each week. Emmett's admiration for the old man knew no bounds.

But one day, over a year into Emmett's employment— summer of 1893, this was—Oskar barked at him fiercely for a minor error. Emmett had been chiming a rack of lamb with a small meat saw, cutting through bone that was less than an eighth of an inch thick. As often happened to anyone undertaking that task, the bone snapped when he cut slightly too much toward it. Oskar looked over at him and roared, "What the feck are ya doin', boy? Can't ya cut a rack? Maybe we should only let you use those brawny arms and that thick head of yours to work on pork and beef! Now, you've ruined that rack!"

Emmett's eyes grew huge at this outburst. He stammered. "But this often happens. We turn them into lamb chops. What's the problem, Oskar?"

"The problem is people can't afford chops! The racks are cheaper." Even as he was saying this, Oskar realized the ridiculousness of his argument and knew that the snapped rack wasn't the cause of his outburst.

"Then sell the chops to them at the price of a rack! What difference does it make? It's the same cost to you!"

"It's the principle of the thing, you eejit."

Emmett put down the saw, took off his apron, and walked out the back door, where he lit a cigar and tried to figure out what had happened. Oskar had never exploded at him like that. And it was about something so trivial. Emmett could make no sense of it. Soon, Oskar came out and stood at his side. "I'm sorry, Emmett. I shouldn't have yelled at ya like that."

"What's goin' on, Oskar? I notice you've seemed stressed lately."

Oskar groaned. "It feels like the world's falling apart around us."

"You're talking about the economic panic?"

"What else! This is a bad one, Emmett. And it's only going to get worse. The damn farms produced too much wheat, and the damn mines produced too much silver. Now, we're all in trouble. Food costs are dropping, so I have to lower my prices. But if I do that, I'm not going to make enough money to pay the bank what I owe on my loan for this place. I worry that I'm going to go under."

Emmett knew Oskar was right: the times were perilous. The newspapers were full of reports of businesses failing, banks closing, people losing their life savings. The booming Denver economy that had drawn him west was unraveling fast. Even the venerable Union Pacific railroad had declared bankruptcy. The ore smelter, the biggest employer in the city, shut down, affecting half the fellas at the boarding house. Virtually all building construction had stopped cold. Thousands of men, including Tom, were out of work. To make matters worse, miners had poured into Denver from closed mountain mines. But there were no jobs for them in the city and no help for them. Rescue missions couldn't keep up with the constantly growing number of unemployed people.

Emmett knew that the anxiety he could see in the old man's sad eyes must be mirrored in his own. "What are we going to do, Oskar?"

Oskar looked up. Deep lines creased his face. He blew out his breath. "Hang on as long as we can, son. That's all we can do. Hang on as long as we can."

Chapter Nineteen

Unlike Alice, Nora was immensely interested in men, entranced by the male of the species. Although she could be cool and sometimes seem aloof, she was extremely vital and eager to experience what life had to offer. She wasn't convinced that one had to wait until marriage for that. And because men had always been described to her as unbridled, predatory animals who would try to get away with everything circumstances and women would permit, that's what she expected.

But, to her astonishment and disappointment, she had found that this was not in any general sense true. A good case in point was Patrick Flaherty, one of the young men who had been visiting her sales counter. He called on her at home, took her out, brought her candy, flowers and books. He would hold her hand, squeeze her while dancing, kiss her in dark corners with an air of diabolical daring. But he never departed from this timid, stale formula of courtship. He appeared to believe that Nora was not the kind of girl from whom more than a stolen kiss could be gotten. How wrong he was!

His yearning for her was so evident. The last time they rode together back to Capitol Hill after an evening out, Nora could see a faint tremble in his hand upon the seat. She knew that he longed to reach out and touch her, and that his touch —his first touch, at least—would be as innocent as a babe's. But he hesitated, as though afraid to put his desire to the test.

When the taxi stopped, they got out at the Flannery's residence. On the porch steps, in the deep shadow of the climbing rose, he hesitated again. He stood a step below her, holding her hand, looking up at her. She knew that he was going to ask her to let him stay awhile. If he had pulled her down to him then, she would have fallen into his arms like ripe fruit into a basket, for she was in the mood to kiss. But he merely stood there looking up at her with his adoring gaze. Not enough! Not nearly enough! Disappointed and frustrated by his timidity, she turned on her heel, ran into the house, and closed the door behind her.

She supposed she could have taken matters into her own hands. She could have thrown herself brazenly at the timorous creature, opened her arms to him and said, "Patrick, if you want me so very much, you may have me." But Nora wanted him to take the initiative. She wanted a dominant male. She craved a lover who, driven by his desire, would carry her away as a cherished prize.

To Nora's great surprise and delight, her romantic life took a much more positive and exciting turn when Tom Quinn came courting. She wanted this man and he wanted her. He was tall, virile, handsome. It's true that his occupational status as a tradesman was not at all to her liking, but she pushed that out of her mind when she was with him, refusing to acknowledge its impact on her. She relished Tom's passionate pursuit, finding his honest, deep feelings irresistible.

When he would come to visit her in the evening at the Flannerys' house, they were intensely conscious of the vibrating tension between them, wanting each other so urgently that they could barely speak. When the evening would grow late and Mary Flannery would say her final good night, bidding Tom to soon be on his way, Nora and Tom would wait until the footfall upstairs grew quiet. Tom then would rise and go to Nora. When they would kiss, they felt as though their separate beings were disintegrating and rushing together in the heat of desire.

One evening, Tom seized her more eagerly than usual, and each time she lingered longer in his arms and pulled away more reluctantly. There was a settee in the dimmest-lit corner of the parlor that seemed to wait for them as though by appointment. At last, as though by an impulse perfectly shared, they went to it and fell back among its cushions in each other's arms. They stayed there for the longest time, breaking down whatever invisible barrier had hung between them. This contact was a blazing discovery to them both, igniting in each of them a desire for more. Just then, Mary

Flannery's voice rang out from the top of the stairs, "Nora, dear, it's getting awfully late. Perhaps Tom should go now."

Unable to find the privacy at the Flannery house that they needed, they tried to find opportunities elsewhere. But it was incredibly hard for them to be securely alone. They would walk to nearby parks, hoping to find a secluded spot, but policemen patrolled the park with a special eye for amorous couples, and interested peepers seemed to lurk behind every bush. They went on a boat ride at Elitch Gardens, but a searchlight roamed the deck of the boat and picked out spooning couples for the uproarious amusement of the passengers. But they achieved many stolen kisses in spite of all these handicaps.

It was Nora who suggested that they rent a carriage so they could escape to the foothills beyond Golden or Morrison. In that world of fecund green forest, spangled with white blossoms and filled with the scent of bud and flower and the voices of birds, they found it impossible to keep their hands off each other. Here were no policemen and no prying, curious eyes. Here, the lovers found the peaceful, private sanctuary they'd been seeking. Here, the ardent spirit of youth seemed to charge the very air with an exotic quality of abandon.

They spread a blanket on a soft bed of pine needles. Tom tucked his folded coat under Nora's head. She relaxed in his arms, laying with her eyes closed, as though she had fainted, breathing softly, lips parted. Under Tom's slow but persistent prodding, her skirts gradually rumpled upward, revealing the silken shapeliness of her trim, bare legs. Warm, waiting and

96

tremulous, she soon was the image of abandon. He bent over her, blood pounding in his ears. For a moment, desire hung poised like a hawk in the air. Then it gave way to another feeling that neither of them could have named. When it was over, they opened their eyes to each other and smiled.

Chapter Twenty

Like the thousands of other men in Denver who'd lost their jobs in the Panic of 1893, Tom searched daily for work, competing against not only his former coworkers but the tidal wave of out-of-work miners and other unemployed men inundating the city.

Beggars filled the streets. Tensions mounted in Denver as residents worried about the tent cities that had sprung up in dry washes and gulches. People thought they were breeding grounds for disease and crime. Tom himself, having been forced to leave the boarding house, which he could no longer afford, lived in a tent city that had sprouted in Riverfront Park along the South Platte River.

Many schemes emerged to try to ease the sudden surge in population and the oversupply of jobseekers. The chamber of commerce gave a gift of lumber to the homeless camped in tents, hoping they would build rafts and float away. Many did. Railroads offered reduced, and in some cases, free fares out of Denver. Efforts such as these, along with the pervasive hardship itself, eventually led to an exodus. Denver's population began to drop. As the number of men declined, the prospects of finding work improved slightly.

By a stroke of luck, one day Tom heard that unskilled laborers were being hired for day jobs on the construction of the new Colorado State Capitol building. It was the only big project that hadn't been shut down or slowed by the depression. The exterior was largely completed, but much interior work remained. The contractors needed men to shuttle sand, lime, and masonry cement by wheelbarrow from outside piles to stone masons working inside. They needed other men to clean finished portions of granite and marble.

Tom got hired and consecutively rehired for such a long period over months that his work there took on the character of permanence. Foremen of several of the trades working on the building noticed his hard work. One of them was Frank O'Rourke, who supervised a team of scaffolders. He'd noted Tom taking special interest in his crew's work.

As the construction of the building was getting into the short rows, O'Rourke asked Tom if he'd ever thought about working as a carpenter.

"Matter of fact, I worked as a woodpecker before the panic shut everything down."

"I wondered that. My employer, Jack Anderson, is eager to bring on two men at a beginning wage. Would you be interested?"

"I would, aye."

Tom Quinn's employment by Anderson's firm was a turning point for him. Although his wages were low initially, they were sufficient to get back into real shelter and to start eating better. His self-confidence, decimated by the effects of the depression, began to recover. With each passing month, Tom liked his carpentry work more and more. He looked forward to each day on the job. He enjoyed working with his hands—and his brain. The work required skill, precision, and focus, especially for complex projects. Paying attention to the details helped him slow down, develop patience. And he put his heart into his job. So at the end of most days, he felt good about the work and about himself.

But even as he was coming out of the misery of his work life, the misery of his love life continued. He had not seen Nora Butler in many months. When he'd been down and out, he could not bring himself to call or visit her. He had been embarrassed and humiliated by his economic situation, and it simply wouldn't do to be in touch with her until things improved.

But now that his life was back on a more even keel, he resolved to try to renew his relationship with her, perhaps even to woo her into marriage.

So, one Sunday afternoon he decided to head to Capitol Hill to visit her. He presented himself at the door of the Flannery home. Mary told him that neither of the Butler sisters was home at the moment. He asked her to tell Nora that he had stopped by to say hello.

On his way down Seventeenth Street, he happened across Alice, who was walking up the hill.

"Would ya look who it is? Thomas Quinn!" she yelped,

with unconceated excitement. "We haven't seen you in donkey's years! How are you?"

He took off his cap and ran his hand through his thick brown hair. "Hello, Alice! I had a hard run of it, I did. But things have been better lately. And you? Still working away at the telephone company?"

"I am, so I am." Alice had a sudden thought. "Where are you coming from?"

"I was up to the Flannerys' in hopes of seeing Nora."

Just as she figured. Now all-overish, Alice hemmed and hawed. "Oh, she's out and about for the day, she is. I'm not sure where."

Being no fool, Tom suspected from Alice's demeanor that *where* Nora was at the moment was less important than *with whom*. So he asked. Now, Alice's color turned crimson. She stammered and stuttered some more. Tom, taking pity on her, said, "I'm guessing she has a beau. Is that the case? Might she be with him?"

Alice looked at the ground. She scuffed the toe of one shoe with the sole of the other. "Might be, yeah." She saw a crestfallen look envelope Tom's face. She hurried to soothe his troubled spirit. "But only because she hadn't heard from you in yonks and had no way of contacting you. She was so disappointed to lose touch. She truly likes you, she does. But she's had suitors in the past months. And one of them has been especially ardent."

Now Tom was the one staring down at the ground. "I fell on hard times when everything shut down. I was as poor as Job's turkey. It was all I could do to stay alive. I thought of Nora often, but I was living no better than an animal. I couldn't for the life of me show up at the house to say hello to her. I couldn't let Nora see me in the state I was in. And if I'd shown up at the department store to see her, the store detectives would have given me the bum's rush."

"We knew most construction had shut down, and we knew it must've meant hard times for you. I'm so sorry to hear you were pulling the devil by the tail." She looked up at this tall, good, handsome man and thought what a shame it would be for Nora to let him pass out of her life. But it was not a matter for Alice to decide.

"Thank you. I got through it and am doing better now." A pause. "So, is Nora serious about this man?"

Alice decided it would not be a service to either Tom or Nora to be disingenuous in her answer. "She is. Aye, Tom. I think she is."

"Do you like him?"

Did she like him? Alice wasn't sure. In any case, the more relevant fact was Nora liked him. "I've only met him the once, but he seems an okay sort."

Tom paused for a long while, then said. "That's good." Another pause. Finally, he asked, "How are you, Alice? Do you ever see Emmett Kelly? I'm sorry to say that he and I have lost touch."

"Oh, I haven't seen him in many months myself, Tom. He must be busy. But so am I."

Tom smiled. "Well, if he were ever so inclined to try, he'd be a mighty lucky fella to snag you, Alice." He put his cap back on. "You Butler girls are about as good as they come, I reckon. First-rate and a half! Well … take care of yourself. And please give my regards to Nora. Slán." And with that, he turned and walked on down the hill. Alice figured that might be the last she'd ever see of Tom Quinn.

<hr>

IN THE FOLLOWING MONTHS, Tom went about his life in the depths of despond. He deeply mourned the fact that Nora Butler would not be a part of his life again. He knew that it had been foolish of him to imagine that she would still be available when he finally emerged from the ravages of the Panic. Naturally, a vital young woman like Nora would be snapped up by some other man in no time at all. But the memory of their time together tortured him every day. His relationship with Nora had quickened every phase of his being. In every place he went, in every thing he saw, he found her—her dark hair in evening shadows, her eyes in stars, her voice in wind and water. In his loneliness, it was Nora he craved.

With Nora gone from his life—out of reach, in the arms of another—Tom suffered long nights of aching loneliness when he walked the city streets feeling depressed beyond description. But even his loneliness had a new character. It was less a mere emptiness and more an active despair. He achieved a sudden crushing realization of his own mortality —of the fact that he was daily walking toward death and nothingness.

Chapter Twenty-One

By late 1895, it appeared Röhr's Meat Market and Grocery would survive the financial panic, but barely. Oskar Röhr had poured every fibre of his being into the effort to keep the store open, and he was utterly exhausted by the struggle. At about 7:30 one evening, he and Emmett had dismissed the help and were alone in the store, getting ready to count the day's cash. Emmett had started to empty the cash register when a burly chap with a dark brown mustache opened the door. Emmett shoved most of the cash under the counter, then shut the drawer. The stranger looked around for a moment. He asked to buy a piece of beef. Oskar cut a steak, wrapped it, and placed it on the counter. As Emmett rang up the sale and the cash drawer flew open again, the visitor drew a revolver and commanded, "Hands up. Give me the money in there."

Poor Oskar, startled almost half to death, threw his hands

up in the air and trembled as the man swung the gun's barrel back and forth between him and Emmett.

Emmett, calm as a pound of liver on a platter, leveled his gaze at the man. "You've come at the wrong time, mister. You shouldn't disturb us now."

"Give me the money, or I'll blow your brains out."

Emmett drew a rueful smile on his face, giving the man his best imitation of someone feeling true disappointment at a turn of events. "We just now paid all our help and sent them home. All we have here are the receipts of only a few minutes, but you can take what's here." He stepped back to allow the thief room to tap the till. The robber injudiciously put his gun into his pocket. He was about to take the cash when Emmett's bulky fist landed on his jaw, flooring him. When Emmett stepped over to soothe Oskar, who was shaking noticeably, the thuggish intruder managed to recover from the stunning blow. He legged it out the door like a deer at full chisel.

Oskar and Emmett watched him go. Emmett locked the door. He led Oskar to a chair in the back room and got him a glass of water. Oskar was still shaking. He took the water gratefully and looked up at Emmett. "In all the years I've been in business, that's the first time anybody has pulled a gun to rob me."

"I'm surprised it hasn't happened more over the past couple years. There are a lot of desperate people out there. Times are hard." Oskar brought his hands to his face and kept them there a long time. His shoulders trembled. He didn't want Emmett to see his tears. Oskar finally looked up, a weary resolve in his eyes. "I don't reckon I can shoulder it any longer, Emmett. The burden's become too much—the constant worry, the debts piling up, the stiff competition from that new Jewish market down the way. And now this ... it's the final straw."

Emmett was at a loss for words, his heart going out to Oskar. He'd seen the toll the years had taken on the man, how the store had aged him beyond his years. Yet, the future of the market hung in the balance. "If you're up for it, Oskar, I'm here to listen, to understand what's going through your mind."

Gazing down, Oskar seemed to gather his thoughts. When he looked back up, there was a hint of resignation in his eyes, the kind that comes with hard decisions. "I've decided to sell, Emmett. It's time I stepped away. Elsa's against me running myself ragged here. And truth be told, I'm weary of it myself. Our daughter in Trinidad's been asking us to go live with her. I think that's our next chapter. I've had my fill."

"So, you've been mulling this over for some time then?" Emmett asked, trying to hide his surprise.

"I have."

"Got a buyer in mind?"

"Nothing set in stone. But Chaim Kupner has shown interest. He's keen on setting up his own place and asked if I might think about selling."

"Chaim? That's unexpected. He doesn't strike me as the shopkeeper type."

"And what type might that be?"

"Someone like me, perhaps." Emmett replied.

"You? That would be a bold step at your age, Emmett."

"But haven't you always said you're pleased with my work?"

"That I have. But there's a world of difference between being a right-hand man and carrying the weight of the whole enterprise on your shoulders. Why would you want to take on such a burden so young?"

Flipping the question, Emmett asked, "Did you not once stand where I am, Oskar? Keen for a chance to steer your own ship, to build something from the ground up? I see the hardship, sure. But I also see what you've built, the pride in your work. That's what I'm aiming for—to look back on my life with the same pride."

Oskar considered him for a moment "How about getting us both a glass and that whiskey bottle over there?" Emmett did as asked and then poured them each three fingers of spirit. "Emmett, let's get down to the nut cuttin', my boy. How would ya buy this place from me? I know what I pay ya, and it's no king's ransom."

Emmett smiled, a mix of nerves and resolve in his eyes. "You know my wages, but not my savings. I've lived sparingly, saved diligently. And with the banks easing up, I reckon I could make a strong down payment and settle the balance over time."

"Is that so?" Oskar said, intrigued, sipping his whiskey thoughtfully.

"And would Kupner be able to pay up front, in full?"

"We've not discussed particulars."

Emmett, sensing his moment, pressed on. "I'd wager not. My proposal likely wouldn't be far off from what you'd arrange with him."

Oskar nodded, considering. "There's merit in your words."

Emmett laid his cards on the table. "Oskar, this is more than a business to me. It's a dream, a chance to carry on what you've built. If you're passing on the torch, I can think of no greater honor than to take it from you."

Touching Emmett's shoulder in a gesture of respect and perhaps, approval, Oskar said, "Let's talk more. You've got the makings of a fine businessman, Emmett. I'd be glad to see the market in your hands."

Chapter Twenty-Two

While big change was afoot in Emmett's work life, the change in his social life was that he had met a pleasing young woman named Clara Gibbons. She was so unlike Alice Butler, the only other woman outside of the tenderloin district he'd spent any time with in Denver. Clara was so good looking that Emmett liked to parade her about, taking her to the city's second-tier restaurants (the top tier being beyond even his growing reach). In a low-cut gown of some dark material that set off her china-white skin to the best advantage, with a wide picture hat upon her thick brown hair and the largest chrysanthemum or rose she could buy pinned at her breast, Clara was a striking figure. And she keenly enjoyed this display of herself, sweeping through a room with the proud, disdainful bearing of a young woman aware of her own beauty.

When the cafés had closed, Emmett and Clara would go out upon the almost empty streets—joyful, singing snatches of Scott Joplin or Arthur Collins songs, and search for a place for further merriment. When they first were seeing each other, the cheap hotels along upper 16th Street accepted them without question. But when a new police commissioner of strong Christian belief started a crusade against immorality, the city cracked down on hotels accepting amorous couples looking for a place to cavort, and rooms became harder to let. Finally, one of these houses was raided, and after that, none of them would admit couples unless the man carried a suitcase and the woman an air of respectability, while others of them catered to men only. "Have you any baggage?" was the inevitable question, and in default of baggage, no room was to be had.

For a short time this caused Emmett and Clara great consternation—as it did Denver's other amorous unmarrieds. But then the word got around that "private dining rooms" were the thing. Denver had certain small cafés whose upper floors were devoted to these exclusive rooms, and soon the number of them multiplied. This continued for a few months, and then the order went out from the police headquarters that the doors must be taken away from all of the private dining rooms in town. Illicit love was once more homeless.

Emmett was soon weary of playing this furtive game. He saw clearly enough that in this, as in other matters, those with greater means, were unmolested by the law. If one had money enough to rent an apartment, he could do as he pleased. Now was not the time to spend money on an apartment—not if he were to purchase Oskar Röhr's market. Yet it would hardly be appropriate for a man of that stature—a shop owner!—not to have such a place. He resolved to have one. His attitude toward this, as toward most such matters involving money, was just go ahead and get it. To Emmett that was the only way to go about it. Dithering and worrying about the money was a losing game for cowards. As always, his view was: get the goods first and then look around for the money afterwards.

After a careful search, he found just what he wanted. It was a place of two rooms and a bath on the top floor of an old remodeled residence on Seventeenth Street. The ground floor was occupied by a real-estate office, and the two upper ones had been recently refinished in the form of four small apartments. It was in a good neighborhood and yet a quiet one, where a discreet man might do as he pleased without attracting undesired attention.

He bought the furniture with great care and on an installment plan. Through observation, he had acquired a very definite ideal of bachelor smartness, which he sought to realize. An imitation oriental rug covered most of the floor. There were two Morris chairs, a heavy square table, and a leather settee with many pillows. A couple of English hunting prints showing men in bright red coats galloping after black and white dogs gave the correct artistic touch, he thought, for he had seen such pictures in fashionable clubs. In a small cabinet, he installed a decanter of whiskey, some glasses and a box of good cigars, which he would not smoke himself, but would have on hand for a visitor whom he might want to impress.

When all this had been done, he was greatly pleased with himself and his new environment. Reclining comfortably in his Morris chair, smoking a pipe, he let his imagination dwell upon the social advantages such a place would give him. He pictured himself receiving some man of influence there, offering him a drink and twenty-cent cigars. He dreamed also of beautiful women coming to his door, discreetly veiled. He had provided himself with the image of smart prosperity— the setting and appearance—and he felt sure that the reality of it would follow.

Meanwhile, he was paying about a third of his salary in rent and installments on his furniture, and he thought hard about how he could pay for all this and the Röhr market as well. From the various groups of men around town with whom he played games of poker or bridge in empty offices or the hidden backrooms of stores and cafes, he selected ones who had the most wealth and least skill in games of chance, and invited them to a poker party at his flat. This gathering soon became a regular Saturday night event with drinks and other refreshments. His first guests brought other guests, and the game grew in size and fame. Good poker players were never invited twice, but youths who who lusted for excitement and had wealthy papas were always welcome.

One of the brightest stars of the game was a youth of Spanish blood named Trujillo. A lean, handsome fellow with fiery black eyes and a hot head, he was the son of a wealthy sugar-beet magnate and he gambled like a fiend. Stud-poker was his favorite game. He nearly always won at first and nearly always lost in the long run because his victory inspired him to believe that he was the beloved child of fortune and could not lose. Emmett very profitably demonstrated to him again and again that such was not the case.

———

Clara Gibbons came to Emmett's new apartment frequently—whenever he summoned her or whenever she hungered for a bit of carnal fun. To Clara, Emmett was a fun companion and an accomplished man. He filled her small mind and satisfied her senses. She longed to possess him wholly and exclusively—longed for him to give her the same level of devotion she gave him—and feared that neither would ever happen.

For a time they were very happy. But gradually, Clara's dissatisfactions became too much for her. One evening, when Emmett took her out to a nice restaurant for dinner, she said to him in a fit of pique, "I can't go on like this indefinitely." She was near to tears, and Emmett was as uncomfortable as a man sitting on a tack. It was clear she wanted him to marry her—and that she was now offering him the choice between that and losing her.

One powerful instinct urged him to hold on to her. They had that bond that unites a man and woman who have truly and fully known each other—a bond that can never quite be severed or forgotten. He wasn't a man of fine emotions, but he was bound to her by the force of his rich, sensual vitality. Also, he came from a long line of men who had married and raised families. So, both flesh and tradition alike urged him to hold on to this woman who had become his mate.

But against all that was the even stronger impulse toward independence and autonomy which was the most distinctive thing about him. He was unusually self-sufficient and fear-less. He feared for his future if he were to go down this path with Clara. He would be the owner of a little bungalow, an endless mortgage hanging over his head, Clara holding him in legal bonds, whiny children disturbing his peace and demanding his attention. It seemed to him suddenly that he was sitting in a trap, with a tempting bait before his nose, and that the trap might shut at any moment and hold him forever.

In an instant, he was on his feet and holding out his hand. "Clara," he said, speaking quickly and without compassion, "I wish you luck! I'm afraid this must be the end for us."

She stood facing him, pale, with trembling lips. "Oh! Emmett!" she cried, her voice trembling with distress. Tears streamed down her cheeks. None of that had any impact on Emmett, who seized her by the shoulders, kissed her hard on the mouth, pushed her away, and hurried out of the restaurant. He ran all the way to the street car line.

Chapter Twenty-Three

In May of 1900, Maggie Sullivan had been in Denver all of four weeks, having recently arrived from New York City, where she'd lived for five years, working as a transcriptionist —taking dictation, then transcribing her stenographic notes with a typewriter. Although she looked younger, Maggie was twenty-six years old, and although she achieved a convincing manner of sweet innocence, she had some bitter knowledge of life and men. Three years earlier, she had sincerely fallen in love with a young Texas lawyer in New York who was a regular client of the transcription service where she was employed. Their engagement dragged on month after month, toward a wedding which was to be sometime when the young man was making enough money. Maggie was romantic and a little reckless. She endured for a long while the tri-weekly course in furtive petting, which was considered appropriate to such a situation, and then surrendered herself in a moment of desperation. Unfortunately, the young man soon went back to Texas to practice law. He wrote to Maggie for a while, then the letters stopped.

Thwarted in love, Maggie turned all her energy and imagination toward building a new life based on satisfying, successful work. She had moved west as had hundreds, indeed thousands, of young women before her who longed for a new beginning. Her plan was to establish her own independent transcription business, which she would operate out of her home. But until she could build up an adequate client base, she took whatever transcription work she could find.

One such job took her to the headquarters of the local carpenters' union, where she was tasked with typing up letters and pamphlets of various sorts. It was there that she saw him, a man of about her age, perhaps a year or two older, on the far side of a teeming group busily folding pamphlets and stuffing envelopes. He was tall and lean and stood out from the crowd like a sapphire in a heap of pebbles. Her gaze encountered his wide blue eyes—bright, expectant, challenging. She looked away, then back. He was still staring at her. They exchanged more glances, and once or twice, faint surreptitious smiles. Across the room, they acknowledged a mutual interest. When she next looked up, he was heading into a back room with a group of other men for a meeting, and he had not come out when her work was done and it was time for her to leave.

On a Sunday near the end of May, Maggie did not wake up until mid-morning. She had slept long and dreamlessly, and she rose with a splendid feeling of peace and good health. She was in a mood to enjoy the mere fact of being alive. She took a hot bath and rejoiced in the silver water tickling her skin to a rosy glow. Having bathed, she admired herself naked, noting with pleasure how good her color was. The fresh air here at the foot of the Rockies was certainly favorable to her constitution!

She sipped her coffee slowly and lolled over the newspaper a long time, reading even the want-ads to prolong this pleasant idleness. Then she prepared to go to Denver City Market. Usually she regarded marketing as a nuisance. But in her current mood of serene idleness, she looked forward to going to the large market, exploring its offerings at her leisure.

As she arrived at the marketplace, feeling open and at ease, she was captivated by the vibrant spectacle before her. The rich colors of the scene struck her in a way she had never appreciated before. A fruit stand caught her eye, with deep red Winesap apples nestled beside sunny California oranges. A nearby huckster's cart was a work of art, adorned with the vivid pink of freshly washed radishes and the lush green of parsley. Even the fish stalls, when viewed from a distance in the sunlight, possessed a certain beauty, their white marble slabs adorned with splotches of speckled silver and gray, and crowned with bright pink mounds of shrimp.

Inside the building, an array of butcher stalls stretched out before her, each one laden with raw meat in shades of deep red and purple, contrasted against the perfect ivory of lifeless fat. Gleaming chocolate-colored liver and the feverish pink of sweetbreads added to the display, while yellow plucked fowls hung by their necks. The air was filled with a subtle, rich, and strangely invigorating scent of blood. Presiding over this scene were rows of plump, red-faced, beefy men clad in white aprons marked with blood stains. The older these men were, the more they seemed to resemble their own wares, their appearance increasingly corpulent and fleshy. One could not help but imagine a grotesque fate befalling them, a slow metamorphosis that would transform them into great slabs and quarters of beef, ultimately to be suspended from their own hooks, chopped up with their own cleavers, and sold piecemeal over their marble slabs.

And through this neat shambles, among these tons of red raw flesh, wandered women with baskets—many of them dainty, pretty women who could not have brought themselves to wring a chicken's neck. Maggie wandered amongst them. She bought a porterhouse steak, choosing it with care, and materials for a salad, and eggs, potatoes, and peaches and cream for dessert. She had still to buy a vegetable. About the vegetable she hesitated. She looked at almost all the vegetables in the market—carrots, turnips, squash, spinach. She couldn't find a thing that was really good. The carrots and turnips were too big, and the spinach was full of sand that would never wash out. But she found some luscious-looking beets. Beets, it would be.

Chapter Twenty-Four

Solidly back on his feet financially, Tom Quinn had found a nice apartment to rent in the Curtis Park neighborhood to the northeast of downtown. The area was a mix of housing that had been built over the preceding twenty years —large and lavish houses mixed in with small and modest ones. After the Panic, some of the big houses in the area had been divided up into smaller living units.

It was near Curtis Park that fate led Tom to her. On a Sunday afternoon, after leaving Denver City Market, where he'd picked up some fresh produce from local farmers, he noticed a young woman on the other side of the street, slightly ahead of him. There was something familiar about her. She was tall and slender, but with a provocative contour and a brilliant vividness of color. Her abundant, bright, strawberry-blonde hair cascaded to her shoulders and seemed to dance with each step she took, as if whispering to him, *Follow me, lad.* He was almost certain it was the young woman he'd exchanged glances with at the carpenters' hall.

At the next corner, she juggled several packages, struggling to maintain her grip. Quickening his pace and crossing the street, Tom was soon at her side, cap in hand. "Beg pardon, miss. Might I lend you a hand with your parcels?"

Startled, she spun around. "Oh, Jesus, Mary, and Joseph! It's you! The union man! You nearly gave me a heart attack. I didn't catch the sound of you coming up behind me." She gazed at him now with frank astonishment and no small amount of delight.

With a gentle smile, he apologized, "I'm sorry for the fright. Wasn't my aim to startle you, only to offer help with your load. Seems we're both bound for Curtis Park. I'd be glad to carry some of that for you."

Relieved, she passed him half of her burden. "That's mighty kind of you. I'm much obliged, Mr....?"

"Quinn. Tom Quinn."

"Maggie Sullivan. And I have this terrible habit of buying more at the market than I can manage, all because I don't care beans for the long walk to and from the market. Though, I can't say I often run into a gallant gentleman willing to rescue me from my own miscalculations."

He chuckled. "Well, Miss Sullivan, I can't promise you've met such a gentleman today, but I'm here to assist. Whereabouts are you headed?"

"27th and Arapahoe," she shared.

"That's not far from me—I'm over at 29th, by the church. How long have you called this neighborhood home?"

"Only about a month. I'm still getting to know Denver."

"Just off the boat, then?"

"No, I've been in the states for five years now. Hailed from Ballincollig, near Cork. Spent my days in New York City but couldn't stand it any longer. A newspaper piece painted Denver in such good light, I thought I'd try my luck here. Guess I'm what you'd call a wanderin' cailín."

"You're not gonna believe this, Miss Sullivan—"

"Please call me Maggie. And I'll call you Tom. I'm not big on formalities. My wanderin' has busted all that outta me." She glanced over at him, gauging his reaction to her forwardness.

His grin only widened. "Well, then, Maggie, as I was about to share, my roots are in Kinsale. I'm a Corkonian, like you! And like yourself, I had a stint in New York before casting my lot here in Denver."

"Now, you're tellin' a thumper, Tom Quinn!"

"It's true as the day is long!"

Teasing him, she said, "I won't be codded by some handsome young dandy, even if he is carryin' my groceries!"

He laughed. "Oh, is that so?" He feigned a move to drop the eggs. "Maybe I'll just let these fall and see how that suits ya."

"If you do, you'll be short an arm come mornin'."

"You'll be goin' to work tomorrow with one less arm, if ya do."

"Ah, you're grand fearsome, ya are!" With a gleam in his eye, Tom took one of the eggs out of the package. He tossed it high into the air. They watched it come down on the street with a splat.

"Sure now. That was a mistake." Quick as a fox, she

stomped on his foot. "One toe for one egg. Cross ten, and I'll start on your eyes." Tom's laughter had him collapsing onto a nearby step.

Once his laughter subsided, he looked up to find her with a victorious smirk. "You're a feisty pup, Tom Quinn. I like that in a fella. How about helpin' me home with my eleven eggs and other goods, and then treating me to an ice-cream soda at Baur's?"

"Baur's? You're still finding your way around, yet you know of it?"

"Aye, I'm not a thick gobshite. Heard tales of Baur's back in New York! Barely washed the journey off me before I was there, tasting Denver."

He chuckled. "Good on ya! But what would be makin' ya think I'd take ya for ice-cream soda?"

"Because, Tom Quinn, your pulse is already racin' from bein' with me. And I'll tell ya a little secret." She leaned toward him and whispered in his ear. "And mine is doin' a bit of a jig, too."

As THEY SAT SMILING across at each other at a little table along one long wall at Baur's, Tom said, "Coincidences like this—bumping into each other today—almost make a mystic out of me. It's as if I made it happen by wishing hard enough for it. When I saw you at the union headquarters, I said to myself that you were the most beautiful woman I had ever laid eyes on, and I wished I could see you again—that I could see you alone. And here we are! Now, isn't that wonderful?"

Maggie laughed. "Oh, I can see that you are trouble, Tom. Quinn. I'm guessin' a woman has to be on her guard around you. She might just get swept off her feet real fast with your flattery and sweet talk."

They talked steadily, excitedly, staring into each other's eyes. She had a curiously he provocative way of opening her eyes wide at him and then narrowing and lowering them again. She asked him questions about his life, his family, his work, and he returned the attention, learning some about her time in New York, her work as a typewriter, and her near marriage to the young lawyer.

"Did that whole experience sour you on the idea of marriage?" Tom asked.

"Oh, no, I don't think so. I guess I want to get married sometime. I don't want to be an old maid. But I can marry any time. I want to get myself established here and have some fun first."

"You think marriage can't be fun?"

"I suppose it can be, if one is lucky enough to find the right person."

"And what kind of person would that be?"

"Someone lively, unconventional. I wouldn't want a staid, traditional marriage of the sort that becomes stagnant within a year. How perfectly awful. Most men are such sticks! They just talk and talk and talk and never do anything. I want someone who appreciates fun—and laughter. I want things to happen! I don't want to go through life dull and sullen."

"Making things happen is my specialty," Tom said. "Just what do you want to happen?"

"Oh , I don't know," she countered, looking at him through narrowed eyes. "Something exciting and lovely ..."

"Your order is taken, Miss," he assured her, going through the motions of writing on an imaginary order pad.

She threw back her head and laughed delightedly. "How perfectly w-o-o-o-nderful!" she said, with a long sweet falling inflection on the last word. "What forms of payment do you accept?"

Tom let out a guffaw at that, and regarded Maggie with frank admiration, perhaps even awe. He had the sense that something had arrived in his life—exactly what, he wasn't sure. But it was as though a door he hadn't checked in a while had blown open, and even without going to look, he know it had.

Chapter Twenty-Five

With Clara Gibbons now out of the picture, Emmett turned his attention again to Alice Butler. He wasn't certain why, but she provoked his curiosity. She irritated him because he could not ignore her as he wanted to do. She was not a great beauty like Clara, yet not at all unpleasing to the eye. Her figure was growing fuller, but was still decidedly good and was set off by trim ankles. Her smile showed perfect teeth. All this was to the good.

But it was her game he couldn't figure out. Full of schemes himself, he believed that others were as well, and he was always trying to discern the secret schemes of others. He couldn't conceive that other people might not be scheming at all or that they might have motives different from his own. He believed every person is driven by their self-interest, as he was. So, Alice had to be up to something. What was it?

She was pleasant to him, but not the least bit flirtatious.

She appeared still to be true to her claim of several years earlier that she was uninterested in marriage, so he was not fearful that she was setting a matrimonial trap in his path. He liked that. But her lack of interest in flirting with him hurt his vanity. He was quite convinced that he had a practically irresistible appeal to women. So, the presence of a woman who showed no interest in him was as uncomfortable as a pebble in his shoe.

After Emmett had taken Alice on Sunday afternoon strolls in the park several weeks in a row, Alice invited him to dinner the following Saturday evening at the Flannery house. To Emmett's surprise and disappointment, the dinner turned out not to be just the two of them, but very much a family affair. Mr. and Mrs. Flannery were there, along with their six-year-old granddaughter and two-year-old grandson—the boy sitting in his high chair and demanding the attention of everyone by hammering on the table with a spoon.

To quiet him, Mary Flannery gave him the leg bone of a chicken to suck. Soon, he was inspired to pat Emmett affectionately on the head with this. Being reprimanded, he went on the warpath, threw the chicken bone at his grandfather, and was promptly carried up stairs, raging against a world that seemed determined to ignore and thwart him at every turn. A short while later, Mr. Flannery took the granddaughter up to bed, too—a mission from which the sleepy gentleman never returned.

After Alice and Mrs. Flannery had done the dinner dishes, Emmett sat in the living room with the two of them, Mrs. Flannery carrying the bulk of the conversation. Emmett listened politely to his hostess and kept his eyes with difficulty from Alice, who wore a blouse of cream-colored Georgette crêpe which left her splendid neck fully exposed and revealed faintly the tender tints and contours of her flesh.

Mrs. Flannery finally, reluctantly, followed her husband to bed. Emmett and Alice adjourned to the porch and sat in the swing. The neighborhood was quiet, the yellow glow of lights peaking through windows here and there. The street was lined with elm trees which rustled softly in the night breeze, filling the air with a soft murmur. Far away some one was playing "The Sidewalks of New York" on a piano. Emmett drew closer to Alice and put an arm around her shoulders. After a while, with his other hand, he took hold of one of hers. When she still did not resist, he kissed her on the cheek. Although she was not encouraging him, she also was not resisting, so he turned her face to his and kissed her on the lips. She turned her head away, but after a while, looked back at him. He kissed her again. To his surprise, her lips stayed a bit longer this time.

Suddenly a distant bell began to toll. Alice jerked upright like she was awakening from sleep. "Good Lord! Eleven o'clock," she exclaimed. "You must go, Emmett. Mary'll give me the dickens. She never goes to sleep as long as I have company."

Emmett accepted his fate for the evening. There would be nothing more than this modest canoodling tonight. It would only be a losing proposition with this woman to protest that the evening was still young, to try to capture Alice with ruthless insistence. He did not want to antagonize Alice or Mrs.

Flannery. He knew the latter considered herself Alice's guardian and counselor.

Emmett still wasn't certain if he wanted to pursue Alice Butler, but he knew that if he were to do so, it would require patience and delicacy, which Emmett believed he possessed in abundance.

Chapter Twenty-Six

Emmett had been running his market for a year and a half at the same location where Röhr's had been. Business was good, but not fizzing. One day, Jedediah Pinsker showed up at the store and asked Emmett for a moment of his time. Emmett alerted his assistant that he'd be unavailable for a bit. He and Pinsker stepped outside. "What can I do for ya, Jed?"

"I've decided to call it quits, Emmett. Times are changin' so fast these days you have to run hard just to stand still. And I'm tired of the runnin'. So, I'm gonna close down my shop and shuffle off into the sunset." With his characteristic gesture, he spread his thumb and index finger, running them down the sides of his mustache. "I reckon I better do it before I lay down the knife and fork." His thin face looked more sunken than usual. There were deep hollows at his temples.

"I 'spect you've more than earned that right, if that's what you're wantin' to do."

"The reason I'm here is I remember our conversation when you came to me last year for advice about shopkeepin'. I told ya then that one of the best things you could do was to locate on the busiest street you could find—location and traffic being prime ingredients to retail success."

"I remember that. And I said it sounded like a grand suggestion, but I wasn't in a position to relocate."

"Might ya be now?"

"I don't know. What do you have in mind?"

"You know where my store is. Colfax is the busiest east-west thoroughfare in the city. I had a modicum of success as a small businessman not because I have special aptitude for the work—hell, I'm nothin' but an old bull-whacker!—but because I was lucky enough to open up at that location. I believe you'd do well in that spot, too. Better than you're doing here."

Emmett knew that was true. The site of Pinsker's store would be perfect for Kelly's Meat Market and Grocery. There were no other food merchants along that broad stretch of Colfax heading in either direction from Pinsker's shop, although the two-story buildings that lined the street did include other kinds of stores, saloons, a restaurant, a meeting hall, and a hotel. And Jed was right: Colfax was as busy a thoroughfare as one could find, since all traffic enroute to Denver from the agricultural communities of Golden and Morrison converged there.

"My building is somewhat bigger than this one, so you'd have room to grow. And what you may not know is that I also own the vacant lot on the corner, next to my store. That lot wasn't available for purchase when I built. I bought it later, thinking I might expand someday. You'd have that, too, giving you even more potential for expansion."

Emmett hadn't given a moment's thought in the preceding months to growing or moving. It had been all he could manage the past year and a half to take over the ropes of Oskar's business and make a go of it. He'd made the last payment to Röhr for the property and furnishings. But listening to Jedediah, Emmett felt his heartbeat quicken. A bigger market!

"Another thing for ya to consider, Emmett, is that my building has a second floor, unlike this one here. You could live above the store. I swear to ya that lessens your daily worries and makes life easier for a shopkeeper in many ways. And I don't know what your plans are, but the space above is plenty big enough for a young family, should ya be thinking of starting one."

Now, Emmett smiled. Indeed, he had begun to think that a man of his position in life probably should have a wife, but the question of where to house a family was one he hadn't managed to resolve. A relocation to Pinsker's place would settle that issue. "Jed, I don't know what to say. You paint a mighty appealing picture. But I don't know that I could afford it."

"You don't know that yet. We ain't discussed finances."

"That's true. But let me ask ya this: why would you sell such a prime location to me? You must have friends or relatives who'd lick their chops to get their hands on your spot."

"No relations. And all my pals is old like me. Nope. I

decided that when I close up, I want to sell to a young buck like you. So, I thought to myself, why not you! And here I am to talk with you. How about getting your shop assistant to take over for you this evening? I'll take you out for a good meal and we can discuss what I have in mind for a financial arrangement that might suit ya."

And that's how Emmett Kelly became the owner of a prime spot of real estate on West Colfax Avenue for Kelly's Meat Market and Grocery.

Chapter Twenty-Seven

To say that Maggie and Tom were sparkin' would be understatement. They'd been all sparks since that first afternoon they met and went to Baur's. Thanks to their proximity to one another in Curtis Park, they spent almost all their non-working hours together. They took picnics to various parks and to Elitch Gardens. Rode all the city's streetcar lines for the fun of it and to see Denver's skin and bones.

At the new zoo in City Park, which had supplanted Elitch Gardens as the premier zoological park in the city, they delighted at the antics of the baboons and laughed at the rhesus macaques. A large, hulking man was standing before the cage of macaques and, in defiance of the rules, was feeding them. He would give a macaque a peanut and then eat a peanut himself while the macaque ate. He and the macaque looked at each other with mild, friendly interest. The macaque captured a flea. The man scratched his head.

He tossed the macaque the last peanut and shuffled on. The macaque shrugged.

Tom and Maggie moved on to the bear den where they laughed again at the funny behavior of an American black bear cub named Billy Bryan. And they joined a growing knot of people watching a rumbling love affair in progress between two adult black bears. Maggie laughed when an excited boy yelled to his mother, "Oh, look, mama! The bears are fighting!"

The woman blushed and said, "Yes, dear. They are." She pulled at the sleeves of her son and hurried him past the bear's den. Glancing back regretfully and with amusement, she said, "Let's go look at the monkeys now."

One of their favorite activities together was bicycling, for they were no more able than other people to resist the allure of the latest craze. Ever since the "safety bicycle" had displaced the old high-wheel model a few years earlier, the streets of American cities had been full of people on the new contraptions. Denver was no exception. For her 27th birthday, Tom presented Maggie with a beautiful new bicycle from the Monarch Bicycle Company. He bought himself a slightly different model.

Every Sunday, weather permitting, they would go for a long ride, exploring Denver's growing reaches to the south and east. Their bicycles were their escape, their instruments of fun and frolic. When out on their bicycles together, they lost track of time, forgot about their cares and duties. Sunshine filled their souls.

But riding their bicycles wasn't a risk-free endeavor. Bicy-clists packed the streets. Many (mostly wild young men) sped along much too fast for everyone's well-being. Adolescent girls were often menaces, too. They'd convinced their papas they should have a bicycle to save on streetcar fares, but they rode with no apparent respect for life and limb.

One day, Tom and Maggie rode into Washington Park behind a Denver Water Company cart. It was of the sort that had a horizontal panel of nozzles on the back to sprinkle water along a pathway to diminish the amount of dust churned into the air. Finding the park road inconveniently crowded, Tom and Maggie continued to pedal slowly along behind that vehicle. Without warning, the driver applied his foot to the lever, and water spouted out. Maggie managed to swerve away to the right. Tom tried to do the same thing to the left, but his bicycle slipped on a wet patch. Down he went, in such a position as to be the object of the cold-water douche.

A pedestrian's shriek had led the driver to stop the cart. But unaware of what had happened, the operator hadn't released the lever, so water continued to spray on poor Tom. At least ten more seconds elapsed before the pedestrian could explain to the driver what was happening. The operator finally released the water lever.

Maggie, at the side of the path, was laughing so hard at the situation she was in tears. Tom sat in the middle of the path, his clothes soaked through. He watched Maggie shake with laughter and made a decision. He swiftly went to her, lifted her over his shoulder like a hundred-pound bag of flour, and carried her to the edge of the park's long lake. "Now you'll be sorry."

She laughed. "Put me down, you brute!"

"'Brute'? I think you could use a dowsing yourself!" He tossed her in the lake. She stayed there for a minute or so, joyfully spraying water from her mouth like a fountain. Then she pushed her long wet hair away from her face and emerged from the water, her biking bloomers stuck to her legs.

"Ooh la la," Tom said. "Look at those drumsticks! You are the jammiest bit of jam!" "Take a good look, you rotten egg. These wet clothes are as close as you're gonna get to a look at my body today. You'll not see me in the nip, you won't."

But that wasn't true. As soon as they got back to Maggie's apartment, they turned to their favorite post-ride activity, retiring to Maggie's bed, where they would spend several hours giving each other pleasure.

On one such lazy Sunday, as they lay intertwined under the sheets, both flushed and smiling, Tom gently running his fingers through Maggie's strawberry blonde hair, they knew it was time. And before they got up to make an early dinner, they had decided to get married.

Chapter Twenty-Eight

The West Colfax area underwent a transformation in the wake of the financial panic, as people who could afford to do so moved to outlying areas of Denver. Migrants from the eastern United States, as well as recent immigrants from central and eastern Europe began to move into the neighborhood and enlarge the Jewish community there. They opened food markets, dry-goods shops, pharmacies, and other kinds of stores throughout the area.

No sooner had Emmett settled into Jedediah's former market on West Colfax than the printer's shop right next door closed down when its proprietor was killed by a cable streetcar. And what new business was going to take over the space? Federman's Grocery and Kosher Meat Emporium. Emmett couldn't believe his bad luck.

Like Röhr, Emmett had always done his best to meet the needs of the Jews in the area. He understood the demand from Jews for kosher meat that complied with the strict dietary standards of Hebrew law. He'd hired a schochet to perform the slaughter of animals, the draining of the blood, and the deveining, salting, and rinsing of the meat. Kosher meat took a lot more work to process. The price Emmett had to charge for it reflected that extra labor. At least he felt he was doing all he could as a responsible butcher to cater to the needs of a large group of his customers. But now he was going to face direct competition right next door.

For six months or so, the two merchants managed to coexist peacefully. Federman's operation didn't seem to have cut too badly into Emmett's business. But gradually the situation for Kelly worsened. Jewish customers who'd long bought their kosher meat from Emmett started going next door to Federman.

Emmett believed that Federman was passing off non-kosher meat as kosher, undercutting Emmett's own prices. Emmett wasn't going to stand for it. He felt a fight was in order. Always fight when someone's doing you wrong.

So, one day, Emmett shared his concerns about Federman with Rabbi Shlomo Rosenstein, the rabbi who supervised the schochets in the area and attested to their worthiness. Emmet had worked with Rosenstein for a long time. The two knew each other well, and trusted each other. So Emmett was blunt in his comments to Shlomo about Federman. Emmett was only slightly surprised when the rabbi responded by saying he'd often had the same thought about the untrustworthy Federman. "He's a greedy little chazir. I think it's time to take him down."

Thus began a fight over kosher meat that split West-Colfax Jewry wide open. Rosenstein spread word in the Jewish community that Federman's kosher meat wasn't to be trusted. Federman immediately responded by finding a different "rabbi" to certify that his "kosher" meat was indeed kosher. He was doing plenty of business, his schochet working day and night. Many of Federman's customers remained loyal to him despite the claims about his behavior. The Hebrew Ladies' Aid Society mobilized in support of Federman, who, for a while, seemed to have the upper hand in the battle.

By this time, Emmett had come to despise Federman. "That greedy fecker's tighter than a camel's arse in a sandstorm," Emmett said to his burly assistant, Gus McGrath. Emmett decided to join the battle in the most visible and outlandish way he could muster. Emmett went to Rabbi Rosenstein and got him to paint four signs in Hebrew, each reading "Federman's Kosher Meat." Emmett and Gus then took four unclean hogs—fat and abhorrent to Talmudic law—and hung them by their chins outside Kelly's store. Around their stretched and opened waists, Emmett tied the rabbi's signs. Then he went back inside his store, rolled up his sleeves, and announced, "Now let 'em come, Gus. They got themselves a meat war. Let's watch things hum."

"Vos is dis?" Federman yelled when he stormed into Kelly's store a few minutes later. His bloodshot eyes gleamed in fury. "Vos is dis you done?"

"Why, Gus and I are givin' the good folks of this community an idea about the nature of the 'kosher' meat you sell,

Federman. Now get out of here before your friends have to carry you out in an eternity box." Emmett made a quick move in Federman's direction to scare him, and the little whiffet scurried out of the store like a frightened baby pig.

Watching from inside the store, Emmett and Gus soon saw children gather around on the sidewalk to gawk at the hogs. Whiskered elders tsk-tsked and issued bass gutturals. Agents of the Hebrew Ladies' Aid Society brought their cupped palms to their mouths in horror. "Strike up Garryowen, Gus. We're going out to chaw up the enemy!" With that, he picked up a bung starter and a cleaver. And Gus, grinning joyously and flexing forearms that would fetch a good figure in Omaha, moistened his palm with a gob of spit, then also gripped a cleaver. They headed toward the door.

Outside, frantic children scattered at the sight of them. The buzzing old men hobbled away, and the Ladies' Aid Society adjourned with shrill screams. Emmett laughed. "Looks like they've got to get home to start supper, Gus. ... But they'll be back. We'd better bring in our pals." They brought the specimens of "Federman's kosher meat" inside and set them up in the shop windows, the hogs still wearing their insulting signs. As anticipated, the agitated crowds eventually returned, so Emmett and Gus sat up half the night on guard.

But the next morning, the tide of the battle swiftly turned when some of Federman's troops became turncoats and went public with their condemnation of Federman and his market. The schochet and the "rabbi," both apparently having had their consciences pricked by the genius of Emmett's stunt and by their own complicity in Federman's wrongdoing, took to the street to inveigh against him. The community responded with the appropriate horror at Federman's fraud. Soon his market went out of business. A victory for Emmett Kelly. And an affirmation of his motto, always prosecute a fight.

Chapter Twenty-Nine

Over the following months, one of the many things Tom had come to love about Maggie Sullivan was that he could talk with her about anything. She was a brilliant conversationalist—vivacious, curious, opinionated, well-informed on a broad array of topics. When Tom commented on these traits, she deflected his compliment, then slyly went on to acknowledge the truth of it by saying it came from two things. First, her own Da was that way. She'd committed herself early on to trying to be like him. Second, her work as a transcriptionist exposed her constantly to information of an astonishing variety, and she was a good learner, remembering much of what she took in. Tom himself would add a third thing: she read voraciously, consuming anything and everything she could get her hands on.

So, it was no surprise at all to Tom to find that she was a perfect discussion partner on his increasingly favorite topic of conversation, trade unionism. Lately, they'd been talking a lot about what he'd been rolling over in his own head: how radical unions should be. Tom didn't think of himself as a radical, but the many months of extreme hardship he experienced in the wake of the Panic of 1893 taught him, as perhaps nothing else could, that sometimes people were down and out through no fault of their own. And he was more convinced than ever that American notions of individualism and self-reliance were wrong-headed. He thought everyone would be better off if they looked out for one another more.

Some of his union brothers (influenced by miners in Leadville and railroad workers in southern Colorado) had begun to favor a militant brand of labor radicalism. Tom did not. He was open to thinking about it, but for now he preferred a more pragmatic strategy toward employers and government, emphasizing the basics of unionism: higher wages, shorter hours, and better working conditions. He liked that the union itself looked out for its members by providing burial insurance, sickness leave, unemployment insurance, and strike benefits.

Maggie had listened carefully as she sipped her beer, still recovering from the fatiguing struggle of getting Mike and Annie into bed after Tom had riled them up with too much rambunctious playtime. "Look, I know how seriously you take this, Tom. But I'm still of the mind that we've each got to be architects of our own fates. I'm keen on steering my own ship, keeping it afloat on my own terms. Don't get me wrong—I've nothing against the unions, and you know well I don't. But there's something to be said for standing on one's own two feet. I suppose it comes from working on my own, setting my rates based on the quality of my work, not on some organization's say-so.

"But I know where you're coming from on this. You're not some fella straight here from the Emerald Isle, newly arrived in Denver, barely managing to get by. But you're not at the other end of local Irish either—not some Dennis Sheedy or J.J. McGinty, living up on Capitol Hill, having dinner with the governor or the mayor at the Denver Country Club, enjoying the good life in every way. You're in the middle. You came here with nothing, like our imaginary friend. You started out fine. But then you went through a horrific period, through no fault of your own. And now you're doing better than okay. You're doing well. You've started your own carpentry business. Your savings have put us well down the path to having our own house. You don't see John Mullen and Dennis Sheedy as oppressors. You see that maybe someday—with grit, and determination, and luck —you could have what they have. Or at least a level of comfort and security you hadn't dared to imagine. So, no wonder you don't think the whole social and economic system needs to be overturned. Yet, you still believe in what unions can do to support and protect their members."

Tom understood the logic of Maggie's observation about his personal attitude. But as the new president of the local carpenter's union, Tom found himself caught between traditionalists who favored a bread-and-butter unionism that was cautious, craft-conscious and unadventurous and the progressive reformers who were more radical, even militant. Denver's labor scene was evolving, and Tom was at its heart, advocating for the unrepresented and the unskilled, driven by his belief in equality and fairness.

It so happened that Tom had come to his position of union leadership at a moment in time when Denver's labor movement, long dominated by skilled craft unions like his own, was undergoing dramatic changes. Responding to the appeals of labor radicals, large numbers of Denver's unskilled workers had rushed to join new industrial unions organized under the umbrella of the American Labor Union. The ALU had a strong following in the city, with active locals among butchers, grocery clerks, laundry workers, cooks and waiters, hack drivers, and mattress makers.

Tom wholeheartedly favored that movement. He believed those workers desperately needed organized representation. There was still no socialist movement to speak of on the political horizon in Colorado, so Tom figured that if unskilled workers were to have their interests represented in any way —have any chance of advancement and protection—it would have to come through the ALU.

"You're an egalitarian, Tom," Maggie said. "That's what you are, in your heart and in your head. Think about it. You actively supported the Populist Party in this state from the moment you arrived here. And because the two socialist parties in this state aren't worth a plug nickel, you're bound to support the ALU! Where else can a man with your sensibilities turn?"

Tom knew she was right about the ALU and correct about his being an egalitarian at his core. So, he decided to make that the center of his approach to unionism. He began to stake out positions that embodied his principles. He took on four-square the decades of anti-Chinese and anti-Japanese agitation within the American labor movement. In speeches to his own union and before the ALU, he argued that continuing to exclude Asian-American "splits the ranks of workers and thereby injures all."

His position provoked heated debate and was far from acceptable to many workers, including Irish-Americans. That particularly rankled Tom, who took to reminding his Irish-American brothers of the discrimination their people had faced earlier. "Some of you who came directly to Denver from Ireland have never experienced the level of bigotry and intolerance that our people faced in lots of eastern American cities. The Irish there didn't like it and didn't deserve it. The Chinese and Japanese don't deserve it either. We have to do better."

Tom's leadership on the issue was so persistent and persuasive that at its convention in Denver that year, the ALU adopted a resolution Tom proposed that read: "We extend a hearty welcome to the Chinese and Japanese, and all other wage earners to become members of our organization."

Because that was among the most egalitarian positions yet to be staked out in United States labor history, it made news all around the country. Locally, the newspapers featured prominent articles about the ALU's stance and about the man who had taken the lead in forging it. Tom Quinn was a bit of a celebrity. He was now a hero to many, but of course a villain to others. In the latter camp fell Emmett Kelly.

Chapter Thirty

After he'd vanquished Moshe Federman in the great Colfax pork war, Emmett's business turned brisk. Demand in the neighborhood for meat and groceries was fierce. The small building that had housed Federman's operation was still for sale. Emmett decided not only to buy it and add it on to his own store, but to build as well on the vacant lot to his other side. Jedediah had been right when he'd pushed Emmett to buy that lot as part of his purchase of the store: the lot was a perfect size for an add-on and would also give Kelly's Meat Market and Grocery the extra advantage of a corner location. Emmett's shop would stretch the length of three storefronts. He wanted the corner portion to have a prominent architectural element that would draw attention to his store. Perhaps an ornate gable, a stepped parapet, or even a turret.

But first Emmett had to build, something he'd never done before. He found the whole prospect daunting. For advice, he turned, of course, to Jed Pinsker, who in recent months had been faring poorly, suffering from diarrhea, vomiting, and abdominal pain. The medical men thought he probably had a parasitic infection in his gastrointestinal tract.

"I'm sorry you're so indisposed, Jed. That's nasty business. Anything I can do for ya?"

"Nah. … What brings you here, Em?"

"I need a bit of advice. I'm ready to build on that corner lot I bought from ya. And now, the storefront on my other side is available, too. I'm gonna buy it and extend my store. But I don't know what the hell I'm doin'. I can't do that work myself. Do you have ideas about where I might turn for help?"

Jed winced at a sudden pain in his lower belly. "How big ya gonna go? Puttin' in a concrete foundation?"

Emmett liked the looks of the buildings he'd seen with the new concrete floors, but he considered them an unnecessary extravagance, not necessary for a market. "No. That would be gettin' too high for my nut. No need for that. All wood."

"That makes it easier. You only need to hire yourself some nail benders."

"I understand. But I don't want to hire union men. I refuse to pay their premium so they can have a better brand of whiskey to drink themselves to sleep. Do you know of some nonunion carpenters I can approach?"

Jed looked at Emmett. "If you go down this path, you're gonna put yourself crossways with your old friend Tom Quinn. You sure you wanna do that? "

"I haven't seen Quinn in years, Jed. I don't care about

him. Or his union. I want to get something built, and I want to do it without laying down extra cash unnecessarily."

Jed reached across the table where they sat, grabbed a stub of a pencil, and wrote a name on a corner he tore off a page of the *Rocky Mountain News*. "I've used this fella before. Not for a project nearly as big as what you're talkin' about, but I'm sure he and his boys are up to the task. He'll take care of ya."

"Thanks."

"Don't poor-boy it, Emmett. Go the entire animal. Do yourself a favor and spend money to put in more windows. Letting in more natural light will make the place more inviting to folks and will save you money down the road on electricity. And put in a wooden plank sidewalk all the way across the front of your building. Women, in particular, will appreciate that."

Emmett laughed. "Now, you're chewing up all the savings I'll get by avoiding union men!"

"Some of it, maybe. But it'll be money well spent. If you're gonna do it, do it right. You want to look like a class act, even if when it comes to knowin' about buildings, you can barely find your ass with your own two hands." He laughed, then clutched again at the pain in his belly. "Then again, what do I know! If I was a building, I'd be condemned."

"Your illness is making you both funnier and more cantankerous, Jed."

"No. I've always been cantankerous. My illness is making me more honest in my fuckin' speech."

Chapter Thirty-One

"How exciting, Nora! I'm so happy for you. When will you get married?" Alice hoped she'd adopted a tone of voice sufficient to mask the disappointment and anxiety she felt at this news.

"J.P. wants to have a wedding in late June."

"You mean this year? But that's only a month away. You can't get married that soon! That would rob us of all the fun of thinkin' and plannin'." In truth, Alice didn't give a fig for planning a wedding, her own or anyone else's. But she knew that Nora would be high on such doin's.

"I know! So, I told him next month would be too soon. He said, 'Don't you want a June wedding?' I said, 'It *is* traditional. So, let's wait until next June.'"

Alice laughed. "Ah. I bet the thought of waiting that long sent him into an agony. But he's been lallygagging along all this time. Why's he now in such a hurry? A sudden grand fire in his loins, maybe?"

Nora knew that wasn't the case. She tended those fires on a regular basis. The real reason was one she didn't yet want to share with Alice because it would cause her no small amount of pain: in October, she and J.P. would be moving to Colorado Springs, where he was to start a new job as second-in-command of the Colorado Springs Rapid Transit Railway.

Alice had an idea. "What about September? You know the saying: 'Marry in September's shine, your living will be rich and fine.'"

Nora thought for a moment. "September might be perfect." And keeping with the veneer of innocence she liked to maintain, she added, "I'll keep his fires burning for a few months, but not so long the embers die out."

Nora wrote to Mam and Da, whose reply, when she thought hard about it, was what she should have expected: "We wondered what was takin' so long. Thank God! Here in Ireland, you'd be out of the marriage market at your age. Good on ya', girl. Sorry we can't be there to see you wed. Please tell Alice not to tarry. Herself's not getting any younger!"

After the engagement had been announced, J.P.'s parents invited the young couple to their home for dinner, along with other family members and several close friends. The Ritter house was one of the finer homes on Capitol Hill, an elegant Romanesque and Queen Anne residence built out of red-orange Manitou sandstone. It had Corinthian columns and a majestic circular porch, with a fanciful turret rising above it. When Nora first found out that this was the Ritter family home, she'd said to him, "Jaysus! I knew you were doing well for yourself at the streetcar company, but I didn't know you'd also grown up amidst that kind of wealth."

Now, as J.P. led her up the steps to the house, Nora's uneasiness soared, and she said to J.P., "What if your parents find me lacking?"

"They'llNow, Nora's uneasiness over the evening rose to new levels.

"Just breathe easy. They don't bite."

In fact, both Mr. and Mrs. Ritter were thoroughly charmed by Nora, who captivated them with her wit and grace. J.P.'s mother was ashamed of herself for being surprised to find these assets in an Irish immigrant girl. Mr. Ritter thought how lucky his son was. If only he himself had found a woman so winning and enchanting! His wife had been agreeable in her day, he thought, but she'd been no Nora Butler.

Mr. Ritter rose to offer a toast in honor of the newly engaged couple. He lifted his glass. "I propose we drink to the health and welfare of J.P. and Nora, the delightful young woman he has decided to add permanently to our family."

Then J.P. stood and said, in his earnest but charming manner, "Thank you. I don't have to tell you how lucky I am. The thing for me to do is to prove, if I can, that Nora has not made the mistake of her life by agreeing to marry me. And I hope it won't be long before we see you all at our own table, with Nora at the head of it and I, where I belong, at the foot."

Chapter Thirty-Two

With the completion of the expanded new Kelly Market (including its larger and improved living quarters on the second floor), Emmett felt that the time was right for him to drape himself with another important element of social respectability—marriage. He supposed it could only be to the good if people thought of him as a solid family man as well as a successful merchant. He didn't care about marriage for its own sake, but only for the extra burnish it might impart to his image. And although it would not be accurate to say he didn't care at all whom he married, he also wasn't willing to spend a lot of time worrying about that. He figured that a wife—any woman who was his wife— would merely be an ornament on the edges of his existence, not a romantic mate. He put little stock in romance. And although sex was important to him, he had no intention of looking principally to a wife for those pleasures. Indeed, he had every intention of continuing the sexual relations he enjoyed with Sadie Ferguson at Mrs. Barker's.

It was with all this in mind that Emmett settled on Alice Butler as the woman he would ask to marry him. He believed Alice was a likable enough person, for a woman. And since he gave no quarter to notions of lasting love, he figured "likable enough" met the standard that mattered. She was also attractive and presentable, as well as competent in all important respects. She'd even taken a six-month class in bookkeeping. That alone made her appealing. The bookkeeper he had was not inexpensive.

On the other hand, he dreaded having someone—anyone! —around all the time. And Alice was not without her drawbacks. She had become something of a health nut about food (at least, in his opinion). The thought of having to listen to Alice natter at breakfast and in the evening—with her talk of healthy this, nutritious that—made his soul die a little. And he also knew she'd be after him to take less of the drink and do more church-going. Those thoughts made his spirit wither a little more. But, on balance, Emmett believed Alice Butler to be as sensible a choice for him as any other he might consider.

He was realistic enough to know that if he were to secure Alice's agreement to wed, he would have to approach her with something approximating romantic affection. So, over the course of about six weeks, he called on her in the evening about ten times, each time bringing flowers or candy—sometimes not only to Alice, but to Mrs. Flannery, as well. Emmett took Alice to the summer stock theater at Elitch Gardens to see the celebrated New York actress Blanche

Bates star in the Augustin Daly comedy, *The Last Word.* He took her on carriage rides and horseback riding.

When, finally, he felt he had laid the foundation for making a proposal, he sat with her in the Flannerys' parlor one evening and said, "Alice, I trust that I am not mistaken in thinking there is a strong connection between us. From the first moment I met you on the train between Omaha and Cheyenne, I had a feeling that we were somehow destined to be a part of each other's life. And every time I've been with you since then has only confirmed that initial impression. I must say that I have become steadily, increasingly, attracted to you and fond of you."

Alice smiled at this, but kept her eyes focused on her hands, which were folded in her lap.

"I think you know, through our conversations, that marriage was, for a long time, not something I concerned myself with. I work hard and long hours. And I think you know what kind of life I lead and what my aspirations are. It's not the kind of life that appeals to everyone, I know. But I know you have strong feelings about food and nutrition, so maybe it's not a stretch to imagine that you might like to associate yourself with a food market and butcher shop. I feel like you could be a real partner to me.

"To be honest, before I met you, I never thought I'd find someone like that, and I probably would have stayed single for the rest of my life. But now, I can't help but hope that maybe this was meant to be.

"I know I'm not perfect, but I can honestly say that I have no skeletons in my closet that would make you regret choosing me. I can promise you that I would take care of you and devote myself to you. So, what I'm asking is, if you feel the same way about me, would you do me the great honor of agreeing to be my wife?"

Through this whole speech, Alice had kept her head down, but the slight smile on her lips never wavered. As she listened to the progression of his words, it was apparent where they were headed, and her mind raced ahead of him, thinking of him as a potential husband. She considered Emmett likely to be a good provider. He already enjoyed a fair amount of economic success, even as a relatively young man. She saw no reason to believe his business wouldn't continue to grow and thrive. And she liked the fact that he was an Irish Catholic—something important to her and, she knew, to her parents. Although he had told her once that he only attended Mass sporadically and grudgingly, she thought she could change that.

And she supposed it was an advantage that he was so close to her in age and that, although he worked hard and put in long hours, his job did not put his life at daily risk, unlike so many in this wretchedly industrialized economy. For both reasons, she figured, she was less likely than other women to end up a widow at an early age.

It bothered her somewhat that apart from this unusually expansive proposal, he was not much of a talker. Indeed, until recent weeks, she would have said he had no real interest in being with her. From what she could tell, that posture of indifference was typical of men of Irish heritage. So, she figured that was what she'd have to accept if she wanted to marry within her own culture. If she were honest with herself though, she would wonder why she stayed so committed to that path, when Nora's experience with J.P. Ritter was so enchanting. That man, of German and Lutheran heritage, positively doted on Nora!

She looked up for the first time since Emmett had begun his little speech. She took his hand in hers and said, "You have surprised me with this marriage proposal, Emmett. And you have given me much to think about. I hope you will favor me with the time to do that thinking. I promise not to prolong my deliberation."

She gave him a "yes" a week later.

Chapter Thirty-Three

Now that he was a married man and the proprietor of a prominently located, successful store in the state's capital city, Emmett began to cast his vision beyond his own business to larger affairs. His visceral hatred of the trusts led him to greater involvement in the Retail Grocers' and Butchers' Association.

The latest object of his enmity was the meat trust. For years, he'd despised the big meatpacking companies and did everything he could to avoid dealing with them. He'd formed close alliances with the strongest anti-trust packing houses in Denver and other western cities. He retailed meats almost as cheaply as they could be bought at wholesale from packers who belonged to the trust. He bombarded his enemy with low prices, and he supplied his customers with the best-fed meats in the market. But it was a constant struggle, for the trust was mighty. The four big firms that constituted it (Armour, Swift, Morris, and Hammond) were always looking for ways to fight back against rebellious retailers like Emmett.

Their latest stratagem, aimed at securing for themselves the retail as well as the wholesale trade of Denver, involved placing stationary refrigerated train cars on the side tracks near the Union Depot in downtown Denver. They sold meat right out of the cars to consumers at retail prices. Two of these cars, one belonging to Armour and one to Hammond, were on the track at the foot of Eighteenth Street, and one belonging to Swift was at the foot of Fifteenth. These were heavily trafficked areas at the confluence of many electric streetcar lines. Markets like Emmett's felt a fierce sting from the competition. The big packers also sold to small retailers at cost, in an effort to kill off Denver's anti-trust packers. Emmett considered the situation untenable.

He'd never been active in the local trade association of grocers and butchers, but he decided this was the time to get involved. He pushed hard for an emergency meeting of the association for the purpose of organizing a war on the great eastern packing houses. He proposed a resolution (which passed overwhelmingly) that no local butchers or retail grocers would have any dealings with the packers until they agreed to sell only to dealers, not direct to consumers. The big dogs backed down and ended the selling at retail from train cars on the side tracks near the Union Depot. Emmett's prominence within the butchers' and grocers' association took a noticeable leap forward.

His next effort to mobilize his comrades came a couple years later in response to actions of the sugar trust. Colorado at the time had a burgeoning beet-sugar industry. The

Eastern cane-sugar trust that controlled the production of granulated sugar tried to destroy the new beet-sugar industry by dumping cane product into Colorado at a low price. Producers of beet-sugar had no hope of competing.

Again, Emmett swung into action, urging an emergency meeting of the grocers' and butchers' association. It unanimously adopted Emmett's proposed resolution that members would handle nothing but beet sugar as long as the cane-sugar trust persisted in its treacherous plan. They vowed to lower the price of beet-sugar at their stores, absorbing some of the loss themselves. Just as the meat trust backed down, so too did the sugar combine. In the wake of this victory, the prominence and respect Emmett enjoyed among the state's grocers and butchers took another step upward.

But not long after this glorious triumph, Emmett allowed the other big issue that vexed him—the power of unions—to undo all his gains of stature among his peer retailers. The matter at hand involved the closing times of markets. The grocery-clerks' union was demanding a closing time of 6:00 p.m. rather than the then-prevailing closing time of 6:30. The grocers' association decided to fight the union over this, declaring their intent to stay open until 6:30 in the evening. The grocery clerks then announced they would go on strike starting the following Monday.

The grocers' association held yet another urgent meeting to determine a course of action. Emmett argued strenuously that it would be a mistake to give in to the union. But he lost. The grocers voted to close at 6:00 for six months in winter and at 6:30 for the six months of summer. In response, Emmett unleashed a flood of indignation, rebellion, and denunciation on them for not having grit enough to stand by their first decision to close shop at 6:30.

"I think a wagonload of sand from Cherry Creek might help you fellows over this yellow streak," he shouted, his face florid with anger. "I want nothing more to do with an association that votes unanimously to close at 6:30 and then is scared out of it by threats of a strike. Henceforth, I am not one of you! I will open and close when I please and sell at prices to suit myself. And I am out of your sugar combine! Tomorrow, I will sell twenty pounds for a dollar." He started toward the door, then turned around for a final volley. "This association has no backbone and is at the mercy of the union. Shame on you!"

As he stormed out of the building, Emmett felt good about having called the feckers on their cowardice. He figured they were all still sitting there, stunned by the truth of this outburst. Surely, they were feeling embarrassed by their spinelessness. He thought he probably looked like a golden thoroughbred in their eyes.

He was wrong. To them, he looked like a jackass.

Chapter Thirty-Four

Maggie nursed eleven-month-old Annie and laughed as she watched her seven-year-old son Mike mimic his father. The boy had rolled a piece of paper into the shape of a cigar, which he "smoked," occasionally spitting out imaginary stray pieces of tobacco. "This cigar tastes like rinse water from a Chinese laundry." Mike complained, his voice a spot-on imitation of his father's lilt.

"Good one, Mike. Now do what he says when he's tired." Maggie prodded.

Mike swiped his wrist across his brow. "Jaysus, what a day I had today! I'm knackered." Tom had come to the door of the front room at this point and watched this scene. He walked across the room and smiled at his little impersonator. "Fair play, you pup."

Mike spun around. "Look, Mam! Here's the oul fella now!"

Now, both Maggie and Tom laughed as Mike marched

around the room, imitating his father's stride. "Why do you only slag me?" Tom feigned indignation. "Why doesn't your mam get the same treatment?"

"To do Mam, I'd have to carry Annie around, and I don't wanna. Half the time Annie smells manky."

Maggie frowned at Mike. "I do things other than take care of Annie."

"Not much, you don't."

"Hey, now, mister. I work like a blue-arsed fly around here. Maybe I'll stop taking care of things and then you'll take notice of all I do!" She playfully made her hand into a fist. "Or maybe I'll give you a bonk on your smeller."

Mike assumed a boxer's stance and danced around the room, slugging an imaginary sparring partner. Tom grabbed him up. "Or maybe we should toss him out the window for talkin' to his Mam that way. What do you think, Maggie?"

"Grand idea. See if he can fly."

Now, Mike laughed and flailed and shouted "No, no. Put me down! Put me down!"

At the window, Tom noticed a street vendor had turned the corner and was coming in the direction of their house. "Raaaaaspberrrries! Blaaaaackberrrries! Apples! Fresh apples here!"

Tom fished in his pocket for a quarter. "Mike, run down and get us some raspberries." "How's she doing?" he asked Maggie when the boy had left the room.

Maggie looked down at Annie, who'd stopped nursing. "Poor baby. She had a hard time of it earlier. I wrapped her in a towel wrung out in tepid water, then wrapped it in a woolen blanket. She soon fell into a quiet sleep. She woke up for her feeding a half hour ago. I think her fever has broken."

"I hope so, for both your sakes. It's not easy to care for a wee one, especially a sick wee one. … I'm sorry, Maggie, but I have to head out to the union meeting. I shouldn't be too late." He leaned over and kissed her on her forehead.

She watched him go. Maggie was so proud of her husband. He'd truly found his puddle. He'd become an exceptionally fine carpenter and built his own successful business. And he'd been re-elected repeatedly as president of the local carpenters' union. He enjoyed the esteem of others in his trade who respected his equanimity, his leadership skills, his intelligent grasp of how to advance the cause of trade unionism.

She thought, too, about what a good father he was. He was kind and gentle to Mike, giving him gobs of attention and affection. Maggie knew that some of her friends disagreed strongly with the parenting style she and Tom had forged. "You're too attentive and lenient," their next-door neighbor had said to her one day. "And it's a mistake to treat Mike almost like an equal. You'll ruin that child."

Maggie knew their style was contrary to the reigning child-rearing philosophies and norms of the day. But she and Tom wanted happy, enthusiastic, playful children—not timid, banjaxed creatures, cowed into submission by dour parents. She wondered what the neighbor would think if she'd witnessed the scene just now in the parlor—Mike making sport of his father and talking so directly to his mother. She didn't care. He was a good, happy boy. And this was a good, happy family. Her family. Her fun family. She would handle things her way.

The same was true of her relationship with Tom. It was unconventional. She knew that. But neither she nor Tom gave a damn about social conventions or expectations. He supported her desire for a measure of independence, her preference to keep working after marriage and even after the arrival of children. She'd worked independently, on her own, from home, since her arrival in Denver. The work was grand, and she made good money. She didn't see a reason to stop. "You provide well for us, Tom. This isn't about you. And it's not about what other people do, about social norms. This is about me. I want to work when I have the time for it. Might as well. Every extra dollar helps." She was right. The money did help. But, more important to her was that her work was constantly educational; it helped her keep up on this rapidly changing world. Tom saw no reason to object, as long as the children were her priority.

Their marital relationship also was atypical. From what she could tell, most marriages were sad, lonely affairs: the aloof, superior husband patting the subservient wife on the head occasionally, perhaps complimenting her on the night's baked chicken. That wasn't for her. From the moment they'd met, the cement that bonded Maggie and Tom was laughter. They constantly gave each other the gifts of gaiety, wittiness, and high spirits— he sweeteners of life. They were consid-erate of one another, looked out for one another. And they took delight in their sexual relationship. Maggie pitied women whose attitude about sex was that it was necessary for reproduction but not otherwise to be engaged in, much less enjoyed.

"Sex wastes a woman's vital spirit," her neighbor Lurleen said to her one day.

"So, you think it's wrong if Tom and I sometimes have sexual congress twice on the same night?" Maggie asked, taking delight in shocking Lurleen. "I tell ya: I myself feel fairly vital after that! Tom and I take horizontal refreshment as often as we can!" She laughed when her neighbor's eyebrows rose toward her hairline. So what if that shocked Lurleen! It was true. They did.

Chapter Thirty-Five

Alice sat by the window, basking in the warm autumn sunlight as she opened the latest letter from Nora. She eagerly unfolded the crisp stationery, taking in Nora's familiar looping script.

"My dearest Alice," the letter began, "the area around Colorado Springs is simply magnificent this time of year. The aspens have already turned golden, and the mountains nearby already are snow-capped. They make me think of whipped cream floating atop hot chocolate—so white and fluffy against the crisp blue sky."

Alice could practically see the scene Nora described—the quivering aspen leaves glittering like coins in the crisp mountain air, the endless expanse of sky stretching on for miles. How different from their childhood in Loughrea!

"We took the horses out last weekend and had a picnic by the river. The water flowed so clear and cold over the rocks. We dipped our toes in and laughed like children."

Alice could perfectly imagine Nora's wavy hair blowing in the mountain breeze, her skirts hiked up as she waded playfully in the stream.

"J.P. takes such good care of me," Nora continued. "He wakes every morning before dawn to stoke the fire and brew coffee. By the time I rise, there is a perfect cup waiting for me, just the way I like it with a dash of cream."

Alice chuckled, recalling Nora's predilection for sleeping in late. How delightful for her to have a doting husband who accommodated her sluggish morning habits.

The letter went on. "He truly is wonderful, just wonderful! He surprised me yesterday evening with a moonlit carriage ride into town and tickets to the theater. The show was entertaining, but nothing compared to having his arm wrapped around mine as we sipped champagne between acts."

Alice smiled, shaking her head. Even in writing, Nora was dramatic as ever. But she couldn't deny she was pleased that Nora seemed so happy with her life in Colorado Springs, with her married life and doting husband.

Alice thought she might very much like a fella such as J.P. doting on her, but she wasn't so certain she wanted that from Emmett. Too much attention from Emmett might not be a good thing. After now having lived with him for a year, she had learned that he tended to dwell on the negative. He was the sort of person who thought he saw rat droppings in a nice raisin pie.

Weighing heavier on Alice's heart than Emmett's negativism were some of his other personal traits that had not been evident to her prior to their marriage. For one thing, he was too quick tempered. She never feared that he would harm her; she'd never seen any inclination of that on his part. But she regarded an inability to maintain one's composure as a weakness. She didn't like weakness. More to the point, his temper caused occasional problems, as when Emmett threw a wall-eyed fit at one of his most valuable employees, calling him a "waste of skin" and causing him to quit right on the spot. And while she regarded ambition as a good thing, she sometimes wondered if Emmett's unbridled determination to succeed might lead to difficulties. She'd seen people get in trouble when their aspirations got the better of their moral sense.

She knew what was behind Emmett's yearning for success. He spoke occasionally of how his father had constantly belittled him, telling him he'd never amount to anything. She supposed that kind of talk by a father to his son might result in the son deciding it was true and thus never having a single ambitious thought. Or, the son might spend his life determined to prove the father wrong. Emmett clearly fell in the latter category. Still, knowing where his aspirations came from did nothing to dispel her anxiety about how they might lead him astray.

An example of this occurred one day when Emmett got ejected from a street car for improper use of a transfer. He'd boarded the car at Arapahoe Street instead of Larimer Street, where he should have made the transfer. The conductor refused to accept the slip of paper and tried to put Emmett off the car at Larimer and Seventeenth streets. Emmett hurled vile language at the conductor and then struck him on the head several times with an umbrella—an action he claimed was in self-defense. "He laid his hands on my person," Emmett said to the policeman who arrested him at the scene for assault and then threw him in the cooler for four hours.

The next week he sued the Denver City Cable Company for $5,000, claiming he'd been peddling live fish by the depot —and that all his fish had died during the four hours he'd been locked up because he wasn't there to tend to them.

"That's nonsense. If I understand it correctly, you used a transfer slip improperly and then lost your temper when the conductor called you on it." She looked up from her work, sewing patches on the knees of Joey's trousers. "And this poppycock about fish? That's just a lie. You weren't hawking live fish there at all."

"Who's to say that?" he shot back.

"I am. And it's wrong, that's what it is. Pure codology. But it's also daft. Who in their right mind would believe you had $5,000 worth of fish on hand? You'd either have needed Loch Ness on the back of your cart to hold that many fish— or you'd have had to been selling the crown jewels of the sea. Emmett, I doubt there were $5,000 worth of fish in the whole city of Denver that day. The judge will toss your claim out on its ear for being pure balderdash You'll be the talk of the town, and not in a good way. This is nonsense."

"I'll tell you what's nonsense: you thinking you know the first thing about how the world works! Keep your beak out of it. It's none of your wake."

"I know how the world works just as well as you, Mr. Kelly, if not better," she retorted, a lump in her throat. "Maybe better."

A month or two later, it gave Alice no small satisfaction when a judge not only dismissed Emmett's case for being frivolous, but fined him $100 for wasting the court's resources with his suit. This whole episode gave her concerns about his ethical compass. The man seemed incapable of resisting the impulse to scheme, cut corners, manipulate institutions and systems to his advantage—he was incapable of doing the clean thing, drawing a straight furrow.

And as they sank deeper into married life, Alice found that his constant belittling of her drove her to stand up to him more, answering sneer for sneer.

She found lately that his constant belittling drove her to stand up to him more, answering sneer for sneer. "You think you're so clever fighting with the beef trust so you can sell your tenderloins and porterhouses and rib roasts for a few cents less per pound. What you should be doing is offering your customers alternatives to all that by selling oatmeal and barley, cracked wheat. Figs and dates. Dried fruits. All sorts of goods you don't bother with."

"And what makes you think there's a call for that?"

"I see them flying off the shelves in other shops! Sometimes you've got to lay out the goods, and the buyers will come."

"Ah, so now you're the grand economic scholar! A wonder, it is, that the A&P got as big as it did without Alice Kelly to tell them how to run their business! You don't know what you're talking about, woman."

But the fact was, Alice did know. She had continued to educate herself about the health benefits of certain foods, the best means of food preparation, the most favorable combinations of foods for easy digestion, and the like. Emmett felt her views were all a bit of hooey—and frequently told her so—but Alice was ardent and unswayed from her convictions. At Kelly's Market, she prided herself in guiding customers to the right food choices and offering them tips on recipes and preparation methods. Emmett himself saw her efforts less as helpful guidance than as intrusive, patronizing meddling.

One day he overheard her talking to a woman who frequently came into the store and was a profligate spender on all sorts of things.

Alice said to her, "You really should be buying and eating less meat. Americans eat too much of it. In the amounts most of us eat, it's simply not at all good for us."

Emmett was flabbergasted to hear Alice talk this way. When the woman left the store, he took Alice aside. "Are you off your chump? You do know this is primarily a meat market, don't you? That's what I'm here to sell. Why would you tell that woman she should buy less of it? She's one of my best customers."

"Because it's true. People should eat less meat, more fruit and vegetables. Medical men are clear about that."

Emmett ran his beefy fingers through his hair in frustration. Why did talking with Alice always make him feel like he was trying to eat soup with a fork! "I don't mind if you give customers suggestions about recipes or how to prepare foods, but I would ask you not to discourage them from buying things. Can we agree to that?"

She nodded, but wasn't wholeheartedly committed to an agreement on that. And on some related issues, she refused to budge an inch. For example, she felt so strongly about the

172

repugnant qualities of oleomargarine that she had made that one of her main issues.

"Remind me what you have against it," Emmett had said one night after dinner, his hand to his head, as he heard her for the fourth time on the subject but obviously still had not listened to her.

"I know you don't wish to give your ear to me on this subject, Emmett, so I'll boil it down to a point for you, just like oleo manufacturers boil down their goo: Oleomargarine is made from the slag of the butcher shop; it's more fit for the soap boiler than for human consumption. People should not be eating it. It's bad for their health!"

"You've bought in to the propaganda of the butter producers. People buy oleo and like it. Why do you think that is?"

"Two reasons: first, they're poor, and oleo is cheaper than butter; second, they're ignorant, and they're unaware how harmful oleo is to their health. No person of sufficient means and right mind would eat oleomargarine."

Emmett laughed at her. "It's curious that an immigrant woman in Denver is now the world's greatest expert on what's good or bad for people's health."

Alice had learned to steel herself to his unkind slights. "I don't give a bedbug's behind what you think about my knowledge of the subject, Emmett. I know I'm correct about this. And if you stock oleomargarine in this store, I will throw it out into the dusty street—every single day, if I have to." Emmett didn't doubt that she would, so he was one of the few grocers in the area not to stock the butter substitute.

He grabbed his hat and stomped down the stairs and out

into the night. While he traveled across town to Mrs. Barker's on Market Street to spend some time with Sadie Ferguson, Alice sat in the parlor and fumed. The man was so stubborn, so fixed in his ways and his thoughts, so convinced of his rightness, so resistant to the opinions and ideas of others. And not good at hearing anything he thought smacked of criticism.

She'd begun to think perhaps she'd made a mistake by marrying him. After all, she hadn't cast her eye very broadly. Denver had been thick with available young men, but she'd pretty much grabbed at the first one who came along. Perhaps she'd have found a kinder, gentler, nobler man if she'd waited longer. Then again, maybe she'd have ended up worse off. She decided to wet the tea and turn to the account books. She liked absorbing herself in the details of the business. At least that was something she understood. Besides, "what-if" thinking never did her any good. She'd found that the more time she spent considering paths not taken, the more miserable she became. And she was miserable enough already.

Chapter Thirty-Six

Jed Pinsker passed away, his health severely compromised by persistent gastrointestinal issues, which left him weak, vulnerable to the pneumonia that ultimately claimed his life. His passing was notable enough to merit coverage in both of the city's leading newspapers, highlighting his status as a storied bullwhacker and longtime Denver retail proprietor. The *Rocky Mountain News* penned an affectionate piece that paid homage to Jedediah's vibrant use of language, showcasing his unique flair for communication:

"In the tapestry of Western history, where cowboys are celebrated for their romantic allure, bullwhackers carved out their own niche. Known for their reliability, expertise, and adept handling of oxen, they were perhaps more infamous for their mastery of colorful expletives and raw vernacular that could make even the sturdiest of souls wince. Jed Pinsker exemplified this tradition to the fullest. With little to no provocation, he could envelop his surroundings in a blue and sulfurous cloud of vivid curses and invectives. Anyone intent on experiencing the most profane harangues and tirades to be heard in Denver need only have stepped foot in Pinsker's Emporium and cock an ear for a few moments."

An ink slinger for the *Denver Post* took a different tack, focusing on Jed's appearance rather than his coarse language:

"Pinsker was an imposing figure. His long, ragged, unkempt beard and his exceptionally tall, lanky frame made him a distinctive figure even from afar. His gait had a peculiar lean to the—a result, he always claimed, of having been kicked on his backside by a surprised mule. During his adventures along the Deadwood Trail, he earned the affectionate moniker "Shorty Jed" among his fellow bullwhackers. This nickname came about from his being frequently asked how tall he was. Jed would quip that he was '"merely five feet, eighteen inches tall.' Shorty Jed was a titan in both stature and spirit, a spinner of yarns as lofty as his own height. Yet, he was a kindly and noble man, deeply committed to this city, leaving an indelible mark on it with his larger-than-life presence."

When Emmett arrived at Riverside Cemetery for the funeral, about fifty people were already there. He figured the crowd must be a mixture of Jed's old friends and people who'd come into contact with him through the store. Walking toward the gravesite, Emmett heard a man say,

"Emmett Kelly." Emmett turned to see Tom Quinn. "I thought I might see you here."

"Of course I'm here. Jed was a kind and generous man. I want to pay my respects." "I only saw him a few times after that last evening you and I visited him together. I calculate you stayed in closer touch with him."

"He sold me his place on West Colfax when he decided to close up shop. Gave me a good price and the opportunity to grow. I'll always be grateful to Jed."

Tom couldn't let the topic pass. "You expanded that place into a fair-sized building. And I understand you used non-union carpenters and painters."

Emmett released an indignant sigh, but made no further response.

"You've ratcheted up your opposition to unions over the years."

"What do you mean?"

"I understand you gave considerable support to Peabody in his run for governor."

"True, I did."

"Was it his promise to wage a "war on unionism" that drew you to him?"

"It was."

"And is it true that you're one of the men behind the Citizens' Alliance here?" Citizens Alliances had sprung up all around the country with the aim of breaking the power of local unions. The Alliance in Denver struck fear into the hearts of local labor leaders like Quinn because it had enrolled nearly 3,000 individual and corporate members within several weeks of its creation and had a huge war chest.

"Where did you hear that?"

"It's still a relatively small town, Emmett. That's the scuttlebutt."

Emmett didn't like it at all that word of his involvement in the group had gotten out. The organization was clandestine in character. Its inner workings and membership were supposedly enshrouded in deep secrecy. Apparently not. Think how upset Quinn would be to know that Emmett was one of the main organizers of it, along with Jimmy Craig.

"I wouldn't have thought you were the kind of man to traffic in idle rumor, Quinn."

"Not idle rumor. Good intelligence. You never were a friend of union labor, were ya, Kelly."

"No, I never was. We talked about it long ago, and I gave you my reasons."

Tom looked over at his one-time friend, his companion on the journey to Colorado and through their first few years in Denver. "And wretched reasons they were. You're a self-interested man, Kelly. It's an unattractive trait."

Emmett scowled at him. "Every man is self-interested. That's human nature. 'Self-interested men' made this country. I have nothing to be ashamed of."

They'd reached the gravesite at this point, which was fortunate because their discussion had been on the verge of boiling over into something more fiery.

After a rabbi read a few psalms, several people spoke, including an old friend of Jed's who knew him from their days together as bullwhackers. The old man stood, hat in hand, and looked out at the throng of people standing before the grave.

"Jedediah was one of the friendliest and most sociable men I ever met. He would strike up a conversation with a tree stump if that was the only thing around to talk to. No one could know him and not like him. But that's not to say that the feeling was always mutual. He got into more than his share of scrapes when we was runnin' bull trains. Many was the fella who regretted thinkin' he could get the best of Jed Pinsker.

"There was one whole category of human beings he couldn't abide: Jed absolutely despised Indians I could go on all day telling you stories about Jedediah and the Indians. I'm choosing only one, because it says a lot about what kind of man Jed was—about his courage and his character.

"One afternoon the Indians had made several attacks on us. They'd killed three of our men and wounded some others. They had us all corralled on a high hill where we spent the evening and the greater part of the night gettin' ready to defend ourselves and the stock we had left. We estimated that several hundred Indians had us surrounded. We knew our chances of getting out of that fix alive were slim unless we could get help.

We needed a volunteer to risk his life by riding to a fort five miles distant to get us relief. Nobody volunteered. After a long moment, Jed stood and said, 'I'll go.' The rest of us breathed a sigh of relief, ashamed of our own lack of courage, but happy that Jed had stepped forward. We knew he would get us help, or die trying. It's the kind of good-wooled man he was

"We spent an anxious night. Not an eye closed. Every one of us stayed awake, with rifle or revolver in hand. Just at fore-day, we saw the Indians scattering to right and left of a large body of mounted men. It proved to be two companies of cavalry coming from the fort, with Jedediah in the lead. Those Indians would have killed us all at sunrise if those troops hadn't come to our rescue right when they did. Jed saved our lives. But he never let us talk about it. If anyone mentioned it in the years after, he'd say, 'Pshaw. That weren't fuckin' nuthin.' "

Emmett and Tom waited their turn to shovel some dirt on Jed's pine casket. As they walked back to the road where their buckboards sat, Tom turned to Kelly. "I hope you listened to that last story, Emmett. Among other things, it showed that not every man is self-interested. Jed obviously wasn't. We could all stand to be more like Jed. So long." He put on his hat and veered off to the left

Chapter Thirty-Seven

Like most married couples, Maggie and Tom had familiar lines of conversation to which they returned frequently—their children, Tom's work, family finances, assemblyman, and neighborhood gossip. But unlike most married couples, they also had Maggie's work to talk about, and it was a topic they both enjoyed. Each found it amusing that there was such widespread fascination at the time with the work of female typewriters. Neither could understand why this particular avenue of work for women invited such popular scrutiny. But it did. Newspapers frequently carried articles about female typewriters in the workplace.

And because sensationalism was what newspapers of the day had settled on as their selling point, the particular angle most of them took on this topic was predictable. They explored such pressing issues as: Were female typewriters hired primarily for their good looks? What proportion of female typewriters only went into the trade to find a man and marriage? Were businessmen more interested in sex behind the locked office door or a neatly typed letter?

Every time Maggie or Tom saw such an article in a newspaper or magazine, they'd bring it to the other with delight, like a cat dropping a dead mouse at the feet of its owner. Look what an interesting item I've brought you!

One day, Tom came home from work and placed a large postal card on the table in front of Maggie. Upon it was a drawing of an office interior, showing a business man attempting physical familiarities with his stenographer. An office boy behind them executed a war dance at the sight of the compromising position in which he discovered his employer. Beneath the picture was the following doggerel:

Pretty typewriters are no sin.

They always produce a sultry grin.

Keep them busy, they like that.

Not with boring work chit-chat,

But with kissing and its kin.

"Did you ever have an employer make advances on you?" Tom wiggled his eyebrows. She reminded him that she never worked in an office alone with a man. But before going out on her own, she had worked for a while at a company that employed typewriters in a pool, principally for legal documents. There, men sometimes tried to seduce the girls.

"Some of us worked the front office. We were the cream of the stenographer crop. The room was divided into three wee compartments, separated by plate glass, serving as our dictating rooms, where we took dictation on the spot. All of us quick on the keys and fair with our charges. If a gentleman fancied wasting his coin on chit-chat about the weather or the like, that was his business. But the moment he'd start with any remarks on my looks, the 'deep blue pools' of my eyes, or my 'curvy figure'—I'd let him carry on and run his bill up." She chuckled, shaking her head as if she still couldn't quite believe it. "Men, they never change. Daft, the lot of them."

Another time, Tom showed Maggie an article reprinted from the Providence Telegram:

Miss Lillian Randall was employed in the local free public library, as assistant, in 1888. She left here after a residence of six months, going to Boston, where she was engaged as a typewriter for a prominent business man, named Coburn. After the death of Mrs. Coburn, her husband married Miss Randall. Mr Coburn died recently, leaving the bulk of his property to his new wife. In all, it amounts to over $800,000, including a $100,000 mansion."

"There's your mistake, Maggie. You should have found yourself a situation like that. You'd be rich, living the life of Reilly. Instead, you're stuck with me. If I die, you'll have to start typing all day long, or you and the kids will be eating ants and grasshoppers."

"I typed all day long for years and was fine with it. Don't you worry about me, Tom Quinn. You've provided us with this beautiful new house, and we're livin' like kings, I'd say. Besides, you're tough as the nails you pound. Nothin's gonna get you, oul man."

"I am tough as nails. You're right. Hard as a nail, too." He grinned.

She laughed and palmed the front of his pants. "Oooh, so you are! But that's no nail; that's a railroad spike! Now leave me alone. I have to finish this and get it over to Mr. Samson."

"This evening?"

"He needs it first thing in the morning, and it will be easier for me to get it to him now than in the morning."

In half an hour, Maggie pulled the last page of work out of the platen, looked it over, and slipped it into a brown envelope. She found Tom to say she was leaving.

"I'd be happy to take it over there for you," he said.

"No, I have to chew my own meat."

He smiled. "I understand. Are you taking the streetcar?"

"I think I'll ride the bicycle. I didn't get enough physical activity today. I need some."

"Be careful."

"I always am, love."

When she wasn't back in an hour, Tom grew concerned, but he figured she was chatting with Mr. Samson, one of her favorite customers. After two hours had passed, he felt frantic. He stood at the window, craning his neck to see as far up the street as he could. The telephone rang. The call was from a nurse at St. Joseph Hospital. Maggie had been injured in a bike accident.

Tom asked their next-door neighbor to watch the children while he went to the hospital. The nurse on the phone had balked at characterizing Maggie's injuries, so the whole way to the hospital, he feared the worst. When he found his way to the ward where Maggie had been taken, a doctor took him aside to tell him what had happened.

Maggie had been riding on 17th Street when a delivery

wagon coming up on her right started to veer too close to her. Attempting to stay clear of it, she wheeled too far to her left. Her front wheel got caught in the shallow groove of the cable-car track, making it impossible for her to steer. She fell, and the wheels of the delivery wagon drove over her left hand, thoroughly mangling it—breaking most of the bones in the hand and wrist. She also had a broken collar bone and some lacerations on her head.

When Tom got to her bedside, both of them began to cry. "What am I going to do?" she asked through her tears. "I won't be able to type any more. The doctor said I'm unlikely to be able to do anything with my left hand, it's so crushed."

"Sweetheart, don't worry about that. We'll be fine. Your income has been important to us, but we'll get by okay on mine."

"But I loved my work."

"I know you did. Maybe we can think of something else for you to do. But that's the last thing you should be thinking about now. We have to get you healed. … I'm sorry, Maggie. I should have taken your document to Samson. I shouldn't have sat there while you went out."

"This isn't your fault. I'm a clumsy oaf."

"No. That's not true. The city is full of unexpected dangers. We're all susceptible to them."

Chapter Thirty-Eight

One Saturday evening the following year, Tom and Maggie returned to Denver with their children after a leisurely outing into the near mountains west of Golden. They'd spent the afternoon picnicking by a lake and walking an easy trail. Tom had not been well, so they'd not engaged in their usual vigorous games of tag with the children. But it still had been a grand afternoon.

It was a bit after 6:00 pm, the light of the late-summer evening shining from behind the western peaks. Maggie had started to think about what she'd prepare for supper when they got home. "Dang! I meant to buy some meat yesterday but forgot. We don't have anything at home. We should stop somewhere."

They were on West Colfax Avenue. "There's not much open at this hour," Tom said.

"There's Kelly's. They're usually open late."

"I don't feel like patronizing that monster, and I don't want to go in and have to talk with him."

"Swallow your pride, Tom. We need some food. We can send Mike in to get it." Soon, they came to the intersection where Kelly's Market sat prominently on the corner. "Will you please stop?" Maggie implored.

Tom sighed and pulled their carriage over to the side of the road in front of the store. Maggie gave Mike money and instructions to ask for a pound and-a-half of steak and about 15 cents worth of weinerwurst. The boy disappeared into the market. He emerged six or seven minutes later, clambered up into the carriage, and deposited the wrapped meat in his mother's lap.

"Take a look at it and make sure it's what you want," Tom suggested.

Maggie unwrapped the meat and looked at it. "It's the right amount, but I don't like the looks of this beefsteak. It looks scaldy." She showed it to Tom.

"You're right. That looks almost rotten." Tom scowled. He turned to Mike. "Who sold this to you in there, Mike? A man about my age? Big arms and a scar cutting through his right eyebrow?"

"That's right."

Tom turned to Maggie. "I guess Kelly thinks he can unload rotten meat on a kid. Well, not on my son. Not on my family."

He started to get down from the carriage, but Maggie grabbed his arm. "No, Tom. It won't do to start something over this. We'll send Mike back in to ask for a different steak." So, the child went back into the store with the steak, telling the man that his papa said the steak was no good and he wanted a different piece. The man with the scar told the boy there was nothing wrong with the steak, that it was the best he had in the house, and he could do no better.

He trimmed the steak more tastefully and sent the boy back outside with it.

Maggie and Tom again inspected the steak. "Is this a different piece of meat?"

"No, it's the same one. He said there's nothing wrong with it and he didn't have anything better. He cut off a little of it and wrapped it back up."

Tom grabbed the paper containing the meat, jumped down from the carriage, and went into the store. Mike scrambled and followed his father inside, despite his mother's order that he return to the carriage. Inside, Tom dropped the parcel of meat on the counter. He yelled at Emmett, "Here's your meat, Kelly. I don't want any such meat as that." The other customer in the store looked around in alarm at the shouts from the tall man.

"It's you, Quinn! I didn't know it was you. What's the matter with the meat?"

"It's rotten."

Kelly unwrapped the steak and turned it on the counter so both of them could inspect it. "Now, you show me where that meat's rotten. Be reasonable. That meat's alright."

"'Alright'? You're not the full shilling, Kelly! You can see it as well as I can! It's grayish and covered with a slimy film." Tom grew more agitated. "It has a potent smell, like ammonia."

"It's the end of the day. I haven't any better in the house.

If you're not satisfied, I'll give you the money back and let you get your meat somewhere else." Emmett started to the cash register behind the counter to get Quinn's money.

Tom had a hard time controlling his anger, not usually a problem for him. "You tried to unload some bad meat on my boy, Kelly. That's craven behavior, and I won't have it!"

"Settle down, Quinn. I'm getting you your feckin' money."

"Don't swear in front of my son! What kind of pig are you?" Tom rolled his sleeves and moved behind the counter to confront Emmett, who swung at Tom and landed a punch to his midsection. Tom retaliated with a floorer, knocking Emmett to his hands and knees. Emmett scrambled to his feet, but Tom kept up the barrage with his fists.

"Stop it, Quinn. Stop!" Emmett shouted, even as he also threw punch after punch.

The other customer ran outside and yelled, "There's a vicious fight going on in here!"

Maggie was now standing beside the carriage, holding baby MaryNell, Annie close at her side. Hearing the man, Maggie cried, "That's my husband in there!"

"I'll go back in and see that it doesn't get out of control." The man disappeared back inside. A crowd began to gather outside the store, with people pressing their faces to the window to see what was happening. Another man from the crowd entered the store to witness the altercation.

Inside, the fight had been going on for about five minutes. The upper hand had shifted frequently back and forth between the two men. There was a butcher's chopping block near where they struggled. Upon it rested a number of knives and two cleavers. Each of the combatants worried the other was so excitable that he might grab hold of a knife or cleaver, with dire consequences.

After the exchange of more blows, Emmett managed to maneuver to the block, twist in his entanglement with Tom, reach behind himself, and grab up a knife, which he brandished at Tom. It was a butcher's knife, thin and razor sharp. "I'll use this blade on you if you don't leave the store now, Quinn."

Undeterred, Tom threw a punch at Emmett but missed, causing him to lose his balance and spin half around. Emmett sank the blade through Tom's clothing, deep into his back. Tom made no sound—not when the blade went in, nor when it came back out.

In fact, the blade was so sharp and thin Tom didn't even feel yet that he'd been stabbed. Emmett hit Tom on the head a few times with the butt end of the knife handle. Tom fell to the floor, slipping on a bit of blood that was beginning to collect there.

Emmett stepped back several feet and looked at Tom. "I've stabbed you, Quinn. Let that finish this." One of the men inside the store monitoring the fight stuck his head out the door and yelled, "There's been a stabbing!" Turning back inside, he saw Michael standing there in shock. The man grabbed Michael by the shoulders and steered him outside, sending him running toward his mother.

Tom didn't seem to process Emmett's statement as fact. He managed to stand, gave Kelly a quizzical look, and started for the door. He felt tired. It had been years since he'd tangled with another so fiercely. He'd forgotten how exhausting it was. He stumbled out of the shop.

Maggie screamed and rushed to his side. The crowd had grown larger, people drawn by the noise of the altercation and the shouts of alarm from the men inside the store. The man who'd watched the fight ran to the next corner where he'd earlier seen a policeman. He told the copper what had happened.

The policeman, a fella named Sereno, hurried to a patrol box to call for an ambulance. He then rushed to tend to Quinn, who by now was on his knees, surrounded by Maggie and his children, and painfully aware that Kelly's words about having stabbed him were true.

"What happened?" the copper asked him.

"Kelly cut me," Tom groaned. His breathing was becoming ragged. "I confronted him about a piece of rotten meat he sold my son. We fought." Tom coughed up a little blood. Maggie tried to support his faltering figure. "He grabbed up a knife and stabbed me without any reason at all." Tom grimaced, then slumped against Maggie. Several onlookers, assuming the worst, cried, "He's dead!"

Sereno left Quinn in his wife's clutch, then went into the shop to detain Kelly. "You're under arrest." He seized the burly butcher by the arm.

"How is Quinn? Is he much hurt?" Kelly asked.

"'Much hurt'?" Soreno registered the absurdity of Kelly's question. "Of course, he's hurt. You'll be very lucky if he doesn't die!"

Kelly began to scream and moan, protesting that he hadn't meant to hurt Quinn, that Quinn's own aggression drove Emmett to defend himself. Outside, Maggie and the children bellowed and bawled over Tom's motionless body. By now, several dozen men and women had gathered around. Some began to talk of hanging Kelly right then and there.

Knowing that if the mob got started along that path, he wouldn't be able to stop them, Sereno took the offensive at once. He handed his revolver to an acquaintance in the crowd and told the man to keep Kelly detained. He then drew his club and went after the mob. As fast as one person would cry "Let's hang him," Sereno would club him over the head and kick him out of the crowd, then move on to the next. He managed to hold the crowd in subjection until a patrol wagon arrived with reinforcements.

A police ambulance had also arrived. A police surgeon and two helpers got Tom into the vehicle and and at once started for the county hospital. But at the corner of Tenth and Santa Fe, Tom took his last breath. The patrol wagon switched its destination from the county hospital to the county coroner.

Meanwhile, Emmett Kelly, having narrowly avoided a lynching by the riled crowd, was taken to the city's squat, red-brick jail house, where he spent the night on the dirt floor of a nasty little cell.

Chapter Thirty-Nine

The next morning, Maggie was in shock—numb, devoid of sensation. She sat in the front room with her crying children, unable to find the words to comfort them, uncertain there were such words. She couldn't mentally process the reality that Tom was dead, gone from their lives. How could this be! He was the most lively person she'd ever known. Dead? It made no sense! Killed by Emmett Kelly in a fight over a fifty-cent cut of meat? It was the most absurd thing she'd ever been forced to think about. Yet she had no choice but to think about it. She had to figure out how she'd provide for Mike and Annie and little MaryNell in Tom's absence.

The doorbell rang. On the front porch stood a tall woman dressed in black. "Yes?" Maggie said.

"Mrs. Quinn, I'm Alice Kelly. I am sorry to bother you. I've come to tell you how terribly sorry I am about your husband's death."

Maggie felt her insides roil at the audacity of Mrs. Kelly to show up like this. Maggie looked at the woman, but didn't know what to say. Why would she have chosen to come here? What could they possibly have to say to each other?

As if privy to Maggie's thoughts and feelings, Alice said, "I suspect you want nothing to do with me, so I'll only impose on you for a moment. Your grief at your husband's death is no doubt monumental—"

"I'd thank you not to characterize my grief."

Alice pushed on. "It is matched only by my own grief in knowing it happened at the hand of my husband. I hope Emmett Kelly gets the punishment he deserves." She started to turn away then turned back toward Maggie. "I know your husband was a good, compassionate man. A person of clear grit. I can't tell you how sorry I am the world will no longer enjoy his goodheartedness. I am sorry my wretched husband has robbed you and your children of his presence. God bless the four of you." With that, she turned and walked down the porch steps.

Maggie slowly closed the door and pressed her back to it. The irritation she'd felt at Mrs. Kelly's presumptuous appearance at her door had dissipated, replaced by a strange sense of wonder at what the woman had said. She wanted her husband punished! Maggie had been so absorbed in her loss of Tom that she'd spent no time at all thinking about Emmett Kelly or what would happen to him.

But now she pondered it. Would he be tried for murder? If found guilty, would he be jailed or hanged? The article in the newspaper about the killing said the Kellys had three children. If Emmett Kelly were punished for what he'd done,

Mrs. Kelly would be in Maggie's situation—head of a father-less family. And yet, she said she wished for that! Maggie shook her head, as if hoping to clear it of fog.

She had so much to do. She had to make final arrangements for Tom's funeral.

Fortunately, the carpenters' union local would cover the costs of the funeral, so at least paying for it wasn't a worry. But, she and Tom had not been regular church-goers. They preferred to spend their Sundays in other pursuits. So, approaching Father Mulcahy at Sacred Heart Church was a little awkward, since he knew the Quinns were not regular attendees at Sunday Mass. Still, he agreed to hold the service at the church and to say the Mass of Christian Burial.

The funeral occurred two days later on a glorious August morning—bright sunshine, clean air. Several hundred men filled the church in tribute to their friend and union brother. Most of them also went to Mt. Olivet Cemetery for the burial. After the rite of committal, Father Mulcahy yielded to another priest, Father Tom Malone, a popular local cleric and labor advocate. He was well known and widely admired by organized laborers in Denver.

Father Malone stood at the head of the grave, looked out at the huge crowd, and made his voice as loud as he could. "Friends, Tom Quinn was the very essence of compassion, selflessness, and devotion to egalitarianism. He was wise to the fact that the riches of our modern world are not enjoyed, as they should be, by all classes of society. He saw clear as day that if we judge our civilization by the condition of the poorer classes in our large cities, then it must be considered a failure. He believed that caring for those worse off than ourselves should be the moral compass by which we steer. He taught us we can aim higher, do better. His union leadership showed us how, through our coordination and combination with one another, we can achieve a better life for ourselves and others. Our lives are all the richer for having been touched by Tom Quinn."

Looking out at the crowd, Maggie saw that among those hearing Father Malone's words was Alice Kelly.

Chapter Forty

Emmett had been released on bail, awaiting trial, after the coroner's jury had returned a verdict of "accidental death." Several days later, Alice was reading the *Denver Post* when she came across the following article on page 3:

In an unprecedented move that has sparked widespread discussion across Denver, Local Union No. 43 of the Carpenters and Joiners has publicly condemned Emmett A. Kelly for the death of their esteemed president and fellow carpenter, Tom M. Quinn. The resolution, adopted with fervent unanimity, casts a long shadow over Kelly, branding him irrevocably in the public eye.

Tom M. Quinn, a respected and diligent member of the Denver community, met his untimely demise on August 11, under circumstances that have left the city in an uproar.

According to the Union's statement, the nature of Quinn's death makes it impossible to accept as an accident or justified act, challenging the coroner's jury's verdict that deemed it accidental.

The resolution pulls no punches, stating, "The killing of Tom A. Quinn, a man known for his peaceful and hardworking nature, not only robbed his family of a husband and father but plunged them into destitution." The Union holds Kelly "morally responsible" for the dire consequences faced by Quinn's widow and their children, emphasizing the tragedy's ripple effects on an innocent family.

In a scathing critique, the Union has denounced the coroner's jury's verdict as "a travesty upon justice," an insult to the intelligence of Denver's populace. They urge all labor bodies in the city to join in a collective outcry against the crime of murder, stressing the importance of a united front in seeking justice, especially when the legal system seems to falter.

The resolution ends with a call to action, urging the community to ostracize Kelly, to "close our homes, our hands, and our hearts against him," until he acknowledges his guilt. It's a powerful message of solidarity and moral accountability from Denver's labor community, signaling a new chapter in the city's fight against injustice.

T.F. Hayden, speaking on behalf of Local Union No. 43, articulated the collective sentiment, "Let this resolution stand as a testament to our commitment to justice and our refusal to remain silent in the face of wrongdoing."

As Denver grapples with the implications of this bold stance, the resolution has already begun shaping public opinion, marking a significant moment in the city's labor history.

Alice put down the newspaper. Tears rolled down her cheeks. She looked across the room at Emmett with feelings of profound disgust. "You've succeeded, Emmett. You found a way to bring total, enduring disgrace on yourself and this family. You are savage as a meat axe, unable to control your base impulses. Most of your wrongdoing over the years didn't surprise me, for I think you're a loathsome person. But killing a man wasn't something I ever expected of you." She paused, and when she restarted it was with more vehemence and volume. "I wish you were back in jail where you belong. We don't want you here at home. Not now, not ever again."

He shouted back at her. "Unfortunately for you, this is my house, not yours. You don't decide who lives here. And you can speak for yourself, you useless auld sow, but not for my children. They will never turn against me, no matter what."

"They've already turned against you, Emmett. They want nothing more to do with you. Eileen says she doesn't want to play with her friends any more because she's too embarrassed that you're her father."

"She's only seven and a half. What does she know?"

"She's old enough to feel a sense of shame! She does. So do I."

Chapter Forty-One

Once a jury was empaneled on the morning the trial of Emmett Kelly began in the West Side court, the prosecution team—Assistant District Attorneys Harry N. Bancroft and George Allen Randolph—made their case. Randolph took on the task of the opening statement:

"May it please the court, counsel, members of the jury; this is a case of murder. You are here because on August 11th of this year, that man, Emmett A. Kelly, took a knife and intentionally stabbed and killed an unarmed man, Tom Quinn. We are confident that the weight of the evidence we shall present to you during the course of this trial will establish the defendant's guilt."

Randolph laid out the facts of date, time, place, and sequence of events: the purchase of the meat; the allegation of the meat's taint; the nature of the altercation; the stabbing of Quinn by Kelly; the death of Kelly within a half an hour from the effects of that stabbing. He walked the jury through what the government would try to prove—what Emmett Kelly did, how, and why.

"We will prove that on August 11 of this year, the defendant, Emmett Kelly, committed the crime of murder when he intentionally grabbed a knife and plunged it into the back of the victim. The circumstances leading up to the killing are unimportant except as they flash light upon the characters of the two men in this fatal drama.

"Quinn was a carpenter. There is nothing exciting about the rasp of a saw or the smoothing shear of a plane. Carpenters are quiet, easy-going men. Even in a labor strike they are proverbially conservative and slow to anger. Kelly is a butcher. He is used to the sight of blood. He has dealt many a slaying stroke to young calves and sheep and fatted beeves. One may say he likes the shedding of blood; one may say he has shed blood, time and time again, and become used to it.

"The killing of things! That is the trouble. It seems a predilection, almost an appetite. What does one inured to the use of knives do when affronted? Why, use a knife! The key ingredients for murder were present: anger, an uncontrolled temper, and a knife. And now Tom Quinn is dead." One could hear a mouse breathe in that court room.

The defense—attorneys John T. Richards and Edward Watson—gave the jury its own interpretation of the facts and set the stage for rebutting key government evidence. Watson took on the task of the defense's opening statement, which he'd decided to make brief: "May it please the court, counsel, members of the jury; good day. We are here today because on August 11 of this year, Emmett A. Kelly, in the midst of a fight with Tom Quinn, accidentally killed him.

"In a criminal case, the prosecution, having the burden of proof, presents evidence first. Only after the prosecutors have presented their case will Emmett Kelly have an opportunity to present his. We ask that each of you wait until you have heard from all the witnesses, ours as well as theirs, before deciding what happened. We do not contest the fact that Emmett Kelly did stab and kill the deceased, Tom Quinn, on August 11th of this year. We agree that this happened. That fact, however, is not the issue in this case.

"The issue is whether Emmett Kelly meant to kill Tom Quinn or did so accidentally in the course of defending himself during a confusing, horrific fight that Mr. Quinn started. I am confident, gentlemen of the jury, that upon hearing all the evidence, you will render a verdict in this case that will be fair.

"The prosecution will not be able to prove, beyond a reasonable doubt, that Emmett Kelly intended to kill Quinn as the fight wore on. We will show there is reason to believe the killing was unintentional. We also will show that Mr. Kelly's actions throughout the fight were in selfdefense. We expect that after you deliberate and carefully weigh all the evidence in this case, you will return the only possible verdict, a verdict of innocent. I thank you."

Sitting on opposite sides of the court room, Maggie Quinn and Alice Kelly wept.

Chapter Forty-Two

Fifteen minutes before the start of proceedings on the second day of the trial, Maggie Quinn arrived with Michael; they sat near the front of the observers' benches. Maggie's light, strawberry hair contrasted vividly with the blackness of her mourning dress and cap and the newly dark, sunken look of her eyes. There was a pathetic appeal for retributive justice evident in her bent pose. She was still in shock—numb, devoid of all sensation.

Yet she was doing all she could to rally herself for poor Michael, who was understandably traumatized by witnessing his father's killing. And now, he faced the prospect of having to appear before a group of strangers and talk about it. That terrified him. Maggie knew they had no choice in the matter, so she gone to Tom's bedroom the previous night to talk about what he might expect today. They discussed what would happen in the courtroom and about Michael's fears, which included having to be in the same room with Emmett Kelly. "He scares me, Mam. He looks like a mean man."

"He does, Mike. And he is a mean man. But you'll be safe from him in that courtroom. Don't worry about that. The important thing is that you tell the truth about what you saw happen in that market. Do you understand?"

Mike nodded, tears welling in his eyes.

"Good boy. Always tell the truth, no matter what."

"Ma? What are we gonna do? How're we gonna get by?"

She reached over and pulled him toward her. "I don't know, Mike. But we will. We'll get by."

Now, the two of them sat rigid as the prosecution led off with its principal witness, Leopold Rudek. Tapping nervously at the arms of the witness chair, Rudek described graphically the killing of Tom Quinn, as he saw it. Stolid, and plumb unmoved by all the questions asked him, Rudek stuck tenaciously to his story, reiterating it to the minutest detail. When he first took the witness stand, he had been very nervous, but after a few questions from Bancroft, he told his story simply.

"I was passing down Colfax Avenue on the evening of August 11. Going by Kelly's Market, I heard there a ruckus inside. It was loud enough to wake snakes. I went in and saw two men locked in each other's arms in the middle of the shop. One was Kelly, the owner of the store, whom I knew. The other man was Tom Quinn, who was unknown to me."

"Near where they were struggling stood a butcher block stuck full of knives, and as I stood there I saw that Kelly was pulling nearer and nearer to this block. I didn't understand what he was going to do, so I merely shouted for the two to separate, as I didn't care to risk getting into the midst of the row.

"Suddenly, Kelly began looking out of the corners of his eyes at the block. Then he gave Quinn a quick jerk and I saw one of Kelly's hands shoot out and snatch a knife from the block. Quinn saw this, too, and turned slightly to pull away. As he did so, Kelly stabbed him on the left side of his back. He then drew the knife out of Quinn's body and beat him over the head and shoulders with the handle of the blade until Quinn fell to the floor."

"What happened next, Mr. Rudek?"

"Kelly began to whimper, saying, 'I've stabbed you, Quinn.' I decided to go get help. When I turned around, I saw the boy, young Michael Quinn, standing there behind me. I grasped his shoulder and steered him out of the store, where he ran to his mother.

"I then hurried down to the next corner to hail a policeman I'd seen moments earlier."

Rudek stopped at this point and glanced around the courtroom until his gaze rested on Emmett Kelly, who had been writhing in his seat while Rudek testified. Kelly looked back at Rudek with an intense loathing.

Bancroft said, "Mr. Rudek, would you say that it was necessary for Emmett Kelly to stab Mr. Quinn to subdue him?"

"No, I would not. Kelly was the stronger, more powerful of the two. And Mr. Quinn appeared to be running out of steam at the time Kelly stabbed him. His tail was quite down. The fight was almost over, in my opinion."

"Thank you. Let me ask you about another matter important to this case. Was there an attempt made to bribe you, Mr. Rudek?"

"Yes, there was. On the night of August 28, Martin Doyle, an associate of Mr. Kelly and someone I know, confronted me as I was walking on Colfax Avenue. They offered me first $150 to come onto this witness stand and say that I didn't see what happened well enough to claim that Kelly stabbed Mr. Quinn. 'That's bribery,' I said to him, 'and I won't have anything to do with it.' He then increased the offer to $250. 'What don't you understand?' I shouted. 'I won't go along with this, no matter how much you offer me. This is bribery, pure and simple. I won't be party to your scheme.'"

Bancroft said, "Thank you, Mr. Rudek. You may step down."

When they called Michael to the witness stand, Maggie's heart ached for him. Seated in the witness chair, the small, pale lad's feet dangled a foot above the floor. How vulnerable and terrified he must feel. Maggie had dressed Mike in a suit and tie for the proceedings. The poor boy's voice trembled when he began to answer the prosecutor's questions.

"You're nine years old, is that right, Michael?"

"Yes, sir. Nine and a half."

"And I understand you're the person who went into the store and bought the meat that became the subject of the fight between your father and Mr. Kelly. Is that right?"

"That's right, sir."

"Then, you went out and showed your parents the meat, and your father decided to go in himself. And you followed him in, is that correct?"

Though nervous, Mike's voice was becoming clearer, less

wavering. "Yes. I knew there was going to be an argument. That's why I followed my da into the store."

"Can you tell us how the fight started?"

In a high, childish treble, he gave an accurate description of the start of the fight—Mr. Kelly swearing at his father; his father moving behind the counter; Kelly swinging at his father, hitting him in his midsection; Tom retaliating."

"Michael, the jury may hear from others that your father threw the first punch. You say it was Mr. Kelly who hit first. Are you certain of what you're saying?"

"I am, sir. Mr. Kelly hit my father first. My Da then fought back. After a bit, Mr. Kelly grabbed a knife and stabbed my pa." When he told of his father lying on the floor of the shop with blood flowing from the knife wound, Michael's fortitude gave way, and he ran his hand over his eyes to wipe away the copious tears.

"What happened next?"

"That was the last I saw. A man in the store hurried me out to the sidewalk, where my mother and sisters were."

When the defense attorney then questioned Michael, trying hard to tangle the little fellow, Michael clung to what he knew and reiterated the words, "Mr. Kelly started the fight, and he stabbed my papa."

"Okay. Thank you, Michael. You may go back to sit with your mother."

Police Surgeon Davis, who attended Quinn in the police ambulance and was with him when he died, was the next witness.

Bancroft asked him. "Would you please describe the wound that caused death?"

"It was inflicted right above the left kidney. The knife had been driven forward and downward with such force that it had penetrated the diaphragm, lower part of the lung, and had shattered a rib."

"How, in your opinion, doctor," asked Randolph, "did Mr. Quinn come to his death?"

"By an internal hemorrhage."

"Caused by the knife wound you have described?"

"Yes, sir."

The defense had no questions for the police surgeon. One could have heard a worm cough in the court room when the next witness, Mrs. Maggie Quinn, walked to the stand.

"Mrs. Quinn, would you describe the events leading up to your husband's entry to Kelly's Market?"

She described the family picnic in the mountains, the ride into Denver, the decision to stop to purchase meat, and the consensus that the meat sold to Michael was tainted.

D.A. Randolph asked, "What was the condition of your husband's bodily strength previous to his death, Mrs. Quinn?"

Attorney Watson leaped to his feet, objecting to the question.

"Overruled," Judge Bailey said.

Maggie sat there, tears flowing down her cheeks, biting her lips, vainly trying to keep back the pent-up emotion. "My husband had been sick for three weeks prior to the night Emmett Kelly killed him." Maggie's voice broke. "He can't have given Kelly much of a fight. He was ill and weak at the time he was murdered."

Chapter Forty-Three

When the trial opened that third day for the start of the defense, Attorney Watson called Martin Doyle to the stand. Doyle testified that Leopold Rudek had approached him on Colfax Avenue and tried to extort money from Kelly through him, asking for $150 in exchange for testifying that he had remained outside the market during the fight and saw nothing of the killing,

Then Emmett A. Kelly took the stand in his own behalf. In his testimony, he claimed

Quinn started the fight. Then he gave a graphic description of the fight itself. Kelly said he could remember nothing of the stabbing, claiming it was unintentional.

Kelly's attorney, John Richards, said to him, "I wish to call your attention, Mr. Kelly, to some testimony you gave before the coroner's jury in reference to the struggle with Mr. Quinn in your shop. Did you testify as follows: 'I fell down and he continued to strike me, and when I got up, he clinched me, and we were close to the meat block. I saw him reach for a knife or something on the block, and I pushed him away.' Now, is that correct?"

Kelly glanced around uneasily. "We struggled away from the block."

"I'm asking if you testified to that effect before the coroner's jury?"

"I must have," replied Kelly, in an uncertain voice.

"And was that testimony true?"

"To the best of my recollection."

"Did you also testify to the following: 'After striking me on the head, he backed up against the meat block and I thought he was after a knife or cleaver.'"

"I did."

"So, you believed your life was in danger?"

"I did."

"No further questions, your honor."

D.A. Randolph approached the defendant. "Mr. Kelly, was the meat you sold to Michael Rudek rotten?"

"I wouldn't say 'rotten.'"

"Would you say it was tainted?"

Kelly hesitated. "I suppose so."

"Why did you sell tainted meat?"

"It was still edible, and it was the end of the day. It was the best I had in the house at the moment."

Randolph paused, walked over to his desk and picked up a paper, then back. "Mr. Kelly, you testified before the coroner's jury that Tom Quinn repeatedly hit you in the face and on the head. Is that true?"

"It is."

"And yet, a report by a police surgeon who examined you after you'd been taken to the county jail said he made a thorough examination of your neck and face and could find no bruises or marks of blows. How do you account for that discrepancy?"

"Maybe his eyesight was bad."

There was muted laughter from the Kelly claque in the courtroom.

"Mr. Kelly, you have claimed that you remember nothing of the stabbing and that it was unintentional. Is that correct?"

"Yes."

"And yet two witnesses have testified that after they saw you grab the knife, they heard you say, 'I'll use this blade on you if you don't leave the store now, Quinn.' Wouldn't a reasonable person say that sounds like you had some intent?"

"I don't remember saying that."

"You have said that in the frenzy of the fight, you were not even aware that you had stabbed Mr. Quinn. Yet, witnesses have testified that after you used the knife on Quinn, you said, 'I've stabbed you, Quinn. Let that finish this.' Wouldn't a reasonable person say that sounds like you were aware of having stabbed Mr. Quinn?"

"I don't remember saying that either."

"Officer Sereno testified that when he entered the store to arrest you, you asked him, 'How is Quinn? Is he much hurt?' Wouldn't a reasonable person say that sounds like you were aware of having inflicted severe harm on Mr. Quinn?"

"I don't know what a reasonable person would say. I wouldn't say that."

There was more laughter in the courtroom at Kelly's unintentional slighting of himself. Even Judge Bailey allowed himself a small smile.

"Okay, Mr. Kelly. Since you exclude yourself from the category of reasonable persons, there's probably not much point in hearing more from you. But I have one last question: Based on all we have heard, isn't it true that a reasonable person would conclude that you conspired with your confederates to bribe Leopold Rudek to influence his testimony?"

"Mr. Randolph, I have no respect for you or your attempt to convict me. And I suspect the reasonable people on this jury will agree with me that your case against me is nothing but balderdash."

Judge Bailey said, "Mr. Kelly, mind yourself or I will hold you in contempt of court."

Kelly barely veiled his sarcasm. "Of course, your honor."

Randolph said, "I have no more questions for the witness."

Judge Bailey adjourned the court and said the trial would resume with closing statements at 2 o'clock.

Upon resumption, Judge Bailey said, "As you know, it is the custom now in this state for the defense to present its closing first. From whom shall we hear—Mr. Richards or Mr. Watson?"

Watson stood, buttoning his jacket. "Both of us, your honor. I'll start and Mr. Richards will finish."

"Proceed."

Watson started by reviewing the testimony that had been offered in this case. He first took apart the testimony of Leopold Rudek, trying to pick flaw after flaw in it, hoping to lay it before the jury like combed flax, bleached and tattered. Slowly working to a fevered pitch about Rudek's "nonsensical testimony," he whirled around and pointed at Rudek, who sat in the back of the courtroom, surrounded by a number of his friends and acquaintances.

Pointing his finger at Rudek, Watson shouted, "Leopold Rudek, a lowbrow, Polish Jew! He's like one of the rabble that gathered around the palace of Pontius Pilate when Christ was on trial, shouting, 'Give us the man, that we may shed his blood.'"

A few of the fellows who surrounded Rudek hissed at Watson's simile. A better class of Hebrews, friends of Kelly, occupied the front of the court room. They nodded their heads approvingly at Watson's denunciation of Rudek.

Watson continued. "There is a motive behind every word uttered by this witness against Mr. Kelly—a cold and purely mercenary motive. Mr. Rudek is not possessed of a high order of intelligence, nor is he overburdened with a sense of moral responsibility. He is from Poland, and it was not the salubrity of the climate in Colorado that induced him to come here. He came to make money, any way he could. By hook or by crook.

"We have proved to you, through the sworn testimony of Martin Doyle, that Mr. Rudek approached him, asking for money to renounce his claim that he had witnessed the stabbing.

Watson then took up the testimony of Michael Quinn, son of the dead man. "That poor boy was frightened, and had a natural desire to avenge his father's death, perverting his testimony. Gentlemen, if you let Mr. Kelly go free, when that boy gets older he will thank you. Should you convict the defendant, that boy will go to his grave with horrible regret tearing at his heart—regret for the false testimony he gave on the stand about his father's death."

Now, Attorney John T. Richards, associate counsel for the defense, rose to continue their closing argument. Like Watson before him, Richards made sure to catch the eye of each juryman before he started. He waxed lyrical for a while about justice and fairness. Then, as if the defense couldn't quite decide what strategy to pursue, he made a dual argument that Emmett Kelly's killing of Tom Quinn was both an accident and an action taken in self-defense.

"You heard Mr. Kelly testify that he had no intention of stabbing Quinn—that it happened in the heat of the fight. We have shown that Quinn, in a white heat of anger, went into Mr. Kelly's shop and attacked him, first with words and then with fists. We have shown that Quinn knocked Mr. Kelly down. You heard Mr. Kelly testify that he thought Quinn was angling toward the butcher block to grab a knife or a cleaver. It would be only natural for Mr. Kelly to grab a knife himself in self-defense. Surely, a man may lawfully resist an attack with such force as is necessary to protect his own life. Emmett Kelly had no hatred in his heart toward Tom Quinn. This was a tragic accident that occurred as a man was trying to defend himself." Richards returned to his chair next to Watson.

D.A. Harry Bancroft stood, walked back and forth at the front of the courtroom, then stopped in front of the jury box. He rested his hands on the rail and looked at the twelve men arrayed behind it.

"Gentlemen, Mr. Kelly's attorneys have filled the air in this room with poppy-cock.

During this trial, they attempted to impeach the integrity of the principal witness in this case, Leopold Rudek, by having allies of Mr. Kelly allege that he tried to extort money from Kelly to change his testimony. Just now they have tried to support this outrageous claim by making base slurs about Mr. Rudek's character and intelligence.

"Mr. Watson encouraged you to believe that Mr. Rudek came to America to get money 'by hook or by crook.' He repeatedly called your attention to Mr. Rudek's Polish heritage and his Jewishness. Why? Because he's trying to suggest there is some national bias, some ethnic antagonism, affecting the attitude of witnesses for the prosecution. Yet, there is absolutely no proof of that. So, you should accept the testimony of Leopold Rudek as fair and free of bias."

Bancroft paused. Then, as his colleague had in the prosecution's opening statement, he turned to Emmett Kelly's career as a butcher—and what that apparently immaterial fact meant. "The slaying of live things, the becoming accustomed to the shedding of blood, is not conducive to moderation and self-control. It does not inculcate in the butcher a fondness for the settlement of disputes by aid of argument, reason, or arbitration. It predisposes him to kill."

Bancroft walked away from the jury and drew close to Emmett Kelly, at whom he quietly stared for fifteen seconds or so. He then returned to the rail of the jury box. "Gentlemen, you may find it interesting to know that in the state of Delaware, a butcher is prohibited by law from sitting on a jury, as you're doing. Yes, that's right. An entire legislature has held that the disposition of the fate of a man is not safe in the hands of a butcher!

"This may seem an unjust prejudice against one engaged in a useful avocation that's necessary to the comfort of man. But the law has emphasized the prejudice and crystallized it into a dictum which might be construed as follows: 'A butcher is a good man—a good man to let alone if he differs from you in opinion. He does not argue; he cuts." Bancroft looked each member of the jury in the eye, then raised his voice and said, "Gentlemen, are you going to wash the bloody hands of this man, Kelly, or are you going to answer the wail of the widow and orphan for vengeance?"

He then took his seat.

With the closing arguments finished, the judged declared a ten-minute recess. When the court reconvened, Judge Bailey read to the jury ten closely written pages of instructions. He gave a brief review of the case and instructed the jury on particular points. "It is alleged that Mr. Kelly sold the Quinns bad meat. If this is so, gentleman, the deceased had a right to return said meat, and reasonably express his indignation at such treatment." Bailey went on in that vein and concluded by defining the different degrees of murder and manslaughter. "There will be no verdict of murder in the first degree in this case," he said, as he folded the typewritten pages of instruction.

The jury deliberated for twenty-four hours, discussing and arguing over the case. When the jurymen informed Bailiff Andrew Knight that a verdict had been agreed upon, the bailiff notified Judge Bailey and the opposing counsel in the case. Soon, all gathered in the courtroom and the jury filed in.

T.M. Campbell, foreman of the jury, handed the judge a slip of paper. Judge Bailey read the verdict, took off his spectacles, and asked the defendant to rise. The defendant looked like the most unconcerned man in the courtroom. "Emmett A. Kelly, you are found guilty of involuntary manslaughter."

Chapter Forty-Four

Maggie wept upon hearing that Emmett Kelly had escaped a murder conviction. "There is no justice for me, for my children. How can those men have come to this conclusion?" Maggie said to William Samson, the former customer of her typewriting services, who, along with his wife, had rallied to Maggie's side with support and friendship in the wake of Tom's death.

"I agree with you, Maggie. This is an unjust outcome. It's hard to fathom. I think most people who followed the trial would agree the district attorneys did as well as they could with a difficult case. They're both capable prosecutors. The trouble is that Kelly hired distinguished counsellors with great expertise. I hear Kelly practically bankrupted himself in securing counsel, wiping out whatever tidy sum he'd set aside for old age and the family. Those men were as sharp as Philadelphia lawyers!"

Abigail Samson chimed in. "It obviously didn't help that

there were witnesses who swore to peculiar things and that there were charges of extortion against Rudek."

William agreed. "And there seems to have been a total lack of investigation into those charges and countercharges. Why that is, I can't say. Because Kelly has influential friends? I don't know. I'm not sure how these things work behind the scenes." William paused a while. "Let me ask you, Maggie. Have you thought about filing a civil suit against Kelly?"

"I have. I think I have to do it for the sake of my children."

"It would be foolish not to. Winning a civil case is virtually certain in this instance. Civil liability doesn't require the intent to cause harm, only the harm itself. And there's no doubt that Kelly caused the harm. Plus, your case would have a strong emotional appeal. A jury considering your pain and suffering might well compensate you with a large award— more than whatever you sue for."

"Do you have a recommendation for an attorney I should use? I have a couple ideas, but I'd set store by any suggestions you may have."

"Let me think about it."

A week later, Maggie Quinn filed a civil action in the district court. In her complaint, she set up that: "On the 11th day of August, Emmett A. Kelly willfully and maliciously slew Maggie Quinn's husband; that he thereby took away from her and her family of three children their mainstay and support; and that she and they suffer much mental and physical pain and hardship by reason of Kelly's bloody act. Hence, she prays for $5,000 damages, the same to be secured out of the estate of Emmett A. Kelly."

But Maggie's attorney had warned her that the case could take a long time to work its way through the court system, so she shouldn't count on seeing any money anytime soon. Fortunately, Tom's union brothers from local no. 43 and members of the Denver circle of Women of Woodcraft organized a benefit dance and card party at the immense Denver Coliseum to benefit Maggie Quinn and her children. The event netted $600, which Mrs. Ada Slathawer and Mr. John Weirtham presented to Maggie at her home. That would keep the family going for five or six months, at least.

Chapter Forty-Five

"What are we going to do, Emmett?" Alice's voice was thick with contempt. "You've bankrupted us by hiring those two attorneys to defend you. And now there's this civil suit. $5,000! We don't have that much money left after the trial. What's your grand plan?"

Emmett who was out on bail, pending his sentencing hearing the next day, looked at her. "The system is corrupt, woman. A jury is nothin' but twelve men who decide which side had the best lawyers. If I hadn't hired Watson and Richards, I might be swinging from the gallows next week. They saved my neck."

Although she didn't like the mental picture of Emmett hanging by the neck, Alice felt that would have been the right outcome. "That would have been your just desserts. Your money bought you your life. But spending your money to save your neck has jeopardized the future well-being of your family. I ask you again, what's your grand plan?"

Emmett loathed the woman sitting across from him. What had he ever seen in her? A pretty face, he guessed. But it wasn't so pretty now. Since his fight with Quinn, she had started to look like his own mother—hollow, sunken, gray. "I've asked Hank Cohen to sell the market. He'll get a good price for it."

"And where are the children and I supposed to live?"

"I'll figure that out."

"You'll 'figure that out,' will ya? That's reassuring. I suppose you'll let us know the results of your figurin' from your prison cell, eh?"

Emmett had blanched at her mention of a prison cell, but in truth, he knew that was in his immediate future. His attorneys had told him to expect it. The only question was how long he'd be behind bars.

The next day, he found out. Judge Bailey first denied a motion for a new trial, then sentenced Emmett to one year in jail, the longest term he could give under the limit of the law.

BY THE END of that week, Emmett sat in a cold 8-by-10 foot cell behind a door of heavy steel bars. The cell itself was also solid steel, including the floor and ceilings, not a particle of wood in sight. The building, about twenty years old at this point, had four stories or tiers of such cells surrounding a main rotunda, with balconies overlooking the rotunda on each floor. As jails went, it wasn't bad. It was well lit and fireproof. Still, Emmett felt it was inhumanely cold in there in November and December.

But an even worse cruelty, in his view, was that the jail, at the corner of Colfax and Klamath, was a little less than a mile from his market, his home, his family. What made that hard was that he knew the area like the back of his beefy hand. So, whenever he got a glimpse of the outside, he knew exactly what he was seeing and could picture well what was around, in every direction. He knew well the bustle of life going on right outside the walls that contained him. That was a form of torture.

Numbing routines regimented his life. Three times a day, a team of guards came through the cellblocks to dish out food to the prisoners, slopping the food by ladle through the bars. He was only let out of his cell to perform janitorial or kitchen work, as one of the jail's forty "trusties"—men anxious to make a good record so they'd be awarded parole time (two days from each thirty days of sentence).

By late December, he'd concluded he had to get out. He didn't see how he could stay in that cell for another 10 months. He was certain he'd go insane. He was allowed to write and receive letters, which is how he spent much of each day. He corresponded with friends and anyone he could think of who might be in a position to help him. And despite his troubles, there were plenty of such people, many of them other members of the Citizens Alliance. Good thing he'd decided to help form that group, he thought. Those folks might be able to save his hide.

"What can I do?" he wrote to Jimmy Craig, president of the Alliance. "Do you think it would work to present to the governor a petition, signed by you and other prominent men, asking him to pardon me? Even if it didn't achieve the desired outcome, I don't see what harm it could do."

Craig replied to Emmett that such a stratagem might well work, but Emmett should do the leg work, writing to notable men, asking them to intervene in this manner on his behalf. Emmett calculated that a better, more patient course of action would be to lay some groundwork first before asking the men for their help. It wouldn't do to ask for assistance or a favor right off the bat.

Instead, he would write first not as an act of supplication, but as a gesture of friendship—to inquire as to the recipient's health and well-being, to express dismay if his own recent misfortunes had brought any mortification to the good men of the Alliance. By cloaking his ultimate intentions, he hoped to gain trust and feelings of good will. Since most of these men were superior to him (more talented, more successful, of higher social and economic orders than he), Emmett had to be careful always to approach them in ways that made them feel comfortably superior.

He knew that his name was surrounded with sensation, scandal. But he also knew that along with notoriety sometimes comes power. To many of his associates, he now appeared larger, more interesting, more mysterious than he had before. That could work to his advantage. He understood well that everyone frowns upon the timid and admires the bold.

In any case, he chose not to accept the image that he felt society had cast upon him. He refused to be seen as a killer. So, he set out to reshape his image in the eyes of his allies, casting himself as a champion of causes they shared, as a bold pursuer of his correspondent's goals—someone of far greater use to them out of jail than in.

And he wasn't above a bit of direct investing in good will. He scoured the newspapers for scraps of information he could use. When he read of a birth or a death or a marriage in an influential family, he arranged for Gus to deliver flowers and a basket of fruit and treats. He knew that giving before taking was a way to get what he wanted.

Finally, he was ready to act—to ask, to take. He arranged for the Secretary of the Citizens' Alliance to circulate to fifty of the group's most influential members a petition asking the governor to grant Emmett a pardon and release him from jail. The movement on Emmett's behalf snowballed. Eventually, nearly a hundred prominent men in Colorado—drawn from every important industrial and economic sector—beseeched the governor in writing for the release of Emmett Kelly.

Emmett had another card up his sleeve. The ace was this: in addition to asking his friends to petition for his pardon and release, he asked them to contribute to a fund to secure the financial well-being of Mrs. Quinn and her children. Somehow, Emmett had known that a show of compassionate effort on his part to help his victim's family might ultimately be the key to his liberation from his steel cell. The governor would have to be impressed by Emmett's benevolence.

Chapter Forty-Six

Meanwhile, Alice herself was busy raising money for the Quinn family. Involved for years with two Catholic charitable organizations—St. Vincent's Aid and Good Shepherd Aid—Alice had arranged for each organization to make donations to the Quinns. She further had arranged for she herself to deliver the sums to the Quinn residence.

So, it was on a cold Wednesday morning in January, in the midst of a heavy snow, that Alice again showed up on Maggie's front porch. Maggie opened the door, surprised to see Mrs. Kelly standing there. She hadn't been expecting anyone. But what surprised her more was the appearance of Alice Kelly. The woman standing on the porch seemed to have shrunk. Her skin was sallow, her cheeks sunken, her eyes dead. Maggie tried to conjure the same dismissive manner she'd used to greet the woman when she'd shown up on the day following Tom's death, but found she couldn't muster it. She said, "Mrs. Kelly?"

Alice hadn't known how she'd be greeted, so she'd decided in advance to turn directly to her mission, skipping any preliminaries. "Good day, Mrs. Quinn. I'm here as a representative of two Catholic aid societies to give you a sum of donations made by people in two parishes to aid you and your children through hard times."

She stepped forward and handed Maggie an envelope. "There are two bank checks totaling $500 in here. We hope you'll think of it not as charity, which can wound one's pride, but as a gesture of friendship from your Catholic neighbors. We wish you well." Alice offered a thin smile to Maggie, then turned to go.

It seemed to Maggie that she had never known the passage of a few months' time to work so great a change in anyone as it had worked in Alice. Her face was thinner. It now seemed all eyes, and very grave soft eyes they were. She had a deep and quiet dignity. Maggie could not escape the feeling that one spirit in the body of Alice had been killed, and another and wholly different one had entered to take its place.

Maggie made a split-second decision. "Wait a moment. Won't you come in?" Alice Kelly's whole appearance had plucked a chord deep inside Maggie. She'd wondered from time to time what Alice's life was like in the wake of Emmett's imprisonment, and now she had an inkling that it was hard. Compassion had made her speak.

Hearing Maggie's invitation, Alice stopped in her tracks and slowly turned back. Surprised to be invited in, she stammered and stuttered. "W—well, if you're certain I'm not imposing."

Inside, Maggie took Alice's coat and invited her into the front room. "Please have a seat," she said. "I'll wet some tea." She left Alice alone for a few minutes and returned with a teapot, two cups, and a couple of biscuits on a tray. As Maggie poured the tea, Alice took note of her mangled left hand and the difficulty she had performing even this ordinary task.

Maggie smiled and said, "Please tell me about these organizations. I'm not a daughter of Erin who stayed close to the Church, so I'm unfamiliar with their workings."

Alice spoke of the help the aid societies offered to the elderly poor, to widows with children, to the sick, and to others in dire need. Maggie listened. "And you go around delivering this beneficence?"

Alice coughed. "Not me in particular, but someone does, yes."

Maggie nodded. "I suspect it feels good, what you do."

Alice looked up, wary of some verbal trap ahead. She coughed again. "I'm not sure what you mean, Mrs. Quinn."

"I mean nothing unkind. I mean only that I can imagine it feels good to know you're helping others."

Again, Alice was reluctant to go along with a statement that put the focus on herself. "There are so many people in need through no fault of their own, Mrs. Quinn. If only there were resources enough to aid all those who need it."

"You're doing what you can. That's to your credit. Please call me Maggie."

Alice smiled at the unexpected kindness.

"Mrs. Kelly—"

"Alice."

A faint smile touched Maggie's lips, her eyes softening with worry for the woman before her. "Alice, tell me, how are you holding up.? I know this has been no easy stretch for you either."

Alice's face was a picture of astonishment at Maggie's kindness, a whirlwind of gratitude and disbelief swirling within her. How to respond? She couldn't possibly lay bare the full brunt of her struggles, the dark depths she'd found herself in these past months. "It's generous of you to ask. The troubles my wee ones and I are facing pale in comparison to the suffering Emmett Kelly's deeds have brought upon you. You're in my thoughts daily, wishing I could ease your burden somehow."

Tears had pooled in Alice's eyes. Gently, Maggie reached across with her right hand, giving Alice's a comforting squeeze. "Alice, you bear no fault for your husband's wrongs. It's clear you've a kind heart, a pure soul. I hope you can free yourself from this shadow of guilt you've been carrying. It's been tough on you as well, I can see that."

Alice, overwhelmed by Maggie's unwavering kindness despite her own loss, finally let the tears flow freely. Once she'd composed herself, she managed, "It's shameful, me sitting here, accepting your comfort." She paused, her voice a mere whisper, "Tell me, truly, how do you keep going?"

Maggie exhaled deeply, her fingers tracing the rim of her tea cup. "Life without Tom is a daily struggle. He was the love of my life, brought me nothing but happiness. Ours was a rare bond. I miss him something fierce. But, the children and I are managing, more or less. The carpenters' union has been a godsend, holding benefits that have helped us immensely. And now, this extraordinary kindness from you and your group! So, we're holding up, financially, at least for the moment."

Maggie was attuned to the mix of relief and sorrow in Alice's gaze, understanding well that Alice's pain stemmed from her unique plight. The community's support that she, Maggie, received was a stark contrast to Alice's isolation. Surely there were no organizations holding benefit dances or taking up collections to aid the family of a killer.

"Let me ask again how you and your children are faring." Maggie pressed gently.

Alice's eyes welled up once more, yet she held back the tide of her emotions. "Truth be told, we're in a rough patch. My husband used up our savings for his legal defense, and since the trial, foot traffic's all but vanished from the market. Can't blame folks for steering clear of a place marked by such tragedy. Emmett's managed to arrange the sale of the shop from his cell, hoping to start anew on a smaller scale once he's out. But where that leaves me and the children, in terms of a home or livelihood, I can't yet fathom."

Maggie reached out again, a comforting anchor. "We barely know each other, but you strike me as a strong person, Alice. You'll find your way through this."

Alice managed a weak smile. "I cling to that hope. It's just that right now, I don't see the how of it." She hesitated, then ventured. "Forgive my asking, but your hand…"

Maggie glanced at her gammy hand. A shadow crossed

her face as she recounted the bicycle accident that had marred her life a few years earlier.

Alice's sympathy was immediate. "That's terrible. I can only imagine…"

"It was a cruel twist, it was. The accident forced me out of work. I had a transcription business—stenography and typewriting—that I'd been able to run from home. But that came crashing down, like I did. My clients drifted away, in search of alternatives. I can still do stenography, but that doesn't do me much good without being able to do the typing as well. Usually, people need the two services in combination. … And then losing Tom… it was like being hit by a second wave before I could right myself from the first."

Alice nodded, empathy etched in her features. "To lose your husband on top of everything else … What a cold scald!"

Maggie offered a grim smile. "Yes."

They shared a moment of silence. Maggie, with a hopeful glint in her eye, broke the quiet. "Would you like to know how you might help me further?"

Alice leaned in, eager to offer whatever support she could. "Yes, absolutely. Anything."

"Join me for tea once a week."

Chapter Forty-Seven

Alice put the letter from Nora back in its envelope. She seethed. The man had no shame! One would think that all he'd been through would have taught him some humility, shown him the error of his ways, made it plain to him that he had to accept responsibility for his behavior and bear his punishment. But no. Nora's letter informed Alice that Emmett had written to J.P., now a bigwig in Colorado Springs, and to J.P.'s father, a lumber-industry magnate, asking them to join other prominent men in petitioning the governor to grant Emmett a pardon. The man was so outrageous he could make a stuffed bird laugh!

Nora had written: "J.P. and his father will do whatever you ask, dear Alice. If you want them to join in this petition, they will, for they both care for you. But if, as I suspect, you believe Emmett's latest exercise in brash self-interest is wrong, then they will refrain from participating."

Alice wrote back. "Dearest Nora, Thank you for notifying

me of Emmett's latest scheme. Truly, there are no limits to that man's audacity! Please ask J.P. and his father not to take part in Emmett's machinations. I send you my love."

Then she drew another piece of paper and wrote to Emmett for the first time: "Emmett, I learned through Nora of your latest stratagem. You are a shameless coward of a man. I am giving you notice that upon your release from jail —whenever that is—I want nothing further to do with you. The laws of the Church, for which I have respect, will not allow me to divorce you. But I will not live with a man such as yourself. And I will not allow my children to do so either."

Before she could change her mind, she sealed the letter in an envelope and affixed a two-cent stamp to it. She had no idea how she would carry through on her resolve, but she intended to find a way. She was to be at Maggie's for tea in an hour. She would post both letters on her way there.

Walking the two miles to and from the Quinn residence each of the past few weeks had done Alice some good. The brisk air and strong sunshine had a salubrious effect on her. Even she herself could see that she looked less run down, more vibrant than she had of late. So, she'd been doing more walking, apart from her trips to Maggie's house. And the time spent strolling was conducive to reflection and rumination.

Even before this latest evidence of Emmett's refusal to accept responsibility, Alice had begun to think of how she could separate herself and the children from him. As she'd written to him, divorce was out of the question. So was legal separation, for even that would require his consent. But an informal separation was not. What was to stand in the way of that? He couldn't force them to live with him. But leaving him would mean she'd have to find a way to support herself and the children. Was there a way? As she approached Maggie's house, she vowed to broach the idea that she'd been nurturing the past week.

Seated this time at the little table in Maggie's cozy kitchen, Alice regarded her new friend, whose own visage also had seemed brighter of late. She supposed if she told Maggie of her idea, she'd also have to tell her of Emmett's efforts to secure early release. His plan was adding urgency to her need to find a viable course. So she started with Emmett's latest audacity.

"Maggie, I have to tell you something." Alice unveiled Emmett's scheme. "I obviously don't know what may come of it, but I wouldn't put it past that man to secure an early release from jail. He's as slippery as polished ice."

"Oh." That seemed all Maggie, slack-jawed at this news, could muster at the moment.

"I know. It's horrible." She paused. Do it, Alice. Do it, her inner voice said. "Maggie, I can't live with Emmett when he gets out. I won't. He's not a good man, and I will not spend my life in his company. Nor will I let my children do so."

"What will you do?"

Alice swallowed hard. Say it. "I'm wondering if you'll teach me to typewrite." Maggie's eyes grew large. First she smiled. Then her smile turned into laughter. She stood, pulled Alice to her feet, and hugged her tightly. "Of course, I will!" The two rocked back and forth in the first embrace either of them had felt in months. It was a luxurious, exuberant, life-affirming hug. Finally pulling apart, Maggie said, "What are you thinking, Alice?"

Alice was so surprised by Maggie's positive reaction that she was momentarily nonplussed. When she regained her composure, she said, "I'm selfishly thinking you could help me find a way to support myself and my children."

"There's nothing selfish about that, Alice. And I'll do anything I can to help you. When shall we begin?" They hugged again, swaying together and laughing.

Chapter Forty-Eight

On May 18 of 1907, the *Rocky Mountain News* carried a brief article, under a stark headline: "KILLER RELEASED FROM JAIL." It read: "Emmett A. Kelly, sentenced to serve one year in the county jail on the charge of involuntary manslaughter in the killing of Tom M. Quinn, was granted a full and unconditional pardon yesterday by Governor Henry Buchtel. The statement of facts accompanying the pardon announced that the list of petitioners for the pardon was very lengthy and comprised many well known men."

The article failed to note Emmett's most cunning move: the request to his allies that they contribute to a fund to secure the financial well-being of Mrs. Quinn and her children. It galled Emmett that the newspaper didn't report that part of the story. What good did it do him to be so benevolent if people didn't even know of it!

"He's getting out next Wednesday," Alice said to Maggie the day after the article appeared.

"Then you'd better hurry."

"Hurry to do what?"

"Hurry to move into this house whatever you need for you and your children."

Alice couldn't believe what she'd heard. "What are you talking about?"

"You must move in here, Alice. We have room for you all."

"Maggie, stop spouting nonsense. We can't move in with you!"

"Why not?"

"Foremost, what would Mike and Annie and MaryNell think of that?"

"Ah, they'll be fine with it."

"How can you say that? The family of their father's killer! Moving in with them? Nobody on this earth could countenance that!"

"Along with me, my children are the kindest, most generous people on earth. So there!" Maggie's grin spread across her still-beautiful face.

Alice laughed.

"Maggie, are you serious? How could we possibly make that work?"

Was she serious? What had she done, Maggie wondered. She'd spoken up before giving the idea due consideration. "It's an idea. Possibly a very good idea. I'm not saying it would be easy, especially at the beginning. ... Let's each give it thought overnight and talk about it again tomorrow. For now, let's get back to this lesson."

They'd bought a new typewriting machine, the best one they could find. Alice had taken Maggie's old one home so that she could practice at any time. She'd been slow at first—mostly, Maggie thought, because the learning curve and the machine itself intimidated her. But after the first couple of weeks, Alice's speed improved and her error rate declined.

"Did you time yourself last night?" Maggie asked.

"Yes, several times. My best was 39 words per minute."

"That's very good, Alice! You've only been doing this a short time."

"I know, but I feel I should be improving more rapidly."

Maggie rolled a piece of paper behind the platen of her machine and laid a magazine article next to it. "Let's see how you do with this piece."

Alice sat at the table, remembering to straighten her posture the way Maggie had shown her. She placed her fingers on what Maggie called the home row. "I'm still finding the hardest thing for me is to keep my eyes on the writing material rather than on the keys."

"Everybody struggles with that at the beginning. It won't be long before you're able to do that with ease. Your fingers will know where the keys are. I have a suggestion you might try. Do you know any poems by heart?"

"A few."

"Say them in your head. As you do, typewrite them with your fingers. Just practice moving your fingers to where you know the correct keys are. You can do that anyplace, anytime, even when you're not at the machine."

"That sounds like a good idea."

Maggie laughed. "I did that when I started learning. Then it turned into a curious habit. A quirk. I'd 'typewrite' things without even being aware I was doing it. A thought would stick in my head or I'd read some words on a sign. After a while I'd realize my fingers were twitching. Tom would sometimes be sitting with me and he'd notice my fingers moving like I had a nervous tick. He'd ask what I was typewriting. We always laughed when I would realize what word or words had been going through my head."

Alice found the story thoroughly charming, but also foreign: it had been so long since Emmett had paid any attention at all to her that the idea of having a husband notice such a tiny thing seemed fantastical. Alice smiled. "What a wonderful husband you had."

The comment mystified Maggie because that hadn't been the point of the story. "It's true. ... Now, give that a try. While you do that, I'm going to do some laundry."

Alice started typing. The article was called "The New Woman." As she typed, she realized she must be improving. Usually, she was too fixated on getting the letters and words correct to think about the content of whatever she was copying. But this article had her thinking. She knew the piece was representative of all the talk at the time of "the new woman" —her discontents and her desires for change.

Alice supposed if she were to follow through on her determination to live apart from Emmett—to be a grass-widow—people would cast her as some sort of "new-woman" feminist, intent on putting her own welfare and happiness ahead of her obligations to her husband. Let them. As far as she could recall, the last time she'd cared what people thought of her was when she was thirteen years old and had earned the enmity of the boys in Loughrea by pushing Timothy Shaughnessy into the pit of pig manure.

Chapter Forty-Nine

That evening, each woman considered the idea of blending Alice and her children into the Quinn household. To Alice, the benefits were clear. She had to get out of Emmett Kelly's house. Living there any more was untenable. Moving in with Maggie would mean she wouldn't have to buy new kitchen gear or furniture—other than perhaps beds and mattresses. And she'd grown very fond of Maggie, enjoying her company immensely. The costs included the fact that their living at the Quinns' would probably exacerbate whatever rage Emmett would feel at his family moving away from home.

For her part, Maggie figured she would have to sit her children down and explain to them that what happened to Tom was the fault of Mr. Kelly alone, not his family. It might take the children a month of Sundays to warm up to the newcomers, but she knew it would happen. They needed new friends and companions. And although the house would be a bit crowded, it would not be cramped. The home Tom and his men had built for them was large and roomy.

Plus, Maggie craved the companionship Alice would bring. She'd been so lonely since Tom's death. The two of them had thrived on their togetherness, their lively conversations. She desperately missed that kind of adult contact. Alice was no Tom Quinn in the conversational department, but each passing week had brought Maggie and Alice closer, so that now their talks were more personal, more meaningful, more satisfying. Plus, Alice was funnier than she initially seemed, so their craic was often hysterical.

When they met the following day for yet another typing lesson, the question before them filled the air like a cloud of perfume. "So, did you give my idea some thought?" Maggie asked.

"I did. But I think you should speak first, Maggie. It was your idea. Tell me how you feel about it now that you've had more time to think about it."

"We should do it." Maggie did not hesitate or equivocate.

"You truly think so?"

"I do. I think it's a grand idea."

"So do I."

They shared their thoughts, discussed the pluses and minuses, considered logistics, mulled over what they'd need to purchase, how they might arrange things. After an hour, they were satisfied they had a workable plan.

Maggie decided the time was right to raise her other idea. "Alice, I have another proposal I want to discuss with you." She paused a moment. "I think we should go into business together. Once your typewriting is up to full speed and accuracy—which, I judge, won't be too distant in the future—we should start a transcription business. I'll take the shorthand. You can do the typing. How is that for high?"

"Oh, Maggie. I think it's a marvelous idea! But I can't read shorthand. How could I type from your steno?"

"I've thought about that. Initially, I would read back to you aloud the shorthand dictation I take from a client. But you could study shorthand, same as you're studying typewriting.

Eventually, you'd be able to read my shorthand and would no longer need me to read it to you."

"Do you think so?"

Maggie smiled. "I do. And although all my former customers have moved on to other services, I wager we could capture many of them back. Plus, you have many contacts in the city that don't overlap with mine."

Part of Maggie's calculation was that Alice seemed to be familiar with almost everyone in Denver—or, at least, to know something about them. Alice had explained that it came from her many years working at the telephone company. She'd reached the point in that job where she'd have brief chats with people on each ends of the calls she connected. So, she knew thousands of Denverites by name and voice, if not by face. And they knew her.

"Surely, you could bring in business from your many friends and acquaintances."

Alice grinned. "What would we call our business?"

"Beautiful Maggie Quinn's Universal Business Service." Maggie guffawed, pleased with herself. "I don't know! Something generic, like 'Denver Transcription Service.'" "Moving in together and starting a business together? Sounds stressful." Alice gave herself permission to make the joke that had come to mind. "Maybe this time a Quinn will kill a Kelly!" Maggie stared at her for a moment, then broke into raucous laughter. Alice, relieved, joined in.

Later that day, news reached them of Emmett's orchestration of the fund-raising campaign, which netted nearly $12,500 for Maggie and her family. The two women had different reactions. When Maggie recovered her breath from the surprise, she saw the windfall as a sign that perhaps Emmett was a better man than she'd thought. Alice saw it as the manipulative, calculating wangle it was. But both regarded it as good news. The money would help cover the initial costs of combining households. It also would boost them over the early financial hurdles of starting a new business.

"This will allow us to get our feet under us," Maggie said with a grin. "And then some."

"We're going to do this. And we're going to make a success of both ventures."

"That suits me down to the ground, my friend."

Chapter Fifty

Patrick Riordan, the warden of the Denver County jail, escorted Emmett to the enormous exterior gate. He shook Emmett's hand. "We'll miss you, Emmett. But I hope not to see you back here. Stay out of trouble." Emmett smiled and tipped his hat, "Thanks, Patrick. I'll send your family a ham as soon as I get settled."

It took him only fifteen minutes to walk home. He stopped in the market to say hello to Gus, who was busy with a customer, then went upstairs to greet the family. Nobody was there. And all their clothing was gone. Damn that woman to hell! She'd done it! She'd moved herself and the children out. He thought she'd been spouting her usual balderdash in that letter. Where could she have gone? He hurried downstairs and asked Gus, who knew nothing about it. Later, when Gus thought about it, he realized he hadn't seen any of them around for the past several days.

Emmett was in a rage. Who did the woman think she

was? She had no right to move his children away from him. Was there a way to pursue legal action against her? He called John Richards. The answer was: legal action was unlikely to bear fruit. Richards told him that while Alice appeared to have ended their cohabitation, she had not said anything about intending to end the marriage. The difficult question was whether she had left without justification. Richards said that a judge might decide Emmett's manslaughter conviction was justification enough, suggesting, as it did, an intemperate character on Emmett's part. Richards counseled Emmett to leave the matter alone and try to move on with his life. Perhaps Alice would change her mind when she realized how hard it would be to support the children on her own.

Emmett wasn't the sort of man to let family matters slow him down. Henry Cohen had a deal pending for the sale of the store. But that begged two questions: where would Emmett go and what would he do? Cohen told him of a property available farther downtown that was perfect for a small market.

Emmett abhorred the idea of starting all over, but he didn't see what choice he had. He needed to sell his current store in order to pay off his debts. Whatever he netted from the sale would leave him little to work with, but he supposed he could make a go of it. He only had himself to look out for now, Alice and the children be damned. She's so high and mighty? Then she could provide for them!

Little had he known that his cynical machinations to deliver money to Maggie Quinn would end up feathering his own family's new nest.

Chapter Fifty-One

Just as Alice had feared, the Quinn children were none too happy at the arrival in their home of the four Kellys. Mike, in particular, balked, being the oldest and the most aware of the whole situation. His newly sullen demeanor was occasionally interrupted by tetchy outbursts of uncontrolled anger. Alice was mortified. "Maggie, I'm so, so sorry. Maybe this was a terrible idea."

"It's only been ten days, Alice. It's normal he'd be making strange. Give it some time. He will come around. Besides, look at the others. Annie and Joey are getting along famously; MaryNell and Bridget are attached at the hip. We have to accept that Mike and Eileen are going to have a harder time with this. It's understandable."

"Of course, it is. But I'm still sorry Mike's in distress."

Maggie pulled Alice in for a hug. "It will be all right. I'm happy you're here with us. I truly am." Then she turned to business. "I was thinking today that we should prepare an advertisement to place in the *News* and the *Post*. And we should have a leaflet printed that we could send out to prospective customers."

"Do you think we're at that point already?"

"No, not yet. But we should have such things ready for when we are. It won't be long, I think."

"I copied a list of all Emmett's suppliers. And I asked the Catholic aid societies for a list of their members. They were happy to give them to me. We'd have to spend ten or twenty dollars on postage to reach all those people. But it might be worth it."

"I have a good feeling about this, Alice. I do." She paused. "I feel a need, though, to say, right here at the start, a few things about my convictions, my beliefs about a woman-run business. I say this, mindful that you have plenty of experience of your own, as you helped to run a business. But not one like what we're starting. A woman-run business is a different creature, and special care needs to be taken with its operation."

Upon hearing this, Alice was initially put off by Maggie's attitude of superior knowledge. But she chastised herself for being silly. Maggie did have particularly relevant experience she herself lacked. "I'm eager to hear."

"You may not agree with all this, but … I believe that, hampered by tradition and heredity, women too often hesitate to seize opportunities, fear to take the initiative, shrink from financial risk. We've been trained to hoard money, to 'scrimp and save.' We've not been taught to spend wisely. Your comment about spending ten or twenty dollars on postage is what prompts me to say this. It would be a big mistake not to advertise enough, not to see the wisdom of spending $100 to earn $1,000. Scrimping on advertising to save money is about as useful as stopping a clock to save time."

Alice felt chastened by Maggie's remark. "Of course. I see what you mean. How boneheaded of me not to realize that ten or twenty dollars could yield multiples of that." Maggie laughed and pointed at Alice. "And that there. That self-depreciation you're displaying. That undue, misplaced modesty! That's not productive of success in business. An apologetic, forelock-tugging attitude doesn't convince the public or a potential customer of one's worth. It doesn't bring in patronage. If we're to succeed, we have to have absolute faith in ourselves and in our business. What's more, we have to impress that faith on our would-be customers."

Alice jokingly tugged at the hair growing above her forehead. Laughing, she also bowed a little. "You're right. I'm so, so sorry."

Maggie smiled at the jest and continued. "Finally, we have to be thorough, careful, exacting in the execution of every project we take on. If we produce at the highest quality, there will be a market for our work. Even small attributes are fundamental for success. Things like punctuality, courtesy, willingness to accommodate, alertness, clear-sightedness—"

"Okay," Alice interrupted. She was a bit miffed, but hoped to hide it behind a posture of feigned indignation. She crossed her arms and adopted a stern expression. "You had my attention and agreement until now, Maggie Quinn, when you started to sermonize. What do you think I am, a monkey? An untrained dog? I'm fully familiar with the arts of social intercourse and will represent us well in every respect, even if I am a bit bone-headed about spending on advertising."

Maggie realized Alice was codding her, but also knew she must have tread on Alice's toes with those last comments. She decided to slide by it. "Now, I want to hear your thoughts."

Alice wondered what she could add to Maggie's catalog of good advice. Surely, wise investing, self-respect, earnestness, value, and efficiency covered the topic. Alice looked down at her black muslin dress. A thought occurred to her. "We should dress the part. I'm not saying we should try to pass ourselves off as members of 'the smart set,' or try to mimic the higher classes by adopting their style. But we need to look more appealing. At least, I do. You always look grand. But I'll have to update my clothing and my look. I need a sprucing. You've convinced me with your comments about the attributes necessary for success. I'm adding personal presentation to the list. 'Take a look at me,' my appearance will say. 'This is how good your typescript is going to look!'"

Maggie laughed and applauded. "That's my partner!"

Chapter Fifty-Two

Everything about his new life made Emmett mad as a March hare. His new store was smaller than the old one. The location wasn't as good. He had to travel farther to pick up supplies or run errands. Worst of all, he was just getting by, barely making ends meet. Emmett was down to his bottom dollar. He didn't know how he'd cope if he had four other mouths to feed, four other bodies to clothe. As far as he was concerned, it was good that Alice had taken the children and moved in with Maggie Quinn. They all deserved each other!

To deal with his financial woes, he'd been standing off his creditors, delaying payments to his wholesalers and service providers. He was getting complaints from many of them about that. Sometimes, the complaints grew more serious. The Baker-Vawter Company, a manufacturer of loose-leaf accounting forms and binding devices, filed a civil action against Emmett when he failed to pay a bill of $177. As was often the case with Emmett, that legal problem mushroomed into something bigger when he exercised poor judgment and showed weak self-restraint.

On the morning that case was set to go to trial, Emmett waited in the basement of the courthouse for the case to be called. Down the corridor came Arthur Collier, who had done considerable work for Emmett in arranging a loose-leaf system for keeping the books in the new market. Collier had been summoned as a witness for the plaintiff company.

Emmett approached Collier. He mustered his most menacing look. "If you make trouble for me by testifying against me, Collier, I will give you a brutal anointing. I suggest you keep your bone box shut or you'll be going early to your earth bath." Emmett's mien and demeanor so frightened Collier that he fled the courthouse. When the case was called, the plaintiff's attorney told the magistrate that his principal witness was not in court. The judge issued an attachment for Collier, and the case was delayed for two weeks.

When Constable William Horner presented Collier with the writ, the frightened bookkeeper said, "There's no way I will appear at that courthouse unless I get proper protection." "Protection? Why? From what?" Horner asked. After Collier told him about Emmett's threat, Horner nodded and said, "I'll see to it that you have protection on the day you have to testify." Horner was true to his word.

Collier gave his testimony, and when asked by the judge about his failure to appear in court on the originally scheduled date, Collier repeated the story of Kelly's threat that day in the courthouse basement. "I'm afraid of the man, your honor, as I have heard something about his reputation and I believe that he meant to carry out his threat. That man is so cold-blooded you could get frostbite just bein' near him! I believed from his actions toward me that day that he meant what he said. He would do me up. That was the reason that I stayed away from the court."

Later that afternoon, Emmett appeared in court to give his own testimony in the case. As soon as he stepped down from the witness stand in Magistrate De Lappe's court, he was arrested and charged with trying to intimidate a witness and threatening to kill Arthur Collier. He was released on $1,000 bond for a hearing the following Thursday.

News of all this reached Alice and Maggie through Harriet Gilmore, a friend of Maggie's who happened to have been the court stenographer assigned to the case. She phoned the Quinn residence after court adjourned. Maggie listened to Harriet's tale with amazement at Emmett's incorrigibility. And that was the topic to which Maggie and Alice returned time and again in the following days.

"He appears to have learned absolutely nothing from his time in jail," Alice said. "One would think six months behind bars would have had a reformative effect on the man, but apparently not!" She wondered what mental defect plagued Emmett, preventing him from learning from his own experience and making him prone to repeated wrongdoing. "Where will it end with him?"

Maggie thought it best not to weigh in on the matter, as Alice was doing a good enough job bashing Emmett without her help.

Emmett was in a fix now. He'd have to hire Watson or

Richards again to defend him, and he didn't have the money. Perhaps he could arrange to pay a small amount now and more later. Watson agreed to that, so was at the hearing the following Thursday to defend Emmett. Watson persuaded the judge to dismiss the charge since there was no witness to the alleged intimidation.

Again, Alice and Maggie learned of this outcome through Harriet Gilmore.

Alice knew Emmett well enough to know that this wasn't the end of the matter. Surely, Emmett would find a way to get back at Arthur Collier for causing him trouble. What would it be? she wondered. Within three weeks, she had her answer. One morning, she was reading the newspaper and came across a tiny item at the bottom of page 5.

TRIED TO RUIN BUSINESS, KELLY CHARGES IN DAMAGE SUIT

Efforts to ruin the business of the Kelly Mercantile Company, of which Emmett A. Kelly is president, are charged in a damage suit filed against Arthur M. Collier. The plaintiff asks damages of $2,000.

It is alleged that Collier circulated stories to the effect that Kelly was about to abscond with the proceeds of the company, located at 1230 16th Street. He also is charged with saying that the firm would soon become insolvent.

Alice suspected that Collier had done nothing of the sort, that this was Emmett's retribution against the man. Emmett would probably induce some of his low-life friends to testify falsely against Collier.

Poor Collier. Alice felt for him. In a way, she felt Collier's problems were her fault. She had been Emmett's longtime bookkeeper. The only reason Arthur Collier came into contact with Emmett Kelly in the first place was that with Alice gone, Emmett needed a new bookkeeping system. Poor Collier. Getting drawn into Emmett Kelly's world was dangerous to one's wellbeing.

Chapter Fifty-Three

The new transcription business was slow to ramp up. Customers were happy with the services. But the client base still wasn't big enough. Maggie thought about what they might do to attract more customers. One day, she had what she thought was a brilliant idea. She didn't know if she could sell Alice on it. That night, after all the children were asleep, Maggie broached the subject.

"Alice, I have an idea for how we might get more business."

Alice looked up from darning one of Michael's socks. "Oh? Tell me."

"I think we should see if we can get the *Post* or the *News* to write an article about us. A human-interest story about two women whose husbands were on opposite sides of a death-fight, now living in the same house with their children and running a business together." Alice's jaw had dropped open. Maggie laughed. "Your face tells me what you think of the idea."

Alice laughed, too. "Sorry. I hadn't expected anything like that!"

"But do you think it's a bad idea?"

"Not necessarily. What's your thinking?"

"Such a story would bring us a lot of attention. Some people are attracted by a bit of intrigue, out-of-ordinary circumstances, celebrity. The attention could well bring us business from people who want to meet us, have some contact with us, be associated with us. Does that make sense?"

Alice smiled. "Interesting! How would we go about it?"

"Bill Samson knows newspaper people. I bet he can plant the idea with someone."

"Let's give it a try."

Three weeks later, the *Denver Post* carried an article that started on page one and continued on page five:

WIVES OF VICTIM AND KILLER UNITE IN BID FOR NEW LIFE

We are well into the era of 'The New Woman,' that female of formidable determination and bold autonomous streak. We all know this new model of femininity. She is of a new generation of American women, taking responsibility for her own life, independent from male control.

Two women here in Denver are giving to that term 'new woman' a luminous, unusual gloss. They have formed an unlikely alliance, an unexpected partnership, a close bond that may shock observers who know of their history—one that, in the normal order of things, would never allow such an association. The history? One woman's husband killed the other woman's husband. But now, the two women live in the same house with their total of six children, and they have started a business to provide for their common support.

The article—accompanied by an appealing photo of Maggie and Alice, both nicely clothed and coiffed, standing behind a typewriter—went on to spell out the particulars: the pair's gradual realization of their shared pain, their reciprocal compassion; Alice's determination that she had to live away from Emmett; Maggie's welcoming of the Kellys into her home; the typewriting lessons; the decision to start a transcription service. It continued:

History is replete with unlikely friendships of one-time enemies. The Franks and the Mongols. The Dutch and the Turks. John Adams and f Jefferson. What will become of this newest alliance? Who can say? But there is no doubt we sit now with a burning question: how will the business community of Denver react to this most unusual of pairings? Will these women be spurned for their daring in taking their lives in a bold direction of their own choosing? Or will the community embrace and support the spirit of compassion and the vital spark of self-reliance they represent?

"What do you think?" Alice asked, looking up from the newspaper.

"I think it's good. I'm not so keen on the 'new woman' angle, but I suppose it was inevitable. I believe the article portrays us sympathetically, which is all to the good. Now, we have to wait and see what, if anything, it yields."

They didn't have to wait long. Just as Maggie had anticipated, their new visibility and celebrity translated into business. Oodles of business. Soon, they had more work than they could manage, and they had to hire two friends of Maggie's to help them out.

Chapter Fifty-Four

"Emmett says he doesn't want to see them. He says I've ruined the family for him. I said he did that to himself. What kind of man doesn't want to see his own children?"

"My experience is that people usually live what they learn, meaning he probably didn't have a good father as a role model."

"That's true, Maggie, and you're right: he didn't. But you and I both know there are wonderful men who had a bad father yet somehow learned from that experience. They became good fathers themselves despite the lack of a positive example."

"Did Emmett ever spend much time with the children?"

"No. He regarded the children as a burden, not a joy. He believed the children were my responsibility, outside his domain. He was always too busy with his store, with his own life. That lack of contact had a circular effect. When they were together, he and the children felt awkward. That made it less likely they wanted to engage with each other again.

"When I would try to talk with him about his lack of attention to the children, he'd invoke his financial obligations and his need to make the market a success as justifying his absence from family life. He probably thought it appeared less selfish to blame his financial responsibilities than to acknowledge his narcissistic strivings for success."

"It's strange, I suppose, that you and I have never talked about Emmett at any length." Maggie gave Alice a quizzical look. "What was that word you just used in describing his strivings for success?"

"Narcissistic?"

"I'm unfamiliar with that word."

"I only know it from an article I recently typed for a professor at the University of Denver. His article was about the work of an Austrian named Otto Rank, who recently published a paper about this idea of narcissism, linking it to vanity and self-admiration. This article had me thinking all the way through about Emmett and how perfectly this concept captured his personality. He's so self-centered and vain, with this inflated sense of self-importance."

Alice paused. "Did I ever tell you that after he expanded his store, his advertisements called it 'one of the largest and finest markets in the West'? He always drew the long bow with that kind of outrageous grandiosity. He even liked it when the spotlight cast him in a bad way. That was fine with him as long as he was the center of attention."

"I usually don't like to think about Emmett. But this is interesting. Tell me more." Alice tried to think about what she remembered from the article she'd typed. "These narcissists often have a hard time experiencing empathy; they often disregard and invalidate how others feel. That's Emmett, right there. But at the same time, he's incredibly sensitive to his own feelings. Take criticism, for example: nothing stings him like criticism. If people find fault with him, he'll try to cut those people out of his life or try to hurt them. And his rage can be truly scary."

"What you're describing seems like it goes a long way to account for what happened in that market the night Tom died. Emmett lost control of himself when Tom came in and criticized the steak Emmett had sold us."

"Yes, and I think it goes further back with the two of them. I've thought about it before. This notion of excluding from your life people who criticize you? I think that's what Emmett did to Tom. I remember sitting at the little table in our kitchen one day when Emmett read an article in the newspaper about Tom being elected president of the carpenter's union local. He flew into a rage about it, ranting on about unions and what he regarded as Tom's misguided affinity for them.

"I asked him why he was mad as hops. And in a rare moment of self-revelation, he said the article somehow stirred up an argument he and Tom had one night about unionism. He said he stopped being Tom's friend after that. I hadn't known that, and I'd always wondered what had come between them."

"You're saying there was some deep-seated antagonism Emmett felt toward Tom over unionism?"

"Yes, and it predisposed him to be angry at Tom. That was the bed of white-hot embers that was already there when Tom came into the store that night to return the tainted meat. That criticism fanned those cinders into flames."

Maggie sipped her tea. She looked at Alice over the rim of the cup, then said, "That doesn't make me feel any friendlier toward Emmett Kelly, but it's helpful to have that extra context about the relationship between him and Tom. It's interesting. Why do you suppose

Emmett is so opposed to unions?"

Alice paused to consider the question. "He always spoke of how unions were bad for businesses, driving up the cost of everything, leaving business owners with less money to hire and expand. But it occurs to me, now that we're talking about this idea of narcissism, that a deeper explanation may rest in that. Apparently, narcissistic people have such a high opinion of themselves that they don't feel they need the help of others. They only think of others when they're trying to figure out how others might be useful to them—how they can exploit others when it suits them.

"The whole idea of unionism—of people joining together in common cause for their mutual protection and advancement? That's foreign to Emmett's way of thinking. In his view, he doesn't need anybody. He's so capable, so clever and intelligent that he doesn't need to combine with anyone else."

Again, Maggie looked at Alice over the rim of her tea cup.

"I remember once telling Tom that although I wasn't anti-union, I was a strong believer in self-reliance." She smiled. "Of course, that was before my hand got mangled and my husband got killed. Funny how adversity can change one's mind about needing the help of others."

Alice smiled and reached over to pat Maggie's arm. "I'm so glad we have each other, Maggie Quinn."

Chapter Fifty-Five

Reading the newspaper one morning in early July 1912, Maggie had lost herself in the reports from Great Britain, where a royal commission investigating the sinking of the Titanic in mid-April had wrapped up its work. Finished perusing these stories, Maggie's attention caught on a story lower on page one of the *Denver Post*.

"Oh, no! This is awful." Maggie cried, putting down the *Denver Post* and removing her eyeglasses.

"What? What is it?" Alice asked, alarmed.

"Sarah Platt Decker died yesterday! This article says she was in San Francisco to give a speech. She collapsed from an abdominal obstruction. She was only fifty-six years old!"

"Oh, Jaysus. What a shocker."

Sarah Platt Decker had been one of the most prominent women in Denver. A notable suffragist, she'd also been the first important woman in the city to bring Maggie and Alice under her wing after the newspaper article about their new business venture and the shared life they'd forged. Sarah had pushed for Maggie and Alice to be invited to join the Woman's Club of Denver, an organization that brought together the city's foremost women. Many of the members objected to the idea of including these two immigrant women who lacked college educations.

But Sarah, as president of the club, chastised the nay-sayers, arguing, "If you're at all serious about those elements of our mission which involve promoting immigrant workers and the interests of children and working mothers, then you cannot—you must not!—be opposed to having Mrs. Quinn and Mrs. Kelly join us as members. They've built a new life for themselves and a formidable business! Who among us would have the courage and the internal resources to do what these two remarkable women have done?"

With that ringing endorsement and considerable extra lobbying by Sarah, Maggie and Alice had been invited to join. And their membership in the club had been yet another windfall for their business, bringing in scores of new clients and necessitating the hiring of still more employees.

"Sarah did oodles of good for us. Our business wouldn't be the huge success it is if she hadn't championed us."

"That's so true."

"This article says she will be the first woman to be given the honor of lying in state in the rotunda of the State Capitol. Thursday, it says. We'd better bunk off work and go pay our respects."

At the Capitol later that week, they ran into their acquaintance Sadie Likens, who introduced them to Helen Ring Robinson, a prominent local educator who was running

266

for a seat in the state Senate. Helen was attracted to the two of them like a bee to clover. The three became fast friends. In speeches and at campaign events, Helen often made reference to Maggie and Alice, citing them as shining examples of the strength and resourcefulness of women.

ONE DAY, Emmett was reading a news article about one such speech Helen Robinson had given with Alice and Maggie at her side. He became enraged. He looked across the room at Gus. "Feckin' Christ! These two women are in the papers again! It makes me sick to my stomach, it does."

"Wind your neck in, boss. Why do you let it bother you so much? Just ignore them."

"It bothers me because I see the two of them as responsible for my problems!"

Even Gus, loyal as he was to Emmett, couldn't help but laugh at the flawed reason of that statement. Those women had about as much to do with Emmett's troubles as Gus did with the sinking of the Titanic! Emmett had brought on his own problems. But Gus knew better than to fail to indulge the boss in his desire to vent. "How do you figure?"

"I reckon the Quinn woman was the one to complain about that meat being tainted. She sent him into the market to confront me. And Alice Kelly never did anything at all to stand up for me. She was always about as useless as thumbs on a pineapple."

"She gave you three good children."

"And those kids were about as useless as nails on those thumbs."

"Kids aren't supposed to be 'useful.'"

"Oh, now you're an expert on children, are ya', Gus?"

Gus knew how to deal with Emmett. He'd put up with Emmett for years. Usually he walked away when Kelly got abusive. But sometimes he pushed back. He'd learned to do that when he was a kid and others tried to bully him. Emmett didn't like pushback and usually got more enraged when he received it, but Gus didn't care. Gus was even bigger and more powerful than Emmett, who wouldn't be stupid enough to try to fight him. And Emmett couldn't afford to fire Gus, who was the only thing holding Emmett and his little store together. So Gus pushed back. Hard.

"Not only an expert on children, Emmett. On marriage, too." Gus grinned. "You tell me why you think Alice Kelly should have stuck by you when you never take responsibility for your own mistakes. You always consider yourself a victim, no matter the truth. If something goes wrong, it's always someone else's fault.

"It wasn't only your manslaughter conviction that led Alice Kelly to turn her back on you. She left you, I'm guessin', because being with you made her feel awful. You always put your wants first. You're selfish. You never have anything nice to say to anyone. And because you can't stand criticism, I bet you're about to go off on your ear or make the fur fly!"

Emmett fumed and sputtered. His face was as scarlet as Gus had ever seen it. Emmett slammed the newspaper down on the counter and stormed out of the little store.

Good, Gus thought. I made you look yourself in the mirror.

Chapter Fifty-Six

Newly elected State Senator Helen Robinson had grown accustomed to going to her friend Alice Kelly for advice and counsel on issues relating to food quality and food safety. Alice's information was reliable and up-to-date, her analysis of it intelligent and sound. One of the first issues to come up involved a bill that would repeal the state's prohibition against the sale of colored oleomargarine —a ban that had been in place since 1895. Oleomargarine had been one of Alice's pet vexations. She knew the issue inside and out.

Alice explained to Helen the ban's origin. "It had to do with a war between the dairy industry and the new manufacturers of oleomargarine. The emergence of a new butter substitute threatened the dairy farmers. They succeeded in getting restrictive taxes slapped on margarine and licensing fees imposed on those who manufacture it or sell it."

"I understand. The dairy folks wanted to make it harder

for the margarine folks to compete. But what about the color? I don't get what that's about."

"Usually, as you know, butter is yellow. It gets that color from plant carotene in the milk of grass-fed cows. But margarine, as made in big industrial vats, is white. It's that unappetizing shade of the paste that kids use in grade-school projects. Margarine manufacturers wanted to tint their product yellow to make it more appealing to the public.

"Butter producers objected, saying that coloring margarine yellow was a fraudulent attempt to deceive the public, masquerading the product as butter. And the dairy industry was powerful enough that by 1902 it got the legislatures of 32 states to ban colored margarine. Colorado was a few years ahead of the pack." Helen regarded Alice. "So, what position do you think I should take on this bill to lift the coloring ban?"

"You know full well what I think: you should oppose it."

"You think people are duped by color?"

"I think anything that makes margarine more appealing to people is bad. Anything that makes it easier for people to mistake it for butter is bad."

Alice did not know that her estranged husband was one of the shadowy, back-and-hidden figures behind the political effort to lift the ban. Emmett himself couldn't have untangled his motives behind his involvement in the issue. Some moments, he was certain it mostly had to do with his idea for how he might make money if the ban were dropped. He knew how he could make an enterprise profitable if he could get the state to repeal its prohibition on coloring. And if he could find the money to build a plant.

Other times, he acknowledged to himself that it was Alice's long-standing, strident opposition to oleomargarine that drew him to this issue. It had always irked him that Alice had prevented him from selling the product in his market. Now, he wanted to stick it to her. And that was before he found out that she was counseling this Robinson woman on the issue! After he'd discovered that, his passion for the cause grew intense. Alice and Helen Robinson were the sort of duo that made the stuff of Emmett's nightmares: know-it-all women who wanted to decide what was best for everyone!

On the night the state House of Representatives approved the bill to lift the ban, joining the Senate's position on the matter, Emmett went out drinking with his allies to celebrate. What a delicious victory it was. He could picture how dejected Alice must be. The thought delighted him. He imagined her with that Quinn woman, surrounded by six whiny children, crying in her tea about the outcome. Oh, what a glorious night. He was happy as a possum eatin' persimmons.

After he'd had a few drinks, Emmett left his associates and went to the Palace Theatre, at Fifteenth and Blake, down the street from his little store. Famous throughout the West, the Palace hosted racy stage shows, poured enough booze each night to fill a pond, and arranged gambling tables of every sort.

Emmett often went to the Palace after he closed up shop. Most nights, he had a few drinks. But sometimes he gambled. He always kept in mind what Jed Pinsker had said that night in Cheyenne about playing games of chance versus games of skill. So, if he'd been drinking before gambling, he played craps or the roulette wheel, not poker or checkers. It didn't matter much either way: he usually played for low stakes.

But on this night, he ignored Jed's advice, and despite having had a few drinks, he got in a high-stakes game of poker. Amazingly, he won big. Even more astoundingly, he had the sense to quit for the night, take his thousand-dollar winnings and leave the Palace. All the way home, he smiled to himself, sometimes breaking into euphoric laughter. This was it! Emmett never had won so much at one time. And he knew what he would do with this windfall. He would build that oleomargarine factory!

Chapter Fifty-Seven

Gus McGrath sputtered with exasperation when Emmett finished speaking. "Oleomargarine? Emmett, you are crazy as a goat at mating time! What do you know about oleomargarine? Why would you want to do that?" Gus was a man inclined to careful preparation in all matters, and he often thought Emmett was the very incarnation of impetuosity. Here was a fresh example.

"You think I concocted this plan last night on my way home from the Palace, Gus? You think I'm going it bald-headed? I've been studying this oleomargarine situation for a long time, given it a lot of thought. I think we can make money doing this. You know as well as I do that margarine sales are increasing steadily. Why shouldn't we get in on it? There are no oleomargarine factories this far west. We might as well be the first. There are slaughterhouses and meat-packing plants right here in Denver, with most of their beef tallow fats going to waste. We can get that fat from them for a song. My plan is sheer genius."

"Emmett, the difference between being a genius and being stupid is that genius has its limits and stupidity doesn't. This is stupid." Gus assumed that part of Emmett's attraction to this plan had to do with Alice, whose longtime advocacy for healthy foods and healthy eating now had a prominent outlet through her association with that new woman state senator. Gus suspected Emmett wanted to be the first person in the state to produce the stuff as a way of poking his finger in Alice's eye.

Emmett found an available empty building at Thirteenth and Welton to house his grandiosely named Great Western Oleomargarine Company. With his thousand dollars as a downpayment, Emmett managed to get the Broadway Bank to loan him the money for the building and equipment. The bank's president, Robert A. Handy, was a friend of Emmett's from the Citizens' Alliance.

Emmett and Gus outfitted the space with a 14-horse-power boiler, an ice machine, and the necessary storage tanks, melting tanks, agitators, and pipes. Crude though it was, the operation made Emmett feel as if he were part of the new industrial order.

Soon, he and Gus were churning out oleomargarine. They got their beef and mutton tallow, hog's lard, and refined vegetable oils from local Denver sources. And they pinned down the proper proportions of each to mix in their melting tanks with water. They'd learned how to agitate it all, wash it, and heat it by means of steam injected into the tank through pipes from the boiler. After agitating for the specified time, they'd remove the heat, separate off the water, draw the newly coagulated mass into suitable vessels or packages and allow it to cool. Ready for sale.

Only eventually did it become apparent to Gus how Emmett thought he could make a profit on this venture. It wasn't by being economical and efficient. It wasn't through some miraculous new manufacturing method. It wasn't by selling finer oleomargarine than customers could find elsewhere. No. He planned to evade taxes!

Oleomargarine had come to be heavily regulated and taxed in the United States, thanks to the power of the butter industry and its determination to make margarine less attractive to consumers. The federal government taxed manufacturers of colored margarine at ten cents per pound, and uncolored margarine at one-quarter of a cent per pound. The law also required manufacturers to pay an occupational tax of $600 per year. Retailers had to pay $48 per year to sell colored margarine and $6 per year to sell uncolored.

When Gus asked Emmett why they weren't labeling their product and affixing the stamps that would show the company had paid taxes to the federal government, Emmett said simply, "Because we're not going to pay those damn taxes, Gus. Those taxes are only there at the demand of the butter lobby to make the price of margarine less competitive. The tax is unfair, and I'm not gonna play their game."

"How are we gonna sell this stuff then?" Gus asked.

"You and I both know there are plenty of grocers in this city that will be glad to avoid the extra costs themselves. We'll deliver direct to them."

Gus received this news with the solid hesitation it

deserved. He was no saint, but neither was he eager to break the law. And this was federal law Emmett was talking about violating, not some municipal rule, or even a state law. Gus figured real trouble could bear down on them if the feds caught them. He'd gone along with many of Emmett's crazy schemes over the years (the "kosher" hogs during the Great Colfax Meat War being one of his favorites). But this? Gus was wary. "Emmett, you're swingin' at a wasp nest with a real short stick here. This is a bad idea. "

"A bad idea? I'll tell ya what's a bad idea! Payin' their stupid taxes! And we're not gonna do it, Gus. Not gonna do it! You're the sort who could never make an omelet 'cuz you're too afraid of breaking eggs. Well, not me. Besides, the federal government has better things to do than worry about you and me. We're invisible to them."

"That might've been the case, Emmett, until you got the newspapers to report that Denver was soon to have the only oleomargarine factory between the Mississippi river and the Pacific coast. If you aimed to not pay the taxes, why would you call attention to the fact that you were startin' up an oleo factory? Why put a big sign on the top of this building that says, 'Great Western Oleomargarine Company'? That's idiocy. That's invitin' trouble. Call it a cooper shop or a chandler shop. Anything but an oleo company!"

Emmett didn't like this kind of criticism at all. "Gus, you don't have enough brains to fill a gnat's ear! You think the folks in Washington, D.C. are paying attention to a tiny little oleo producer in Colorado? Friend, you should consult Alice Kelly on your eating habits, 'cuz whatever you're eatin' is banjaxing your brain!"

Gus scowled at Emmett. "You can't trick the federal government any sooner than you can catch a weasel asleep. … And you'll be tryin' to trick them on your own. I want nothin' to do with this. I quit." Gus threw off his apron and stormed out the door.

Unfortunately, Emmett often was certain he knew how the world worked, when, in truth, he was woefully ignorant about it. In this case, he was unaware that at that time the Bureau of Internal Revenue was devoting special attention to investigating operations in the margarine industry. Contrary to what Emmett had assured Gus, the feds were, indeed, paying attention—even to little oleo producers like them.

The factory had only been up and running for a month or two when federal revenue agents began to suspect the company of a scheme to defraud the government by failing to pay the taxes owed. The government had notified Emmett on two occasions of his company's obligation to pay taxes on its oleo. When the company still purchased no tax stamps, revenue agents staked out the plant. They gathered enough evidence to make their case.

A mere four months after Emmett opened his margarine factory, U.S. Deputy Marshals arrested Emmett and Martin Doyle, whom Emmett had hired to replace Gus. The agents seized the plant, shut it down, and sold the remaining stock of margarine to pay off taxes owed. The federal agents charged Emmett and Doyle with federal tax evasion.

The front-page article in the *Denver Post* blared:

FEDS SEIZE NEW DENVER OLEOPLANT — E.A.

United States deputy marshals have seized the plant of the Great Western Oleomargarine Company, 1310 Welton Street, and arrested the proprietor, E.A. Kelly, a well-known Denver merchant, and his employee, Martin Doyle. Kelly was released on $5,000 bond, and Doyle on $500 bond.

The government charges that Kelly has been selling oleo in large quantities without paying the required government taxes on the substance. There were 2,100 pounds of oleo in the plant when the raid was made. This was seized and will be sold by revenue officers to pay the tax.

Alice and Maggie marveled that Emmett Kelly had found yet another outrageous way to get up to no good. Maggie said, "Apparently, the fear of shame, stigmatization, exclusion from the community of law-abiding people—none of that is a deterrent to him."

Alice nodded. "All he cares about is avoiding costs to himself. This time, he's going to end up paying a huge price for his behavior."

Maggie agreed. "I wonder where he got the $5,000 for his bond."

"Good question. Some of his nefarious friends, no doubt."

Chapter Fifty-Eight

Eileen found Alice in the front room, mending some shirts. "Ma, Joey is sick. He says he has a sore throat. He looks pawky, off the level."

Alice put down her needle work and went to the bedroom that Joseph shared with Mike. Joey was in bed. He looked miserable. "Hey there, big fella. Eileen tells me you're not feeling well. What's wrong?"

"Aargh, I have a bad sore throat, Ma. And I feel pure hot." Alice sat at his side and placed her hand on his forehead. "Oh, my. You are hot! You're running a fever, for sure. When did this start?"

"I dunno. This morning, I guess."

"Does your head ache?"

"Yeah."

"Put your tongue out for me, Joey." He did. His tongue had a white coating on it, with little red bumps protruding through the white, giving his tongue a "white strawberry" appearance. Alice's blood ran cold; her fear ratcheted up. Scarlet fever. She turned to Eileen. "Darling, would you please ask Maggie to come in here?"

When Maggie arrived, Alice told her what she was thinking.

Maggie blanched. "If you're right, then we have to keep the other children away from him."

Alice agreed and told Eileen to alert Mike and the others to stay away from Joey. "Tell Mike he can sleep on the sofa in the front room for now. But you all must stay clear of this room, do you hear me?"

"Yes, Mam," Eileen said, before hurrying away.

"What can we do for him?" Maggie asked.

"We should see that he drinks plenty of water. And let's see if he's able to gargle. If he is, then we can give him salty water to gargle. That may ease his throat pain."

"The dry air in here may be irritating his throat, too. I'll boil some pots of water. The steam from them may help."

The hours passed with agonizing slowness. Then, as she'd feared, Alice noticed the beginning of a bright red rash on Joey's face and in the flexion of his elbows and his knees. Over a span of hours, it slowly spread to his torso, then out to his arms and legs. The rash was bright red on his cheeks—red as a boiled lobster!

"Oh, Jaysus. How did this happen? I'm such a bad mother. I should have been paying more attention to my children!"

"Alice, if it's scarlet fever—and, I'm afraid you're right that it is—then you had nothing to do with it, and there's nothing you could have done to prevent it. Poor Joey probably caught it from some child sneezing or coughing at school. You can't blame yourself for this."

Alice recalled what she had read in one of her health periodicals about the treatment of scarlet fever. "I must do more for him. Maggie, would you please go to the drug store for some eucalyptus oil—and perhaps, some carbolic oil, too, if you can find it?"

Alice stayed by Joey's side, holding his hand, putting cold compresses on his forehead and giving him cold baths with a cloth. When Maggie returned, Alice commenced with a routine of rubbing pure eucalyptus oil all over Joey's body, from head to foot, twice a day. She swabbed his throat and tonsils with carbolic oil each day. But despite her efforts, Joey's condition only worsened. He was having a hard time breathing.

Maggie said, "Alice, you've done all you can for him. You've been heroic. But we must get him to the hospital. He's getting worse."

Alice agreed, and they took Joseph to the new Mercy Hospital on 16th and Milwaukee. Over the next couple of days, his breathing difficulties worsened. He began to show frequent involuntary muscle movements and the build-up of collagen fibers on the back of his wrists, the outside of his elbows, and the front of his knees. The physician told Alice these were now signs of rheumatic fever and he feared the onset of rheumatic heart disease.

Alice stayed by Joey's side the whole week he was in the hospital. And she was there with him on the night he died.

She felt she had no choice but to inform Emmett of

Joseph's death. But she dreaded his reaction. Alice knew he would blame her.

And he did. His letter in reply to her own said, in part: "Perhaps if you hadn't been traipsing around Denver in recent months, making a spectacle of yourself as an aspiring big-timer, you might have noticed Joseph's illness earlier, in time to save his life."

Even though she had anticipated such criticism from him, it still cut her to the bone. She knew it was his essential nature to assign blame like this, but it still galled her. Why was it, she wondered, that when something tragic happens, people like Emmett automatically think there has to be a culprit, a well-defined reason. There has to be something that could have been done that would have avoided the result.

When Alice and Maggie talked about this that evening, Maggie suggested the answer again lay in Emmett's narcissism. "He believes he would have seen something wrong earlier. He would have noticed the one thing that would have saved Joey's life. He would never have missed the obvious. That's totally consistent with Emmett's arrogance, Alice. You have to ignore it. Tragedy happens. It doesn't always have a direct cause that we can easily point to. It's too bad that Emmett can't offer compassion rather than heaping salt on your wounds by blaming you. But that's not who he is."

Alice offered Maggie a grateful smile. She set store by Maggie's support and wise words. "You know what makes his blaming so hard to take? I already deal, every day, with guilt—piercing, all-consuming guilt. To this day, I continue to go over every what-if scenario I can think of when it comes to what I could have done differently for Joey—all the way back to my pregnancy with him." Then Alice broke down in tears, her sobs coming wave after wave.

Chapter Fifty-Nine

Emmett was unaccustomed to the discomfort he felt in the weeks leading up to his trial. Usually brash and confident, he knew that the federal indictment for tax evasion was a significant matter. He also knew that the federal district court was not a place where his many connections and allies would do him any good. He wouldn't be able to orchestrate the sort of farce he'd stage-managed for his murder trial. Knowing that the mechanics of the process would be beyond his reach unsettled him. Knowing that federal revenue agents would testify as witnesses against him unsettled him still more.

On the day the trial began, Emmett was further disquieted by the grandeur of the setting. The imposing new federal courthouse, under construction for six years, had recently opened. Occupying an entire city block in downtown Denver and standing four stories in height, this building of monumental scale and presence was no decaying West Side courthouse. With his attorneys, Emmett walked up a series of grand stairs that led up to the main entrance off Stout Street. Sixteen, three-story, Ionic columns graced that side of the building.

His figure had thickened perceptibly in the past few years, and he had raised a small black mustache. There was a gathering roll of fat on the back of his neck that showed when he lifted his chin up. He had a look of solidity and appeared older than he was. threw his head back and laughed. His face was a little more full, a little heavier in the howls. The eyes were habitually narrower. They seemed to express more cunning, and less eagerness.

Inside, the main entry lobby spanned the width of the building. Emmett and his lawyers walked toward U.S. District Courtroom A. Above them was a grand vaulted ceiling, with arches springing from the pilasters. The terrazzo floor under them picked up every click of their shoes, sending the sounds echoing off the ceiling. They entered the still-empty courtroom with its high, arched ceiling and white marble walls. Gold-trimmed black velvet covered the apse behind the judge's bench. Emmett swallowed and looked around nervously at the majestic and dignified surroundings, thoroughly unfamiliar and intimidating to him.

A half hour later, the courtroom was abuzz with life. There were maybe twenty spectators, four or five newspaper reporters, two prosecutors from the U.S. Attorney's office, and thirty men in the back who made up the pool of potential jurors. Soon, Judge Robert E. Lewis entered the courtroom and began the proceedings. Just as with the murder trial, the *voir dire* process for this trial was complicated by the tremendous amount of news coverage the arrest and indictment of Emmett Kelly had received. Emmett's notoriety had made the newspapermen salivate at the thought of another juicy trial involving the rogue grocer and butcher. By the time a jury was seated, it was mid-afternoon, so Judge Lewis decided to adjourn for the day.

The trial began the following morning. The judge took his seat at the bench and looked out over the courtroom. "Mr. Tiernan, you may commence."

"Thank you, your honor. Gentlemen of the jury, good morning. I am United States

Attorney James Tiernan. This is a case of greed. Pure and simple. It is a case of right vs. wrong, of one man's unwillingness to obey the law, simply because he wanted more money. The defendant, Emmett A. Kelly, is charged with defrauding the United States of the tax owed on the manufacture of oleomargarine. The facts of this case are clear, gentlemen. The government will prove to you that Emmett Kelly knew taxes were due, but evaded them by removing oleomargarine from the place of manufacture for sale without coupon stamps showing the payment of a tax and without such tax having been paid or secured.

"Federal revenue agents will testify that they saw Emmett Kelly and his associate clandestinely remove oleomargarine from their factory and take it to retail establishments where they sold it.

"Retail grocers will testify that Emmett Kelly solicited them to purchase from him contraband oleomargarine and that they did, indeed, do so.

"By the time the government rests its case, you will

conclude, beyond a reasonable doubt, that Emmett Kelly is guilty of defrauding the United States of the taxes to which it was entitled. Gentlemen, Emmett Kelly is a greedy man who deliberately set out to evade the laws of this land. Thank you."

Judge Lewis said, "The defense may make its opening statement."

Edward Watson, again Emmett's defense attorney, stood. "Your honor, the defense will reserve its opening statement until after the government has presented its case. Thank you."

"Fine. The prosecution may proceed, Mr. Tiernan."

"Your honor, I call to the stand Clement Jones." A large man with a bald head went to the stand and was sworn in. "Mr. Jones, would you state your occupation for the jury?"

"I'm an agent here in Denver for the Federal Bureau of Revenue."

"How did the Great Western Oleomargarine Company come to your attention?" "The men who established the company arranged for newspaper articles announcing its founding. It was all over the news."

"Why did you decide to scrutinize the activities of this company?"

"The federal government was experiencing tax fraud on the part of oleomargarine manufacturers around the country, so word had come down from on high to pay attention to potential problems."

"So, after the company was up and running, you began to monitor it?"

"I did, along with my associates at the bureau."

"What first tipped you off to a problem with this manufacturer?"

"They'd been operating for a while, but they weren't purchasing any tax stamps. None at all. We issued them a warning, reminding them of the taxes to be paid on colored and uncolored oleomargarine. Still, they purchased no tax stamps."

"What did you do next?"

"We staked out the plant."

"You 'staked it out.' Meaning you placed it under surveillance?"

"That's correct"

"You and who else?"

"Two other revenue agents."

"Misters Thompson and Hodges?"

"Correct."

"We'll hear from them later. Mr. Jones, would you please tell the jury what you yourself observed?"

"By using high-powered binoculars, I was able to see through the windows of the plant of the Great Western Oleomargarine Company. I could see there were no labels on the boxes of oleo the company was selling to the retail trade."

"How do you know they were selling the oleo to the retail trade."

"We repeatedly watched Emmett Kelly come out on the sidewalk in front of the factory, hurriedly glance from side to side to see that no one was watching him, and then hasten off to retail stores with packages of oleo. Those should never have left the plant without being properly labeled and the tax paid to the government."

"Would you describe for the jury the tax stamps for colored margarine that should have been on those packages?"

"Yes, they are about the size of a greenback dollar. The colored oleomargarine stamps are printed in bright orange. They read, 'Tax Paid Stamp for Colored Oleomargarine. In the center of the stamp is a number indicating the weight of the package for which stamp is to be used. For example, 10 pounds, 15, or 20."

"Mr. Jones, is the item I'm holding in my hand a tax-paid stamp for colored oleomargarine?"

"It is. That's a stamp for a 15-pound package. So that stamp would cost the manufacturer $1.50."

"Your honor, may I hand this to the members of the jury, so they can pass it among themselves and have a good look at it?"

"You may."

"Mr. Jones, were the binoculars you spoke of necessary for your surveillance?" "Not really, but they aided us in telling from a considerable distance whether or not the taxes had been paid on the particular packages Kelly carried away. As you can see, the color of those tax stamps makes them highly conspicuous."

"And you are absolutely certain there were no tax stamps affixed to the packages that Emmett Kelly removed from his plant and took to retail stores for sale?"

"I am."

"Mr. Jones, is it possible the packages you saw Mr. Kelly take from his plant contained something other than oleomargarine?"

"We considered that possibility."

"How do you know that wasn't the case?"

"We arrested him as he was emerging from the plant with a package. It contained oleomargarine. And when we finally entered the plant, the only things in it were oleomargarine and the machinery to manufacture it."

"And how do you know for certain that he was selling contraband oleomargarine to retailers and others?"

"We watched him go into establishments with his packages and come back out without them."

"Is that the only way you know for certain he was selling it?"

"No, we also got sworn statements from a number of the establishments he dealt with, admitting that they had bought contraband oleomargarine from Kelly."

"Thank you. No further questions, your honor."

The judge turned to the defendant's counsel. "Mr. Watson, do you have questions for the witness?"

"No, your honor."

Emmett looked up, alarmed by his counsel's answer. He whispered angrily at Watson. "What are you doing?"

"Leave it alone, Emmett."

The prosecutor then called the two other revenue agents to the stand. Each of them provided testimony similar to that of Jones. One of them testified that he also frequently had seen Martin Doyle leave the plant to take oleo to retailers. "Unlike Kelly, at least McGrath had the sense to hide the oleo packages under his coat when he'd make the dash."

The prosecutor then called a grocer named Burton, who testified that he had bought contraband oleomargarine from

Kelly, knowing that it was cheaper to purchase because Kelly had avoided paying taxes on the product. Finally, the prosecutor submitted into evidence sworn statements from ten other retailers, two hoteliers, and four restaurant owners that contained similar admissions. The prosecution rested its case. The judge adjourned proceedings for a lunch break and called for a two o'clock resumption.

Chapter Sixty

Maggie had been in the courtroom that morning. She'd perched in the back row, a wide-brimmed, floppy hat on her head. She was confident Emmett wouldn't see her. Even if he did, she doubted he would recognize her. When the trial broke for lunch, Maggie phoned Alice to tell her what had happened during the morning.

"The man is pure eejit!" Alice was amazed that Emmett's perfidy still had the capacity to surprise her.

"It takes your breath away, doesn't it? Emmett's lawyer didn't even ask any questions of the witnesses!"

"That's not a good sign for him."

"Certainly not."

"Thank you, Maggie. Will you stay or come home?"

"If you don't mind, I think I'll stay for the afternoon to see what happens."

Over lunch, Ed Watson advised Emmett that the government's case against him was strong. Emmett was likely to lose the case. Watson suggested a guilty plea. "The law allows a sentence of three years in prison for this, Emmett. And a fine of up to five thousand dollars. You don't want to spend three years in Leavenworth. You almost went crazy as a loon after six months at county. And there isn't going to be any friendly governor in this case who can arrange your early release. If you agree to plead guilty, we could probably negotiate a reduced sentence, maybe even get it down to two years."

Emmett was so incensed he could barely speak. This wasn't his idea of a defense attorney. "You didn't cross-examine a single witness! And now you want to capitulate? Have me plead guilty? No. Ed, that's not the way I operate. If they want to calaboose me, then let them prove to those jurymen beyond a reasonable doubt that I'm guilty. It seems to me their case is ridiculous—revenue agents playing spy with their binoculars! How silly."

"It doesn't matter if you think it's silly, Emmett. Their witnesses testified clearly to your behavior, and they have sworn statements from people who say you sold them contraband margarine. The government's case against you is rock solid. And we have no defense. The only light at the end of this tunnel is a lightbulb hanging from the ceiling of a cell at Leavenworth."

"I'm not pleading guilty!"

"Okay, but I warn you, our defense is flimsy. So flimsy that I will be embarrassed to present these arguments in front of Robert Lewis. I've known him for years, and I won't be able to look the man in the eye after this. Emmett, you're going to lose. You'll spend three years at Leavenworth."

"We'll see."

When the trial resumed, Edward Watson called to the stand the defense's only witness—a lawyer from St. Louis named Charles Young.

"Mr. Young, am I correct that in 1902 you were one of the lawyers working in

Washington, D.C. for the House committee that wrote the amendments of that year to the

Oleomargarine Act?"

"That is correct."

"So, it's fair to say that you are an authority on what the language of the act means, is that right?"

"I believe that's right, yes. There are few people who know that law better than I do."

"Good. Let me ask you a few questions. Is it true that under section 17 of the statute, the fraud punishable is only that committed by particular persons—that is, to quote the law, 'any person engaged in carrying on the business of manufacturing oleomargarine'?"

"That is correct."

"What is the meaning of that phrase—"carrying on the business of manufacturing oleomargarine?""

"It refers to the people actually doing the work of manufacturing margarine."

"Why does it say 'carrying on the business of'? Couldn't that reasonably be construed to mean managing a business to that effect?"

"It could, yes."

"But that's not what Congress meant? It meant those actually manufacturing the margarine?"

"It did."

"Do we know that Emmett Kelly was "carrying on the business of manufacturing oleomargarine? Did any of the prosecution's witnesses claim to have seen Emmett Kelly actually manufacturing oleomargarine?"

"Not that I recall, no."

"Mr. Young, do you recall what Mr. Kelly's title at the company was?"

"I believe he was president."

"According to your understanding of American businesses, would you say that it is customary for the president of a company to be engaged in the actual production of that company's goods?"

Prosecutor Tiernan jumped to his feet. "Objection, your honor. This witness has not been presented as an expert on American businesses."

"Overruled. I'll allow the question."

"Again, then, Mr. Young, would you say that it is customary for a president of a company to be engaged in the actual production of that company's goods?"

"No, I would not."

"Mr. Young, the government's indictment alleges, does it not, that Mr. Kelly, 'in his several capacities" at the company defrauded the government?"

"It does."

"But, Mr. Young, is that sufficient to warrant an indictment against Mr. Kelly? Is what Mr. Kelly did 'in his several capacities' at this company consistent with the requirement of the law—which you helped write!—that a principal in a case such as this must be actively engaged in the manufacture of oleomargarine?"

"In my view, no."

"No further questions, your honor."

U.S. Attorney James Tiernan's cross-examination of the witness impeached Young's integrity, establishing that he'd been dismissed from the congressional committee staff for incompetence. Tiernan also exposed the preposterousness of Young's assertion that the phrase "carrying on the business of manufacturing" referred only and specifically to the actual production of the margarine. "Mr. Young, isn't it true that the Senate committee report makes it clear that the committee had considered different language for that sentence?"

Young looked uncomfortable. "I don't know."

"I think you do. Isn't it true that the legislators rejected the wording, 'engaged in the activity of producing oleomargarine' in favor of 'carrying on the business of manufacturing oleomargarine'?

After a long pause, Young admitted that was true.

"So, even if Mr. Kelly had no hands-on activity relating to the production of the margarine, as president of the company, he would have been 'carrying on the business of manufacturing oleomargarine'?"

A dejected Charles Young said, "Yes, I suppose so."

Edward Watson put his hands to his face. He turned to Emmett Kelly and whispered, "Leavenworth."

Tiernan asked the judge's permission to call revenue agent Jones back to the stand. "Mr. Jones, how many people did you observe coming and going at the premises of the Great American Oleomargarine Company?"

"Two people."

"Only two people?

"Yes."

"And who were they?"

"Emmett Kelly and Martin Doyle

"Mr. Jones, do you recall what Mr. Doyle's job title was at the margarine company?"

"Yes, he was vice-president."

"So, the only two people you ever saw go in and out of that building were the two who called themselves president and vice-president. Is it reasonable to conclude that, even if you were unable to directly observe Kelly and Doyle producing the margarine, they must have been the persons who did it?"

"I believe so, yes."

"So, even if Mr. Young had been correct in his original assertion, that Congress meant the phrase at issue to mean those persons 'actually involved in making oleomargarine,' those persons must have been Kelly and Doyle, am I correct?"

"Yes."

"The margarine didn't make itself, did it?"

"No, sir."

"Thank you, Mr. Jones. No more questions, your honor."

After closing statements, Judge Lewis gave the jury its instructions. It took the twelve men only thirty-six minutes to return a verdict of guilty. The judge sentenced Emmett Kelly to three years imprisonment at Leavenworth Penitentiary.

Chapter Sixty-One

Months had passed since Joey's death, but Alice grieved for him every day. It wasn't getting any easier to deal with. Harder, in fact. "I still don't know how to live in a world without Joey in it," Alice said to Maggie one evening. "This must be how you felt about Tom for the longest time."

"Any death of someone so close to us is horrific, Alice. And I'm sure everyone deals with grief differently. But I can imagine how awful it is for you that you were robbed of Joey's presence. I know how much you loved him. I saw it on a daily basis. And I know what hopes and dreams you had for him. It's so unfair that he didn't get to grow up and be the wonderful man I'm sure he'd have been. Tom at least got to live an adult life, fulfill his dreams of family and work. Too short, but still …"

"Sometimes I feel so powerless. I wasn't able to protect Joey. What if I can't protect Bridget and Eileen either? And whether or not I can protect them from harm, I end up feeling most days that I'm failing them. I'm supposed to be a fully functioning mother for them every day. But much of the time I don't feel I have the emotional reserves to give them what they need."

"You're beating yourself up. Stop. You're a good, attentive mother to them. They're both doing fine. And I know they miss Joey very much, but even in that respect I think they're doing okay."

Alice smiled. "I hope so. … I think I'll go see what they're doing. I'll be back. Want me to bring you some tea?"

"Aye. Thank you." Watching Alice leave the room, Maggie thought how horrible it would be to lose a child. It must be the very worst of all possible losses. And yet, although she hadn't wanted to say this to Alice, in some ways she thought losing a spouse—at least, a loving spouse—might be worse. She thought of the many different bonds that had linked her and Tom, and the emotional power of those ties. The two of them were co-managers of the home and the family, a "couple" to the rest of the world, joyful companions, sexual partners. All of that disappeared with Tom's death. And although the Kellys' move into her house meant that Maggie had in Alice a close, day-to-day companion, uncommon to the experience of most widows, it wasn't nearly the same.

Then Maggie started to think about Alice's loss not of Joey, but of Emmett. No matter how Alice might feel about that "loss," it was still a huge change for her. And it had meant that both women had experienced one problem in common: how to redefine their role in relation to the outside world without a husband.

They'd handled much of that together, by starting a highly successful business and adopting more visible, public profiles. That had been good for both of them. But since Joey's death, Maggie had noticed Alice pull inward, scale back her civic activities. Maggie understood that. But she also knew how deeply gratifying Alice's involvements had been to her—confidence-boosting and life-affirming.

When Alice returned with the tea, Maggie decided to broach that topic. "Alice, I was thinking: it's been months since you've accepted any of Helen's requests to help her out with various projects or activities. Don't you miss that? Don't you think it might be good for you to find room again in your life for political and civic engagement? It nourished and sustained you."

"You, as well."

That's true, Maggie thought, with a sudden smack of self-awareness. It wasn't only Alice who'd pulled inward since Joey's death. She had, too. "Well, I think it's time for both of us to get back out there. Let's regain our civic footing."

Alice smiled. "Let's."

Chapter Sixty-Two

Two federal marshals took Emmett and three other prisoners from Denver to Kansas City by train, where a fortified prison wagon picked them up for the twenty-five mile ride northwest to Leavenworth. When the wagon turned into the horseshoe-shaped driveway leading to the entrance, Emmett caught his first glimpse of the intimidating building that sat adrift in a great sea of nothingness, dominating the Kansas countryside. He expected a high wall in front, hiding the prison from sight. But the prison's two main cell houses themselves made up the front wall, each seven stories high and more than a hundred yards long.

After Emmett had been "processed," a guard took him to his cell house, a five-story row of 5 by 9 foot human cages. The steel cells, with inch-thick bars, were stacked like a giant honeycomb—side-by-side, one row atop the other and back to back. Each cell facing north had an identical cell behind it facing south. Sunlight filtered through the cell house's cathedral-size windows, casting a grid of shadows on the white tile floor.

Emmett was pleased to learn that his cell was on the top tier. He remembered that at the county jail in Denver, the top floor had been the warmest in the winter. He didn't want any more brutal winters in a cell. What he hadn't bargained for was how hot Leavenworth would get in the summer months. The design of the building was such—two structures, one within the other—that the heat in the cell houses built up to intolerable levels.

Some convicts claimed that the bottom tier was the coolest because it was closest to the ground. Others argued the middle floors were the best because they were nearest the few windows that opened. But everyone agreed about the fifth tier, where Emmett was: it was pure agony in the summer. The air was thick. Convicts on the top tier sat on mattresses at night as if in a narcotic stupor, naked except for sweat-soaked underwear. Their bodies glistened with a thin layer of sweat.

Emmett couldn't decide what was worse, the heat or the monotony. After he'd been in there for a while, he began to forget what it had been like to be anywhere else. Steel doors clanged shut behind him. Hostile guards yapped orders. This, he thought, was hell—a netherworld that became even worse late at night when it was quiet enough inside to hear the whistle of a locomotive going by somewhere in the distance. That was perhaps the lonesomest sound he ever heard.

Daytime at Leavenworth was better than the nights. Cell doors opened at six in the morning. Convicts roamed the large prison compound relatively unrestricted until ten p.m., when they had to be back in their cells for the night. Emmett liked the daytime. At least he could walk around, look up at the sky.

But the sky was all he could see. Leavenworth had a wall unlike any other in the federal prison system. It was four-feet thick in places. Red brick. It rose thirty-five feet above the ground and sank another thirty-five feet below—all this, to prevent ingenious or diligent convicts from escaping. Emmett had no notions of escaping. To him, the wall meant only that it was impossible to see outside the prison. At least at the county jail in Denver, he'd been able to see what was going on outside, painful though that sometimes was to him. Not at Leavenworth. So, even though were more than a thousand other men around him, Emmett still found the sense of isolation overwhelming.

The relative freedom convicts enjoyed didn't mean there was no regimentation. Guards counted every inmate at least five times a day to make certain no one had escaped. These counts occurred at ten p.m., midnight, three a.m., and five-thirty a.m., before the cells were unlocked for the day. Each afternoon at exactly four o'clock, inmates had to return to their cells for the most important count. It differed from the others because convicts had to be standing up when guards passed by to count them. By making the inmates stand, guards could be certain that they were counting a breathing human being, not a papier-mâché dummy tucked under the bedclothes.

One day, out in the yard, a huge, mean-looking fella about 6'3" and 280 pounds wandered over to Emmett. He looked like the trunk of an oak tree shoved into a prisoner's uniform. He said, "First time in a penitentiary?"

"Yeah, I've been in county jail before, but this is different."

"True. This is a different bucket of snakes. It's scary until you figure out what's going on. Where you from?"

"Denver."

"What they get you for?"

"Tax fraud."

"Small potatoes." The fella dropped the stub of his cigar, stomped it into the yard's gravel, and left, as if Emmett weren't even worth talking to. No murder. No bank robbery.

Nothing interesting.

Emmett didn't know what to think about that exchange. "Small potatoes." True. The feds had put him there for avoiding taxes on oleomargarine! He wasn't going to get anybody's respect for that! He should have said he'd been convicted of manslaughter, even though that wasn't the offense that landed him at Leavenworth.

He almost felt embarrassed that he'd landed in federal prison for something he considered so insignificant. The place was full of people who deserved to be there! There was that fella Robert Stroud. Like Emmett, he'd been convicted of manslaughter and had served time in a state corrections center in his home state of Washington. But unlike Emmett, Stroud had turned even more violent in local jail, stabbing a fellow prisoner. He got transferred to Leavenworth. One day, soon after Emmett had landed at the Hot House, Stroud murdered a guard in front of hundreds of witnesses, including Emmett, who watched from only ten yards away.

Now, Emmett thought, there's a guy who deserved to be in this hell hole. Not me.

The walking tree trunk had turned around and come back, looking harder at Emmett. "What kind of tax fraud?"

The fella's whole look intimidated Emmett, who couldn't think of a different story fast enough, so blurted out the truth. "I produced oleomargarine without paying the federal taxes due on it."

The monolith laughed. Then laughed louder. "Okay. We'll call you 'Oleo.'"

Emmett knew by that point that a new arrival at Leavenworth, if he was at all active or mingled freely with the rest of the prisoners, got nicknamed. Other inmates exhausted every effort to familiarize themselves with a new fella's weak points, habits, hobbies, physical characteristics, and the circumstances of his incarceration. Once they found something that amused them about the newcomer, they'd give him a fitting nickname that would usually remain with him for his entire stay.

"Nervous Nick" was a man whom prisoners knew to be restless, uneasy, and given to worrying. "Chicago Stew" constantly talked, fumed, and stewed about his home town. "Lookout" earned his cognomen when he cautioned some prisoners about an approaching guard while they were trying to consummate a trade in tobacco. "Sap Head" unfortunately displayed some poor baseball judgment. "Butterine" once complained to the cook about not receiving a full share of the butter at dinner.

Now Emmett would be "Oleo." The ignominy of it was almost more than he could bear.

Chapter Sixty-Three

———————————

Alice knew that for many of the Eastern-European Jewish friends she'd made when living over on Colfax, their travel all the way to Denver was about more than the allure of freedom and economic opportunity; it was about health. The world's leading cause of death at the time was tuberculosis. Some called it "consumption," others "the white plague," from the wasting effects of the disease.

Whatever name it went by, the disease took a particularly high toll in poor, crowded communities of recent immigrants to America. Jews had special reasons for concern about that. Although Jews actually suffered lower rates of infection compared with other groups, pervasive anti-Semitism saddled Jews with the libel that tuberculosis was "the Jewish Disease." Anti-immigrant nativists denounced the impoverished newcomers as germ-carriers.

To escape the congestion and bigotry of East-coast cities, many Jews flocked to Denver. Many thought fresh mountain air to be the cure—or, at least, a palliative. And Denver was not home to the kind of virulent prejudice common in the East.

But despite the fact that Jews had raised money to build two hospitals in Denver for Jewish consumptives, the problem stretched well beyond the capacity of those two institutions to deal with it. By early 1916, the two Jewish sanatoria were treating a total of about 275 patients. But city health officials estimated the number of Jewish consumptives in Denver at 1,200 men, women, and children, not counting those in the two sanatoria.

It was to that problem that Alice turned her attention. Her personal association with so many of those affected by the disease was behind her involvement. Alice's friend Abe Deitsch was the immediate impetus. Abe, his wife, and their four children had come to Denver from New York. Abe had been a butcher, but after a while the severity of his disease forced him to stop. Now he was a peddler. Alice told Helen Robinson, "his prognosis could not be worse. He's going to die any day now."

"What about the family?" Helen asked.

"There's a son, about 12, who sells newspapers. A daughter about 8 years old has tuberculosis. Two younger children. Abe's wife also peddles and works part time mending dust-laden, second-hand sacks. They receive no charitable assistance or supervision. That family is going to go under, Helen."

Alice and Helen Robinson had met with Denver's mayor, William Sharpley, a number of times over various health-related issues. Sharpley was a physician, a receptive audience to their pleas. Helen urged Alice to secure a meeting with Sharpley on the tuberculosis problem. Alice laid out the difficulty so many in the Jewish community faced. "Mr. Mayor, this has to be addressed."

"Alice, it's not only a Jewish problem. It's more widespread than that."

"I'm well aware of that, Mayor. Please don't assume I'm ignorant of the facts. For example, I'm very familiar with Dr. Charles Bundsen who founded the Swedish Consumptive Sanatorium in Englewood. In fact, the Swedes offer a model that we might emulate more broadly."

"You think we should build sanatoria?" He chuckled. "We don't have the money for that, Alice."

"No, sir. Do you know of Frank Craig?"

"The fella who established the tent city for indigent tubercular men?"

"That's Frank. His idea is what I think the city of Denver should imitate."

"How so?"

"He started that tent colony of his out on the plains of Lakewood. That attracted philanthropy. Former Governor Cooper's wife Jane bought and donated property to the colony. Now, they've built three buildings there, with more planned."

"So, you are talking about building sanatoria."

"No, I'm saying that we should build tent colonies. Over time, they'll attract resources from benefactors like Jane, and we'll end up with more good housing for consumptives. My theory is this: start something, and benevolent resources will soon follow. That's what Frank Craig did. Jane Cooper stepped up. I'm saying that's what the city should do. Someone will come forward to help. And it won't cost the city much to get the ball rolling."

Mayor Sharpley looked across his desk at Alice Kelly. He'd come to regard her as a formidable, intelligent, clever woman. "Alice, if you pull together a group of people to plan out such an endeavor, I'll consider what you come up with." She did. And he did. The city built three tent colonies. And hundreds of thousands of dollars from Denver benefactors poured in to support more permanent treatment facilities. More tent colonies followed. More buildings supplanted them.

Alice's vision and determination—and her skill at following through with initiatives—earned her the respect and ear of city officials.

Chapter Sixty-Four

Leavenworth was its own small city. A walled city, to be sure, but still a city. It had its own power plant, water supply, maintenance shop, hospital. It needed next to nothing from the community surrounding it. Convict labor produced the food at a prison-owned farm. Meat came from the prison's own herd of beef cattle. Facilities inside the plant produced clothing, furniture, and other needed goods. An inmate who wanted work could easily find it.

One afternoon out in the yard, when Emmett was still relatively new to the prison, he was talking with a fella whose moniker was "Politician." Emmett thought the nick-namers had missed the mark with this fella. He was so buck-toothed he could eat a pumpkin through a picket fence. But Politician got his name because he liked to do favors for others.

The buck-toothed man said, "Let me give you some

advice, Oleo. Get yourself a job. It will make the time here go by faster and will give you some satisfaction. And when you're not working, join one of the clubs. You know there's everything under the sun here: chess, painting, band, baseball, basketball, football, checkers, choir, the prison newspaper. You name it, we've got it. Do some of them. You'll be happier. Did you ever play any sports?"

"I played sandlot baseball when I was a kid in Chicago."

"Get on one of the baseball teams. Those men seem to have a good time. They play scads of intramural games, and occasional contests against teams from the outside."

Emmett thought about it that night. The next day, he went to the playing field, where he watched the White Sox (an all-white team) get badly bolloxed by the Booker T's (an all-Negro team). After the game, Kelly walked over to the Sox manager and asked him if they were in need of players.

"We're always looking for men. Our roster turns over all the time because men get discharged or kicked off for a violation. You play?"

"Haven't in decades, but I used to as a boy."

"Come to our practice at one o'clock tomorrow. We'll see if you've got anything." Emmett made a good showing for himself at the practice. He hit almost half the pitches thrown to him, two or three of those a fair distance. His throwing arm was strong and accurate. When the manager asked him to throw some pitches, Emmett initially hesitated, but then decided to give it a whirl. Again, the manager thought well of his arm. "Not bad, Oleo. Not bad at all. Your only real weakness, far as I can tell, is that you're not a very fast runner.

Unless you belt that ball, you're likely to get thrown out at first most of the time. But, let's give you a try."

A sense of delight came over Emmett. He couldn't quite understand why. This was a small thing, making it on the roster of a prison baseball team. Still, the delight was there. Miller continued. "You know the rules. They find you guilty of any infractions, anywhere in the prison, you're off the team. Baseball is the main thing around here, so they're serious about who gets to play it. Even who gets to come watch it. So keep your nose clean if you want to play."

"Right."

"And you may not have been here long enough yet to know that we play all year 'round, weather permitting. There is no 'season,' although we don't get much time on the field in January and February. Some days it can be pretty cold. But most fellas are so happy to play they don't let it bother them."

"Okay."

"Be here at the next practice. And tell Mo over there your clothing size. He'll get you set up with a uniform."

Emmett smiled. "Thanks, Miller."

At the next practice, the White Sox went through typical drills. Then Miller announced they were going to play a five-inning game against another team that had been practicing nearby. Miller put Emmett into the rotation. In the first inning, Emmett doubled to the center wall, sending one man home and advancing another to third.

Two innings later, the best he could do was fan out. But in the bottom of the last inning, Emmett rapped one far into left field, driving in the winning run. After the game, Miller said to him, "That strong upper body of yours is going to be useful for us, Oleo. Keep it up and you'll be a star out there." Again, Emmett felt a curious glow of satisfaction that was foreign to him, something he hadn't felt in many years.

That Saturday, the White Sox played against a skilled team from Kansas City. They were structural iron workers, pulled together by the local union there. The Leavenworth team won, 11-7. The next edition of the prison newspaper carried this item on page 4, its sports page:

SOX WALLOP KANSAS CITY BOLTHEADS

The game staged for the afternoon of June 23 was between the Ironworkers' strong nine, of the Kansas City Union Labor League, and the prison White Sox team. Before we go further, we wish to announce that our Sox put the kibosh on the visitors in a decisive manner, 11 runs to 9, and sent the hundred K.C. rooters—a special train car full—back to the junction of the Kaw and the Big Muddy with worlds of respect for the baseball ability of the prisoners at Uncle Sam's big hotel at Leavenworth. The afternoon was perfect for the big game. Tense was the excitement when Umpire Simpson yelled: 'Play Ball!' Great pitching by Robert Bryson, together with timely swats by his mates at critical moments, gave the game to the white legs by a good margin and created throbs of joy in the hearts of the multitude.

The White Sox played a good tight game of ball and did some timely hitting. They also seemed to be on speaking terms with Lady Luck. Patterson played a fair game at first. Randolph covered third in his usual classy way, and Kelly pulled a circus catch in left that was by far the feature of the game. New man Kelly also had a powerful game at the plate, driving in two runs with a triple in the second, and two more with a double in the third.

The ironheads made a desperate effort to tie the score in the ninth inning. They tallied three runs in their last-chance half, but still fell short.

Emmett couldn't recall a time his name had ever been in a newspaper for something other than an arrest, a fight, or a court case. It felt good.

But their next game against a team of meatpackers from Omaha did not go at all well. The scribe for the prison newspaper ripped the White Sox to shreds. One paragraph read:

The flabby, one-legged White Hose had their skins roasted on Saturday by the Omahogs. The hot-house geezers stood around with gaping jaws, so weak they couldn't lift a glass of feathers, couldn't hit the side of a barn with a banjo, and ran bases like pallbearers at a funeral. Kelly provided a full comedy of errors all by himself and led the rheumatic procession to the morgue.

Emmett seethed at the criticism. Who was this writer? No doubt some puny little, pox-complected accountant in prison for embezzlement. Emmett thought of finding the fella and teaching him a lesson. But that night, he considered all he'd lose if he got even with the lunkhead. No, it wouldn't be worth it. His longtime personal motto—"always prosecute a fight"—might have to give way in this case. The more he thought about that game, the more he had to acknowledge, albeit grudgingly, that the writer was correct. They'd played poorly, Emmett especially so.

Chapter Sixty-Five

War was on the horizon. It had started in Europe two years earlier. The United States had stayed out of it so far, but as the summer heat of 1916 began to lift, Maggie and Alice could feel the pressure building for America to enter the war. They'd worked hard with Helen Robinson to support the Wilson administration's stance of neutrality.

And their efforts had garnered much attention. When automobile industrialist Henry Ford chartered his so-called Peace Ship to take himself and a party of pacifists to Europe to mediate an end to the conflict, he had asked Helen to sail with him.

"You must go, Helen," Maggie implored. This is a huge opportunity for you to make a difference. Go, do your best!" Helen did go, but the effort failed and brought widespread ridicule on Ford, whom many came to regard as an ignorant buffoon.

Throughout the autumn's presidential campaign, Maggie and Alice campaigned hard for Wilson, who'd promised to "keep us out of war." The two women passed out leaflets on the streets of Denver, wrote letters to newspapers and to the state's representatives in Congress. But one month after the start of his second term in 1917, President Wilson went before a joint session of Congress to request a declaration of war against Germany. Alice and Maggie felt so betrayed when they heard that news. At least they were able to convince Benjamin Hilliard, the congressman from Denver, to vote against the war declaration.

Although their pacifism had been their principal motive behind their efforts, they were also worried about Mike. Would he have to go to war? They hadn't thought so. The government seemed determined to move forward with an all-volunteer army. But voluntary enlistment lagged, and Wilson instituted a draft. Their worst fear had come true: Mike would go into the army.

When drafted in the late winter of 1917, Mike was sent to Camp Funston, the army training camp on the grounds of Fort Riley in Kansas, where he was to learn to be a soldier. "It's okay, Ma," he said, trying to reassure a distraught Maggie. "I'm going to be fine."

He wasn't fine, as it turned out. Mike had been at Funston for two months, training hard, when a horrible influenza swept through the camp. Dozens of young men—the strongest, healthiest, most robust young people one could imagine—were struck down as if mowed to the ground by a machine gun.

During a three week period, more than eleven hundred of the 42,000 troops to come through the camp fell sick enough to require hospitalization. Thousands more needed treatment at infirmaries scattered around the base. Like the other sick men, Mike suffered from chills, headaches, and profuse sweats; agonizing pains in the back, legs and joints; and a burning pain under the sternum that was greatly aggravated by cough. Many of the young men's illnesses progressed to pneumonia. Some died. Then more of them died.

When time came for Mike's unit to ship out to Europe, he'd been in a camp infirmary for two months. He was deadly weak. Although the War Department was so desperate for soldiers that it sent many sick men across the Atlantic, doctors deemed Mike much too ill to go. After he spent yet another six weeks in the camp infirmary, the army discharged him and sent him home.

By the time Maggie and Alice greeted Mike at Denver's train station, it was clear to everyone that the influenza he'd contracted was part of a global pandemic. Tens of millions of people around the world already had fallen sick; hundreds of thousands had died. When Maggie saw Mike coming toward her, he was so pale and gaunt she almost didn't recognize him. He must have lost 30 pounds or more. She rushed to him and hugged him. Her arms reinforced what her eyes had told her: he was so thin!

"Oh, Mike! We were afraid we were going to lose you!"

"I was afraid so, too," he said, a rueful smile playing across his peaked face. "The doctor said if I got any worse he'd have to prescribe embalming fluid."

"Let's get you home. Alice has been cooking all morning. We'll get some food into you."

"Can that wait, Ma? I'm tuckered out. I want to go to bed."

"Of course, of course."

Maggie and Alice had been reading everything they could get their hands on about the pandemic. And they were being very cautious. A second great wave of the influenza was starting to sweep across the country, and it appeared much more virulent than the first wave that had come in the Spring. Alice had instructed the children to stay away from large crowds, avoid using the streetcars, stay far away from anyone coughing or spitting, keep their fingers out of their mouths, avoid shaking hands with anyone, scrub their hands before meals. They kept the windows open and spent as much time as possible out in the open air.

Alice also had read that in some cities, people wore masks on their faces to reduce the chances of getting the virus. She and Maggie had been doing that and forced the children to do so as well. But she'd seen only a few other people in Denver wearing them, and there had been no public discussion of it. Alice approached her friend William Sharpley, the physician and public-health expert who'd been mayor of Denver a couple of years earlier and now served as City Manager of Health.

"William, why isn't the city doing something to encourage people to wear masks?" "It would be premature, Alice. We're not even seeing incidence of the disease here at the moment."

"But it would help cut down on transmission once it does hit Denver."

"You and I know that. But many people would resist the idea, and we can't move in that direction until we have cases to point to!"

Chapter Sixty-Six

The prison population at Leavenworth had come through the initial wave of the pandemic relatively well. The first case of the influenza back in April had been a man who transferred into Leavenworth from the Kansas State Penitentiary at Lansing. He'd been sick even before he left Lansing, having pains over his body, accompanied by fever. When he arrived at Leavenworth, he mingled with the 1,400 men who congregated in the yard on Sunday, April 14. He ate in the general mess with them, and at night was locked in the receiving room with about twenty other newcomers. The next day he was admitted to the prison hospital with a fever of 102, chills, and severe aches in his back and bones.

Over the coming few weeks, the flu spread through the prison. At one point, about half of the prison population was ill. During the peak of that outbreak, the number of prisoners seeking treatment had quadrupled in a two-day period.

When normally about 100 sought medical help on a regular day, the first day of the peak saw 400, the second 475. Amazingly enough, of the 101 inmates admitted to the prison hospital, only seven developed pneumonia and only three died.

Serious efforts at quarantine and the banning of large congregations quelled the outbreak. The men in the cells on both sides of Emmett had been sick. Their deep coughs and difficulties breathing had struck terror into him. So, when the crisis subsided over the summer, Emmett felt lucky he'd dodged the virus. That bullet had gone by close enough to raise a blister!

But the epidemic returned to Leavenworth in September, again probably introduced by a new inmate, who'd been there two days before he began exhibiting flu-like symptoms and was hospitalized. He told the doctors that one of the deputies who'd brought him to the penitentiary and who occupied a compartment with him on the night train, had complained of feeling ill with cough, restlessness, aches, and thirst.

By the time the new inmate felt any symptoms himself, he'd already taken several meals with the general prison population and had spent most of his time in conversation with many inmates who were eager to learn what was happening in the outside world. So, the flu spread quickly, this time resulting in over 150 cases, 19 of them leading to pneumonia. Eight deaths. The prison tried to stop the contagion by cancelling gatherings such as chapel services and motion-picture entertainment.

Chapter Sixty-Seven

On September 27, 1918, the Denver newspapers reported that a student at the university died of pneumonia a few days after returning from a trip to Chicago. Within ten minutes of reading that, Alice was on the phone to William Sharpley, who expressed his concern to her with dark, doleful humor. "We didn't have to wait long, did we?"

"You have to act swiftly, William." Sharpley did. He persuaded the mayor and the city council to close all schools, business colleges, churches and Sunday schools, clubs, lodges, pool halls, movie houses, theaters, reading rooms, and dance halls. All music rehearsals were banned, along with all public indoor funerals, fraternity and lodge meetings, and all other places of public assembly. Despite these efforts, the total number of cases in Denver soared rapidly, reaching 1,440 by mid-October.

Just as things had started to improve and the city had

eased up on many of its stricter measures, the war in Europe ended. To celebrate, thousands of Denverites thronged the streets, hotels, and other buildings on the night of November 11. Over 8,000 gathered inside the city auditorium for festivities there.

The next day, Sharpley told Alice by phone, "Of course, I understand the human need to celebrate. And what a wonderful thing to celebrate! But the number of new cases surely will increase as a result of this." Sharpley was correct. A week after the Victory Day celebrations, the toll in Denver averaged a hundred new cases and a dozen or more deaths per day.

By now it was also clear that this was part of that second huge wave of cases that had swept across the world, the first being the one that caught Mike in its wake. In some ways, Mike was lucky, because the disease wrought by this second wave was much worse, much more deadly. As the contagion made its way through the United States, it killed 195,000 Americans in the month of October alone. It killed some patients within days or even hours after symptoms began.

Alice appeared before a meeting of the Denver Health Advisory Board and made a passionate plea for a mask order, requiring Denverites to wear gauze face masks while riding streetcars, when attending church services, when in theaters or any assembly (indoor or out), while shopping, when riding in elevators, when working in a factory, when working in a building to which the public had access, or when visiting a physician. Those who served the public in any capacity would also be required to wear a mask. Her argument was persuasive, and the board issued a mask mandate beginning at 4 o'clock on Monday, November 25th.

To Alice's horror, Tuesday, the 26th brought what the Rocky Mountain News described as "almost indescribable confusion." Throngs of people crowded city hall, seeking clarification of the new rules. Many stores along busy Sixteenth Street were unable to obey the new order, as there simply were too few masks to be had to supply either employees or customers. The Red Cross reported that it was doing all it could to produce more masks, but couldn't keep up with the sudden demand.

The next day, Alice walked around downtown to see what was happening. She saw masks in only a few stores. And the reasons Alice heard in response to her questions were as varied as they were creative. The head of the Denver Dry Goods Company told her, "We have received no direct orders from the health department, and cannot act on the basis of a newspaper report." When Alice approached a salesgirl at Daniels & Fisher who wasn't wearing a mask, the girl said, "my nose goes to sleep when I wear one." Another un-masked shop girl, this one at the May Company, said that she believed a higher authority than the Denver Department of Health was looking after her well-being.

As she had so many times over the years, Alice wondered why people were so determinedly stupid when it came to their own health and well-being. The girl's nose went to sleep! Some higher authority was looking out for the other. Well, good luck with that, Alice thought.

Eventually, under pressure from businesses, Sharpley and Mills cancelled the mask order in favor of more stringent isolation and quarantine orders. While new cases continued to develop in the following weeks, and many still resulted in death, by mid-December, the worst was over. Slowly, by fits and starts, life in Denver began to return to normal. Alice had been instrumental in getting several traditional end-of-the-year social events cancelled out of fear the disease might spread. Much to the chagrin of Alice and the city's students—but to the joy of many parents—the public schools would re-open on January 2, 1919.

During the week leading up to Christmas, Alice and Maggie took stock of their blessings. Yes, Mike had suffered greatly. But he had survived. And the worst the rest of them had suffered was inconvenience. From time to time, the two of them had talked about Emmett and what conditions must be like at Leavenworth. "I can't imagine having all those men together like that. It's a breeding ground for this disease," Alice said. "I'm thinking of writing to him. I don't know why. Just to say that I hope he stays well. It is Christmas, after all."

Maggie wondered at this statement. In all the years they'd been together, Maggie had never heard Alice utter a sympathetic word about Emmett Kelly. And thank God she hadn't, for Maggie didn't know if she'd have been able to stomach that. This was some sort of change in Alice's mindset about Emmett.

Perhaps the epidemic had softened her heart. Perhaps fatigue had done that. Perhaps, like the city and the world around her, Alice was simply exhausted—exhausted by the War, exhausted by the toll of disease. Maggie could understand that. Both of them were tired. They were living in a sick and tired nation, in a sick and tired world. Maggie marveled at how exhausting it was to live amidst a pervasive and overhanging awareness of disease. Maggie figured it wasn't surprising that all this touched Alice's feelings about Emmett.

"Then you should do it, Alice. Write to Emmett."

Chapter Sixty-Eight

Sometimes even the most obvious things become clear only in hindsight. For officials at Leavenworth, experience proved to be a slow teacher. It wasn't until after the September outbreak that they started to place all new inmates in isolation for three days before allowing them to be turned loose in the yard with other men or to take their meals with others. Wise though the quarantine strategy was, the period of isolation wasn't long enough in this initial iteration. They discovered this when yet another flare-up of influenza occurred.

In late November, officials thought they'd contained the September outbreak. So they lifted the ban on large gatherings of men. Sabbath services resumed, and the Sunday moving-picture shows reopened on November 24th after having been closed for eight weeks. After such a long hiatus, there was unusually large attendance at both. For Thanksgiving—Thursday, the 28th—Deputy Warden Fletcher decided to schedule the outdoor events the inmates most enjoyed watching: a track-and-field meet, and several baseball games. Audiences of over a thousand men turned out for the contests.

Within days, influenza flared up again in the prison. The disease had been reintroduced and had been spread at the Sunday picture show and during the outdoor events. Officials found that a new inmate had arrived on November 21st from Chicago, where the epidemic raged. He'd been placed in isolation until Sunday, the 24th. He seemed fine when he was released from quarantine. He took his meals with others and attended the Sunday movies. But by that evening, he had a temperature of 102 and was admitted to the prison hospital with unmistakable signs of influenza.

With this latest outbreak, prison officials implemented further measures, including a longer quarantine period for new arrivals and a mask requirement for everyone in the prison community. While these steps no doubt helped to contain the current contagion and would reduce the chances of future ones, they didn't help the eighty-three men who'd become ill this time—one of whom was Emmett Kelly.

Emmett became aware of his fever at about the time of the 3 a.m. prisoner check on Christmas day. Usually, the sound of the guards going by didn't awaken him, but that night it did. He tossed and thrashed for a long time before he was able to fall back asleep.

When he woke up again, it was about ten in the morning. He ached all over his body. He thought he should get himself to the prison hospital, but when he stood, he was overcome with a weakness so powerful he could barely drag himself in a cold perspiration back to his bed and blankets.

At the 4 o'clock inmate count, Emmett Kelly wasn't standing at the door of his cell, as he should have been. "Inmate missing," guard Hamilton said. Three guards entered Emmett's cell and gingerly approached the lump under the bed clothes, in case this was a trick and a surprise attack was in store for them.

When one of the guards flipped the sheet away from Emmett, all gasped at the sight of his blue-tinged face staring up at them. Each of them had seen this many times before. This influenza caused a person's lungs to fill with fluid. The lack of oxygen would suffocate him and give his skin and lips a bluish discoloration. Hamilton confirmed that Emmett was no longer breathing. He called for a stretcher to take Emmett's body to the prison morgue.

The next day, as prison officials were cataloging Emmett's belongings, a clerk from the prison post office showed up at the cell with a letter addressed to Emmett Kelly. He said, "Deputy Warden, here's a letter that arrived this morning for Kelly. I think it's the only letter we ever received for him."

Deputy Warden L.J. Fletcher, who had been given direct supervision of all baseball activities during the past year and thus had come to know Emmett well, took the letter from the clerk. He looked at the return address: Alice Kelly, 1345 Race Street, Denver Colorado. He opened it.

Emmett,

What a horrible year this has been. At least the War is over. But the influenza epidemic persists. I have thought of you over this past year. I knew that many people in Kansas were sick last spring. So, of course, I worried about you, as you are confined in a space with so many others. And the subsequent waves of the disease have been even more treacherous, giving rise to even greater worries, including for you.

I do not mean this letter to raise your hopes, should you have any, about our eventual reconciliation. That will not happen. Even so, I am now past the point of actively wishing hard times for you. In the spirit of this Christmas season, I am writing to wish you well. I hope your health remains good and that your time at Leavenworth passes quickly for you.

Alice

Fletcher said to the postal clerk, "Thank you, Henry. Leave this with me. At least now we have an address for someone we can notify about Oleo's demise."

Chapter Sixty-Nine

"I'm happy it was such a good Christmas for them," Maggie said to Alice a few days after the conjoined families had enjoyed their ninth Christmas together.

"And who would ever have guessed that it could be? This year was so horrific! But they seemed able to set aside the stress of the past months and enjoy the day together. Even Mike. Incidentally, he looks pretty much like himself finally, don't you think?"

"I do. And that means he looks a lot like Tom. More and more."

Alice smiled. "That's true. He does. A handsome young man!"

Eileen came into the room, carrying a handful of letters. "Mail arrived." She handed the small bundle to Alice, who thumbed through the envelopes with little interest until she came upon one with the return address, "Leavenworth Penitentiary." Her name and address were not in Emmett's handwriting. They had been typewritten. That seemed odd. So it was with mild trepidation that she opened the envelope.

Dear Mrs. Kelly,

It is with great sorrow that I write to inform you of the death of Emmett Kelly on Christmas Day. He succumbed to the influenza, which has taken so many from us.

I personally got to know Mr. Kelly through his various activities in the

Leavenworth community, especially his robust and successful membership on our prized baseball team. A newcomer to it this past spring, he established himself as a star. He was a power slugger and often was the man to drive in our winning runs. More importantly, he was a much-liked member of the team, a man who understood teamwork and cooperation, the value of combined effort.

By focusing on his contribution to the baseball world here, I do not mean to minimize his greater worth to our community. I have enclosed for you an "appreciation" of Emmett that appeared in the prison newspaper. It will give you an idea of the fondness with which he came to be regarded here. Those who knew him from his arrival said he changed for the better.

You will be gratified to know that your letter reached him as his condition still verged on the severe, so he was able to read your words to him and take them with him to the next world.

Please let us know how you would like us to handle the

disposition of his remains, which can either be shipped to Denver or interred on our prison grounds.

Many here share in the grief you must feel at Emmett's passing.

Yours sincerely,

L. J. Fletcher, Deputy Warden

Alice found the small newspaper clipping that had been enclosed:

When the news leaked out into this institution on Christmas Day of the death of Emmett "Oleo" Kelly, our friend and new star baseball player, hundreds of prisoners felt grieved. The sudden departure of their friend and diamond hero cast a pall of gloom on their Christmas day. He will be missed, for he proved his sterling worth to this community. Go, Oleo. Go, friend. Our hearts will be with you.

Tears had come to Alice's eyes. She handed the letter and the clipping to Maggie, who looked up at Alice after the moment it took her to read them. She wasn't certain what to say at that moment, so decided to say nothing. She laid her hand upon Alice's. After a while, Alice spoke. "He changed? He became a better person? Because of what? Prison base-ball?" She uttered that word with all the incredulity it deserved.

Maggie let more time pass, still trying to formulate a supportive thought. "You are a compassionate person, Alice.

And I know you felt sympathy for Emmett in recent months, for the situation he found himself in during this hellacious epidemic. I'm glad that he received your letter in time. At least he had your best wishes at the end."

Alice wiped a tear with a handkerchief. She nodded.

Chapter Seventy

Alice elected to have Emmett's remains shipped back to Denver. She needed to do that for Eileen and Bridget. Who knew how they might feel about their father as they grew older? She arranged for a burial and a private ceremony. The only person she invited outside of the Kelly-Quinn family was Gus McGrath.

Alice knew Gus would want to be there. She also knew that although Gus had been steadfastly loyal to Emmett over more than two decades, the two men had a complicated relationship the past few years. Gus had avoided prison in the oleo case by pleading guilty early and accepting a $500 fine—a decision that Emmett had likened to a traitorous act because it complicated his own defense.

Back at the house after the burial, the adult talk turned to topics other than Emmett. Gus told Alice and Maggie that he and a friend were exploring an idea for a new kind of grocery store. They'd read about a fella in Memphis, Tennessee, who had pioneered an innovative model for grocery shopping. Instead of waiting in line at a counter for a clerk to pull purchases for them, shoppers would do their own shopping, picking up their own groceries from shelves around the store.

"Wouldn't that be chaos?" Alice asked.

"You might think so, but apparently it's not. Upon entering the store through a turnstile, the customer is provided with a shopping basket. He then walks through the store at his leisure, picking out what he wants. Every item has a price tag on it. When he's finished, he takes his items to a check-out stand at the front of the store, where a clerk tallies it up."

"Sounds efficient," Maggie said. "Customers now waste a lot of time waiting for clerks. Such a store would have to be larger, with many more shelves along wide aisles that people could walk."

"That's right," Gus said.

"Do you have financial backing for such a venture?" Maggie asked.

"No. We're only thinking. Probably a fantasy, if you want to know the truth."

"I don't see why you say that, Gus. Sounds like a good idea to me. And you know the saying: 'You'll never plough a field by turning it over in your mind.'"

Gus smiled and nodded. He looked at his pocket watch. "I'm grateful that you thought to include me today. I appreciate it. It's been yonks since you and I've seen each other, Alice. I've enjoyed being with you again. But I'm afraid I have to go now."

"Thanks for coming, Gus. We'll stay in touch."

"THE SUN IS STRONG. It's such a grand afternoon. Let's take a walk," Maggie said. They headed to nearby Cheesman Park and walked its meandering carriage-ways. "Was today hard for you?"

"Oh, I don't even know, to be honest. It's so confusing. I don't know how to describe the feelings I have. Emmett hasn't been a part of my life for ten years. So, it can't be a sense of 'loss' that I feel. And can it possibly be called 'grief' when I didn't want him in my life, hadn't liked him for so long? … Do you know what I mean?"

"Yes." Maggie then stayed quiet for a long moment. "Maybe the 'grief' you feel is around not having had the husband you wanted and needed. Who you wanted him to be is simply not who he was. And now that he's truly gone, you're letting yourself grieve that."

Alice looked at her, nodded, and thought herself lucky to have such a wise, insightful friend. It also occurred to her that in some curious, bizarre way, Emmett's horrid behavior and character flaws had ended up benefiting her: now she had a far richer, more fulfilling life than she ever would have had if she had stayed with him.

When Maggie spoke again, her voice interrupted Alice's thoughts. "I would guess that it's also not easy for you that people know you and Emmett had such a strained relationship in recent years. So they assume his death isn't hard on you. I noticed how Gus was with you. He made no effort to comfort you. It was as if he felt you must not have anything to be upset about. I would guess that feels bad."

Alice looked at her and nodded.

Maggie paused again. "Alice, what I'm saying is that I think dealing with Emmett's death is going to be harder on you than you'd ever have expected. Unraveling emotions you've held on to for years is bound to be confusing. I'm here to talk whenever you want." Alice squeezed Maggie's right hand in thanks and they walked around the park again.

After a while, Alice broke the silence. "What did you think of that self-service market idea that Gus mentioned?"

Maggie's face lit up. "I thought it was fascinating."

Chapter Seventy-One

Over the next half-year, Alice and Maggie made a careful study of the new self-service, cash-and-carry model for grocery shopping. They read of stores on the west coast that were having success with such designs. And the Piggly Wiggly chain—the one Gus had spoken to them about —had opened stores around the country, including in Denver, at a dizzying rate.

Alice said, "A Piggly Wiggly franchise wouldn't be expensive. Saunders wants an advance fee of about one cent per thousand people in the designated territory—a minimum of $500—and a royalty of one-half of one percent of sales, for use of the patented interior design and the trademarks of the Piggly Wiggly system. That's not a high hurdle. I think we should do it."

Maggie looked across the kitchen table. She put down the pencil she'd been using while going through their financial situation. "Alice, you've known me long enough to know that when it comes to business or work, I don't like to be involved in anything I don't control. I'd rather have autonomy than make a fortune."

Alice thought there still might be a way to salvage her plan. "But that's the nice thing about a franchise. We would control it! It would be ours." She knew the argument was flimsy.

"No. We'd have the financial responsibility, but no control."

"Sure we would."

"No, we wouldn't! You read the brochures we got from them! We couldn't change anything at all in the Piggly Wiggly store design. We couldn't advertise or promote on our own authority. There's a list of merchandise we'd be required to stock and another list of thirty-four categories of merchandise that we'd be prohibited from selling. Jaysus, you'd have to sell oleomargarine! I don't call that autonomy!"

"But look at the figures on their franchises' sales and profits. Surely we can sacrifice some control for money like that!"

"Alice Kelly! I never knew you to be greedy!"

"I'm not. I'm looking at a good business opportunity."

"I think the opportunity lies in the idea, the concept—not in affiliation with a big company. You never know what's going to happen with a big company."

"So, you're saying you'd be willing to try opening a store based on the concept? Hasn't Saunders patented the concept?"

"No. He only patented the design of his stores—the

particular layout of the aisles, the appearance of the outside. That sort of thing. He took the idea from someone else. Saunders wasn't the first to come up with it. We'd have to be creative and original in what we came up with to avoid being sued. But that's not hard."

They looked at each other. Both broke into a grin. "What would we call it?" Maggie said.

"Well, obviously, 'Alice's Market.'" Alice was toying with her. "Or maybe "Kelly's Quick Mart.'"

"Sure," Maggie said, rolling her eyes. "Denver still loves the association of the name Kelly with a grocery store! If we were to use the Kelly name, it should truly honor Emmett's memory—perhaps 'Emmett's Self Serve.' The ads would say, 'Where You Take Care of Yourself First.'"

Alice guffawed. "You're brutal, you are. But funny."

Chapter Seventy-Two

Epilogue

Almost six years later, on a Saturday morning in September 1925, Alice Kelly and Maggie Quinn stood on the sidewalk in front of a store at the corner of 23rd and Dexter in Park Hill. A large crowd had gathered around to see Alice and Maggie cut a ribbon and throw open the doors to Denver's newest "Mile High Groceteria." The happy throng rushed past them and into the bright, smartly appointed store with wide aisles and thickly stocked shelves. Gus McGrath stood with them.

Smiling broadly, Gus said, "Congratulations, ladies. That's store number seven! I can't believe I ever had the nerve to doubt you."

Alice said, "Gus, this is as much your accomplishment as it is ours."

"You're kind to say that, Maggie."

"But it's true! You helped us scout out our locations; you helped with the design of the insides. Most important, we could never have done it without your extensive knowledge of what to stock—and how. Your long experience helped make all this possible."

"You're now the biggest grocers in Denver."

"Well, Piggly Wigglys outnumber us."

"But those are franchises. You own and control your stores."

"Our stores, Gus. You're a part owner."

"Don't remind me. It makes me nervous."

Maggie teased him. "Not comfortable being a retail magnate?"

Gus smiled. "I spent so many years working for Emmett or other people that I can't get used to the feeling of being a part owner of something, even if it's a small part."

Alice said, "It seems to me you've handled the change well, Gus. That's not easy to do."

"Change is what scares me. Everything changes so quickly. Who knows what's going to last?"

Waxing philosophical usually went against Maggie's instincts, but she couldn't resist. "Nothing lasts forever, Gus. You know that. The trick is to accept the changes that come your way."

Maggie looked to her right and saw Mike coming out the door, wearing a long white apron. The pin affixed at his chest read, "Mike Quinn, Manager."

Gesturing toward him, Maggie said, "For example, who'd ever have guessed this!" "We could use some help in there," Mike said to the three of them. "But I can understand that it's more fun for you to stand around enjoying some craic than to work." Maggie looked at Alice and raised her eyebrows. "The man has no respect for immigrants!"

"None whatsoever."

She shook her head in feigned exasperation. "Americans!"

The End

About the Author

Thank you for reading *The Butcher on Colfax.*

Reviews are crucial for authors. If you enjoyed this book and have a few moments to spare, please post a brief, honest review or rating on Amazon. That would be enormously helpful in connecting this novel with more readers.

J.T. Tierney writes fiction in several genres. His first novel was *Love, Literally,* a smart romance set on Cape Cod during the early months of the pandemic. *The Butcher on Colfax* was his second. In early March, 2025, he will release his third—a suspense novel, *Extreme Malice,* about local public officials in a small Colorado city being harassed and terrorized by a shadowy group of conservative reactionaries.

The later part of 2025 will see the release of his romantic comedy about a brilliant but socially awkward convention planner, raised in an isolated Arctic outpost by research-scientist parents, who learns to navigate big-city life and the pathways of the heart with the help of an empathetic colleague.

A retired professor of American government, his writings include academic books and journal articles. He was a contributing writer for *The Atlantic* for several years after he left academia. He later turned his attention to writing fiction. He resides outside Chicago with his wife of 43 years and their dog.

To sign up for his newsletter and be the first to hear about upcoming releases, news and special offers, please provide your name and email address in the space provided at JTTierney.com